SUCH A GOOD HUSBAND

ROWEN CHAMBERS

Such a Good Husband

By Rowen Chambers

Published by Waltham Publishing, LLC

Cover Designed by Marisa Wesley of Cover Me Darling

1

"If this dinner tonight doesn't go well," I tell Candace. "I'm taking that to mean I'm meant to be single."

"That's not what it means," she says, pouring a packet of sugar into her coffee. "It means whoever this guy is just isn't the one." She comes up to me, wrapping her arm around mine and leading me out of the breakroom. "You have to meet a lot of the wrong men to find the right one."

"I'm 35. If I haven't met the right one by now, it's not going to happen."

We go into my office and I sit behind the desk while Candace takes a seat on the velvet chair across from me. It was a gift from one of our buyers. The purple is an exact match to the purple on the Adore logo.

"I think you're giving up too soon," Candace says. "Maybe you just need some time away from the apps."

"I'm done with the apps. I never should've been on them in the first place. I don't know why I let you talk me into that."

She shrugs. "I met Tom that way. And Carol in accounting met her husband on an app."

"The success stories are the exception, not the rule. The

whole point of those apps is to keep people on them. It's how they make money."

"Well, you're never going to meet anyone with that attitude." She sips her coffee.

My phone alarm goes off, reminding me of my next meeting.

"I have to go meet with Edward," I tell Candace.

"We can talk about this later," she says, quickly getting up.

"I'd rather not," I mutter as she leaves. I was serious when I told her I'm done with dating. It's exhausting. I can't do it anymore.

Getting up from my desk, I prepare to see Edward. Even though I've known him forever, he still makes me nervous. It's because he expects so much from me and I fear letting him down.

Edward is the CEO of Adore Fragrance. He's an older man who took over when my father died. He was close friends with my father and in some ways reminds me of him. Headstrong. Domineering. Doesn't take no for an answer. Edward can be difficult to deal with, but he's a genius businessman. The company wouldn't survive without him.

I take a deep breath as I walk down the hall to his office. It's on the corner and is lined with windows that look out at the Manhattan skyline.

"Anna!" Edward barks.

Looking up, I see him standing just outside his office.

"I'm coming," I say, picking up my pace.

"We'll need to postpone," Edward says as I follow him into the room that used to belong to my father. Every time I come in here, I swear I can still smell him. His heavy, musky cologne mixed with the smoke from his cigars.

"Did something come up?" I ask as Edward goes behind his desk and sits down in his black leather chair.

"I'm meeting with our attorney," he says. "It appears a

company overseas is selling a knockoff of Adore but using our packaging."

"Oh, then yes, we can meet some other time." I turn to leave.

"Anna," he says in his deep, gravelly voice. "We're not finished."

I turn back. "I thought you had another meeting."

"In ten minutes, which is plenty of time to go over this." He motions to the chair in front of his desk. "Sit down."

Going over there, I take a seat on the stiff, high-backed upholstered chair and wait for him to continue.

"Some women's magazine called me up the other day wanting to interview you."

"Why?"

"Because you're a woman and own a company that makes products for women," he says, like it was silly of me to ask.

"So it's a business article?"

"I suppose it's something like that. She was rambling on. I wasn't comprehending everything she said."

"Why'd she call you and not someone in public relations?"

"Her father and I play golf. I'm doing him a favor."

By volunteering me to be featured in an article? I wish he hadn't done that. Edward knows I value my privacy. I purposely chose not to be the face of Adore when I inherited the company. And honestly, I think Edward and the rest of the board were relieved about that. The Adore brand is about beauty, gracefulness, and glamour. I wouldn't call myself beautiful, I'm not at all graceful, and I'm not even a tiny bit glamorous.

"Here's the woman's card." Edward hands it to me. "Call her and set up a time for you two to talk." He shoos me away. "Now get out of here. Patrick will be arriving soon for our meeting."

I leave, already feeling anxious about this interview. I don't like being in the spotlight. I wonder if I could call this woman and ask her to find someone else.

"Back already?" Candace asks as I pass by her desk.

"He had another meeting," I say, continuing to my office.

Candace follows me in there. "What's wrong? You look like you're going to be sick."

"I'm fine." I sit down behind my desk. "I'm just nervous. Edward arranged for me to be interviewed for some magazine."

"When?" she asks, walking up to me.

"Soon, I imagine. I need to call the woman and set up a time." I pick up her business card. "I suppose I should do it now. Get it over with." I take a breath. "I need to calm down first. I wish I didn't get so worked up about these things."

"Maybe you should take a pill," Candace says.

"No." I sit up straighter. "I'm fine."

Candace is one of the few people in the company who knows about my anxiety and how it can quickly spiral out of control when I'm nervous. I do my best to hide it, because as the owner of a successful fragrance company, I can't appear weak or unsure of myself. But a few weeks after Candace started working here, I couldn't find my anxiety meds and had a full blown panic attack right before a board meeting. Luckily, Edward noticed I was in no condition to attend the meeting and told the board I was sick.

"I'll call her later," I say, setting the woman's card down. "When I've had some time to prepare."

"Changing topics," Candace says, sitting down in the purple chair. "I was thinking about your date tonight. I think you should wear that blue dress. The one that matches your eyes."

I don't like that dress. I only bought it because Candace talked me into it. We went to lunch one day and she saw this dress in a store window and said it was perfect for me and that I had to get it. When I tried it on, I felt it was too fitted around the chest and far shorter than I'd like, but Candace convinced me to buy it anyway. She's 25, still young enough to be filled with energy and enthusiasm, which is partially why I hired her. I thought she might rub off on me. She hasn't, but her enthusiasm did get me to buy that dress and sign up for those ridiculous dating apps.

"I think I might cancel tonight," I say.

"What? No! You can't cancel. It's only a few hours from now."

"So? That's plenty of time for him to make other plans." I get out my phone, feeling relieved I won't have to endure another evening of awkward conversation with a man who I'm sure won't even come close to what I'm looking for in a potential partner.

Candace says I'm too picky, and maybe she's right. But is it wrong to be picky about the person you'll be spending the rest of your life with? Wouldn't it be better to be alone than to settle down with a man who isn't what you really want?

"Just go," Candace says in a pleading tone. Sometimes I think she's more interested in finding me a husband than I am. "It's just dinner. It'll be over in an hour."

"Yes, but it'll take longer than that to get myself ready and to the restaurant. Why bother going to all that work for another bad date?"

"What if it's not a bad date? What if this guy is the man of your dreams?"

I laugh a little. "The man of my dreams doesn't exist."

"Or maybe he does and you just haven't found him," she says with that youthful enthusiasm I wish I still had.

"If he's out there, he'll have to find me. I'm too tired to keep looking."

"Okay, how about this?" She sits up straighter, shoulders

back. "You go out with this guy tonight, and if it doesn't go well, you can go off the apps."

"I was going to go off them regardless."

"Yes, but if you do this, if you keep your date, I'll leave you alone. I won't keep bugging you to find a guy."

It might be worth it to go tonight just for that, to get Candace off my back. The girl is relentless when it comes to finding me a partner.

"If I agree to this," I say, "you never say another word about the dating apps or anything else related to finding me a date."

She ponders that a moment. "Like ever?"

"Yes. I don't want to hear another word about it."

"What if I find a guy who's perfect for you? I can't offer to set you up?"

"No. In fact, after tonight, my search for a husband might be over."

It's sad hearing myself say those words, knowing how much I want that. A husband. Children. A family of my own. I've had that dream since I was a child and assumed it would become a reality far before now, but instead I'm single and feeling painfully lonely and hopeless.

"It's a deal," Candace says, holding her hand out to me. "If your date tonight is a dud, I'll leave you alone. I won't keep trying to find you someone."

"I'm going to hold you to that."

We shake on it and Candace leaves my office. I remain in my chair, swiveling it around to face the floor-to-ceiling windows. As I gaze out at the city, I wonder if my dream man really is out there. He's not, of course. I'm just letting Candace get in my head. She's young and hopeful and doesn't realize life doesn't always give you what you ask for, or that sometimes it gives you the opposite of what you want.

I remember what it was like, being like Candace, believing

I could have what I wanted in life. I used to wish for it every night. I could see my future husband coming home from work, greeting me with a kiss. I saw us living in a beautiful house, having dinner together, talking about our future. Our hopes and dreams.

Unfortunately, wishes don't come true, or they don't for me. My reality is far different from the dream life I imagined. My parents are gone. I spend all my time at this company. And I'm single, with no hope of that ever changing.

2

"Do you have a reservation?" the hostess asks when I arrive at the restaurant.

"I don't," I say, "but the person I'm meeting does. He'll be here shortly, or maybe he's already here."

"Is it Craig?" the hostess asks, looking at her reservation list.

"Um, no, his name is Gary."

She looks closer at her reservation list, then flips to another page. "Are you sure it's not Craig?"

Does she really think I don't know the name of the person I'm meeting for dinner? Gary and Craig don't even sound the same.

"No, it's Gary," I tell her, but then wonder if that isn't his real name. I went out with a man last year who used a different name on his dating profile, saying he didn't want a woman knowing his real name until he'd confirmed she wasn't crazy. I'm not sure how he planned to confirm that. I didn't ask. By that point, I'd already decided I didn't want to see him again.

"Is it maybe George?" the hostess asks. "I have a George, but the reservation isn't for a half hour from now."

I sigh, wishing I'd just cancelled the date like I wanted to. I would've done it if it weren't for Candace and the deal we made.

"It's not George," I say. "It's Gary. And the reservation was supposed to be for seven."

She frowns. "Sorry. I don't see it."

The hostess is young, like Candace, and gives me a look like she feels sorry for me. She obviously knows this was a date and knows I've been stood up, or ghosted, or whatever people are calling it now.

"Do you want to wait and see if he shows up?" the hostess asks in that same hopeful tone Candace uses.

Before I can answer, a man comes up beside me. I glance at him, noticing how tall he is—well over six feet—and handsome. He's wearing a dark gray suit with a white dress shirt and a light blue tie.

"Did you hear from her?" the hostess asks the man.

"I'm afraid not. I think it's safe to say she won't be joining me tonight."

I step aside and feel the man's hand on my arm.

"Pardon me," he says. "I didn't mean to interrupt." He takes his hand off my arm and motions to the hostess. "Please. Go ahead."

"Oh, actually I'm leaving," I say, gazing up at the man's face. He's very good-looking, like a modern day Prince Charming with his thick dark hair and deep brown eyes.

"Her date didn't show," the hostess says, drawing my attention back to her.

Why in the world would she tell him that? This man doesn't need to know I've been stood up, and for the record, I never confirmed Gary was a date. For all she knows, he could've been a friend or a business associate.

"Is that so?" the handsome man beside me says. I feel him looking at me and notice my face getting hot.

"I need to get going," I say, desperately wanting to get out of this restaurant. It's bad enough having my date not show up, but it's even worse when the hostess broadcasts it to everyone waiting to be seated, which includes four couples and the very handsome man at the hostess stand.

"Wait!" The man races up beside me as I head to the door. "I never do this, but given our situations, would you be open to having dinner with me?"

I turn to him, my heart melting a little when I see that the man who seemed extremely confident just moments ago now looks uncertain and a little nervous as he waits for my response. Seeing him vulnerable like this is kind of adorable.

"What do you mean by our situations?" I ask.

"The woman I was meeting. She didn't show up."

"Was this a first date?"

"Yes." He looks down, then back up at me. "Sorry. I shouldn't be bothering you. You don't even know me. I'm sure you think I'm crazy asking you to join me for dinner. I just already had the reservation and thought—"

"I'd love to," I say, smiling at him.

"Really?" He smiles back, hesitantly, as though he's not sure if I'm serious.

"We need to eat and we're here, so why not?"

"Well, then, I feel the need to properly introduce myself." He holds his hand out to me. "Ethan Halstrom."

"Anna Montgomery," I say, shaking his hand.

"It's very nice to meet you, Anna." He motions in front of him. "Please. After you."

I walk to the hostess stand with Ethan right behind me.

"This lovely woman has agreed to join me for dinner," Ethan says to the hostess.

She smiles at him as she takes two menus from the stand. "Right this way."

We're led to a small, round table near the back of the restaurant, which is much quieter than the front. The lighting is dim and there's a candle flickering on the table. It's a very romantic setting for two people who aren't on a date. Or is this a date? I wasn't thinking it was, but perhaps Ethan does.

He pulls out my chair for me, waits for me to sit, then helps move my chair up to the table. No guy has ever helped me with my chair before. It seems old-fashioned, but in a good way. It's nice to be around a man with manners.

Ethan sits across from me, but the table's so small it feels like there's barely any distance between us.

"Would you like a bottle of wine?" he asks. "Before you answer, I should mention that tonight is on me."

"You don't need to do that," I say, picking up my menu. "You don't even know me."

"But you were kind enough to have dinner with me so I would like to thank you by paying the check."

"I think we saved each *other* from having dinner alone," I say, smiling at him. "But if you insist, then yes, you can pay for dinner." I look over the menu, noticing the prices and wondering if Ethan can afford this. "So what do you do?"

"Let me preface this by saying we're not all bad."

I look at him and see a slight smile on his handsome face. "What do you mean?"

"I'm an attorney, which I know is not the most admirable of professions."

"It depends on the kind of attorney," I say in a lighthearted tone. "You're not suing old ladies and taking all their retirement income, are you?"

He laughs a little. "No. Not even close. I'm a corporate attorney. I work for a company that makes nutritional products for infants and children."

That's not what I was expecting him to say, but I'm pleasantly surprised by his answer.

"Does that mean you like children?" I ask, smiling at him.

"Absolutely. I'd like to have several of my own one day. But that day could be a ways off if my dates continue to not show up," he kids.

"So this isn't the first time this has happened?"

"It's happened once before, but she never called back to confirm the date so I wasn't surprised she didn't show. Catherine, the woman I was to meet tonight, initiated this dinner so I'm a little surprised she's not here."

"Maybe she had an emergency, like she got sick or in a car accident."

"I hope it's not something like that." He checks his phone. "I texted her several times, asking if she was okay. I still haven't heard back." He tucks his phone into the pocket of his suit jacket. "What about you? Did you hear anything from the man who was supposed to meet you tonight?"

"No. I'm sure he found something better to do and didn't think it was worth his time to let me know."

"I'm sorry about that," Ethan says.

"It's fine," I say, laughing it off. "It's part of dating, right?"

"Unfortunately, yes, but it shouldn't be. It seems people have forgotten how to be civil to one another. A simple phone call to tell you he couldn't make it would've saved you a lot of time and effort." He glances down at my dress. "You look beautiful, by the way."

"Thank you." I point to my dress. "My assistant picked this out. It's not something I'd normally wear."

"You should. It looks great on you. The blue matches your eyes, which I must say, are absolutely gorgeous. I've never seen that shade of blue before."

"I get it from my father. His eyes were also blue."

Ethan's brows rise. "Were?"

"He passed away ten years ago."

"I'm sorry to hear that. My father passed when I was seven."

"You were so young. That must've been devastating for you."

"It was. I still miss him every day."

"Is your mother alive?"

"Yes, but I worry about her living alone. She says she's fine, but I still worry."

His comment brings back memories of my own mother. She kept insisting she was fine living on her own, but I knew she wasn't. Her memory was failing and she was seeing things that weren't there. By the time she was admitted into a care facility, her mind had failed to the point she no longer knew who I was and would scream at anyone who got near her, thinking they were trying to kill her. She had to be sedated and sometimes tied to her bed to keep her from hurting herself. She died just two months after being admitted to the care facility.

The doctors said my mother had a severe form of dementia with paranoia and delusions. They think it started in her fifties, which is much younger than when it's typically diagnosed. The doctors say it's not hereditary, but I still worry it'll happen to me. I'm like my mother in many ways. I take after her in appearance, and like me, she had severe anxiety in her younger years. I tell myself not to worry, that I won't turn out like my mother, but it doesn't stop me from thinking about it.

Every time I forget something, I worry I'm losing my memory, which was the first sign my mother's mind was failing. Or sometimes I worry that I'm imagining things that aren't true. Like last week, I thought a man was following me home. I thought I saw him again the next day and took a different route home to see if he'd follow me. He didn't. It wasn't even the same man. I was just being paranoid.

But was it normal paranoia, or am I becoming like my mother? Seeing everyone as a threat?

Those are the thoughts that keep me up at night, wondering if I should even be trying to find a husband. I want to get married, have children, and live a normal life, but if I'm going to end up like my mother, why would I even try to have that, knowing how it'll end?

Seeing my mother go through that was terrifying, and then I lost her, far too early. I'd never want to put someone else through that, especially the people I love. And yet I still want it. I want the dream, starting with the perfect husband.

3

"Anna." Ethan reaches across the table, his hand gently grasping mine. "Are you okay?"

"I'm fine," I say, forcing out a smile.

"You're not fine. You're tearing up. Was it something I said?"

"Your mother." I quickly wipe my eyes. "I feel bad for her, living alone without your father."

"That's sweet of you to be concerned." He takes his hand off mine and I find myself missing it, missing his kind, gentle touch.

The waiter stops by our table. "Can I start you off with a drink?"

Ethan looks at me. "What do you think? Would you like a bottle of wine?"

"I'd love one."

I wasn't going to drink tonight, knowing it's not a good idea when I'm out with a stranger, but Ethan is feeling less and less like a stranger.

He orders a very expensive bottle of cabernet, my favorite. The waiter leaves and Ethan's looking at me like I'm the only woman in the restaurant. Usually, the men I go out with are looking behind me or around me, their eyes stopping on women they'd rather be with than me. But Ethan hasn't even glanced at another woman.

"So what is it you do, Anna?" Ethan asks. "Wait. Let me guess." He pauses to think. "A nurse?"

"No," I say, shuddering. "The sight of blood makes me ill. I could never be a nurse, or do any job that involves medical care."

He leans back, rubbing his jaw. "An artist. Perhaps a painter?"

I laugh. "I'm terrible at painting. I even took a class and I'm still terrible at it."

"I've got it." He sits up straighter. "You own a bakery. You make wonderful cakes and pastries and—"

"Sorry, but no," I say, smiling as I imagine myself trying to bake. "I am definitely not a baker. I made cookies once and they were awful. I misread the recipe and they came out looking like flat, little stones."

Ethan chuckles. "I give up. What is it you do?"

I hesitate, not wanting to tell him, because telling him could change things between us and I don't want that to happen. I really like Ethan. I don't want him seeing me as a woman who lives off her father's success. Then again, if Ethan judges me for that, he's not the right man for me.

"I work at Adore Fragrance," I say, picking up my white cloth napkin and placing it over my lap.

His brows rise. "I'm not familiar with the name. Is it local?"

He's never heard of Adore? I assumed everyone had, but I'm biased since I own it. I guess it's not surprising Ethan wouldn't know about women's perfume. Men don't pay attention to those things unless they're married, and even then, it's unlikely they'd know a perfume by name. There's a lot of them out there and Adore is an older brand. Our more recent perfumes are what people recognize.

"It's an international company," I say. "It's quite large and quite successful. They make several perfumes, all with different names, but Adore is the one that made the company really take off, so years ago, the company was renamed to Adore Fragrance."

"Is that what you're wearing tonight? Because whatever scent you have on is intoxicating. I can see why it's a success."

"No, I'm wearing one of our newer fragrances. To me, Adore is meant for someone older, probably because it's what my mother wore. She was actually the inspiration for it."

"Your mother inspired the fragrance?"

"Adore is my father's company," I explain. "I began working there after he passed."

"I see." Ethan leans back in his chair and rubs his hand over his jaw, like he's trying to decide what to say next. His reaction is why I don't like telling people this, especially men. Despite how far women have come, many men still feel the need to be more successful than women and make more money.

"So your father left you the company?" Ethan asks.

"Not all of it, but I own the majority of the shares. Edward, my father's closest friend, owns the remaining shares. He's the CEO." I clear my throat. "If you don't mind, I'd rather not talk about this."

"Why is that?" Ethan asks. "If my father built a company from scratch, I'd want to tell everyone I could about it."

"But it's not his company anymore. It's mine, and men are often intimidated by that. Or some think I don't deserve it since I didn't create it."

"I can assure you, I am not one of those men." Ethan leans toward me, looking into my eyes. "I think it's wonderful your father left you his company and that you didn't sell it off but are continuing his legacy."

"I never even considered selling it. My father built it from nothing. He wasn't around much when I was growing up, which upset me as a child, but now I realize he worked all those hours to make sure my mother and I had a good life. He was determined to make Adore a success, and he did."

"And Adore, the name of the company. You said it's a fragrance?"

I nod. "It wasn't the first fragrance my father developed. It was actually the third, but it's the one that took off and made people take notice of us. It was so popular that stores couldn't keep it in stock." I look down. "My mother wore it every day. Until the day she died."

"I'm sorry. I didn't realize she was gone. Was it recent?"

"She passed a few years ago." I look up at him. "She'd been sick for a while. I knew it was coming." I pause. "Maybe we could talk about something else. Something more pleasant."

"Of course." His phone rings from his pocket. He takes it out and silences it. "I'm sorry about that. I thought it was off."

"You can answer it if you need to."

He slides his phone back into his pocket. "I don't believe in giving my attention to someone on the phone when I'm with someone else, especially someone as interesting and beautiful as the person I'm with right now."

I smile. "I feel the same way about phones. I'd rather give my attention to the person I'm with."

"I'm glad you said that. You wouldn't believe how many dates I've been on where the woman spent half our time on the phone."

"Yes, I've experienced that with the men I've dated. One man even made a date with another woman while he was still on a date with me."

Ethan sighs. "It's sad how disrespectful people can be. I find that's even more true here in the city."

"Is this where you're from? Originally?"

"No, I grew up in Indiana. I went to college in New Jersey

and law school here in New York. At first, I loved the city, but the longer I live here, the more I want to leave."

"Where would you go?"

"I'm looking at places in Connecticut, somewhere close to the city. I'd have a longer commute, but I'm okay with that."

The more Ethan talks, the fonder I am of him. He's more mature than the men I've dated in the past. Unlike them, Ethan seems ready to settle down, get married, and have a family. He's already mentioned wanting children and moving out of the city, things he wouldn't want if he was committed to remaining a bachelor.

The waiter brings our wine and pours it into glasses. "Are you ready to order, or would you like some time?"

Ethan smiles at me. "I'm not in a rush."

"I'm not either," I say, thinking I wouldn't mind if we stayed here until the restaurant closed. I'm really enjoying my time with Ethan. He's smart, successful, polite, and we seem to have several things in common, like being stood up tonight. I was angry about that earlier, but now I'm glad Gary didn't show up. If he had, I wouldn't have met Ethan.

"I'll check back with you later," the waiter says before taking off.

"I hope you're not in a hurry," Ethan says.

"Not at all."

Ethan holds up his wine glass. "To unexpected encounters, and the good fortune they bring."

We clink glasses and I take a sip of the wine, feeling like Ethan is definitely the good fortune he alluded to. If my date had shown up, I'd likely be trying to come up with an excuse to leave. But I have no desire to leave with Ethan here.

"I'm guessing you're a city girl," he says. "Am I right?"

"Yes, I grew up here. I've considered moving somewhere quieter and not as crowded, but being single, it makes more sense to remain in the city. I have a better chance of meeting people here."

"And do you?" He sets his glass down. "Go out and meet people?"

"No," I say with a laugh. "I spend almost every night at home."

"Then what's stopping you? Why not move?"

"It seems odd to buy a house in the suburbs and live in it by myself. I always imagined myself being in a house with a husband and children. I guess I'm still waiting for that to happen." I swirl the wine, watching its movement in the glass.

"I'd like that too," Ethan says. "The house. The family."

My eyes meet up with his. "It does sound nice, doesn't it?"

"It sounds perfect." He smiles and my heart flutters in my chest, like it's telling me this is it. I've found the man I've been looking for, the one I was starting to think didn't exist.

I came here tonight prepared for another bad date, but instead, I might've just met my future husband.

4

THREE MONTHS LATER

"Are you nervous?" Candace asks as she brushes out a section of my hair.

"A little," I say, watching as she wraps my hair around the circular iron, then releases it, creating a loose wave. "But I've heard wedding jitters are normal."

I'm getting married today. I almost can't believe it. I keep looking down at my hand, at the three-carat diamond engagement ring, to remind myself that this is real. I'm actually getting married, to a man who's more wonderful than I ever could've imagined. Ethan is smart, successful, and extremely handsome, yet he doesn't let any of that go to his head. He's not at all boastful or conceited, and although he has a very demanding career, he always makes time for me. When we have children, I know he'll make time for them too. Ethan loves children. He's even on the board of three child-centered charities. It's one of the many reasons I fell in love with him.

"I'd be nervous," Candace says, continuing to curl my hair. "I mean, you've only known him a few months. But I guess if you're in love, there's really no need to wait."

"Exactly. I know I love Ethan, so I didn't see a need for a long engagement. And at our age, we can't afford to wait."

"You're 35. That's not that old."

"It is if you want children. And we want more than one." I smile as I think about that. I can't wait to be a mother. I was thrilled when Ethan said he wanted to start trying right away.

Candace smiles. "I'm really happy for you. I know how much you wanted the whole husband and kid thing."

"I do, and I'm very happy. I couldn't ask for a better man. Ethan will be a wonderful husband."

"I'm taking credit for getting you two together. You never would've gone to the restaurant that night if it weren't for me."

"Even with your encouragement, I almost didn't go. As I was getting ready, I almost messaged Gary to tell him I couldn't make it." I glance at my phone on the bathroom counter. "I wonder whatever happened to him."

"I'm sure he's still on the apps."

"He never blocked me. I thought he might after standing me up so I couldn't message him." I pause. "What if he didn't stand me up? What if something happened to him?"

"Why are you thinking about that guy? You're getting married in a few hours. You should be thinking about Ethan."

"You're right." I pick up my phone and see the last message he sent me, saying how much he loves me and can't wait for me to be his wife. He says the sweetest things. He's very open with his feelings, which is why I found it easy to trust him. I trust very few people, but Ethan's so open and honest with me that I have no reason not to trust him. He even gave me the passcode to his phone, saying I could go through it whenever I'd like. I haven't, but knowing I could just shows that Ethan has nothing to hide.

I'm usually far more cautious with men. In the past, it'd take me months before I'd even allow a man to call me his girlfriend. But I didn't feel the need to be that way with Ethan. The night we met seemed like fate bringing us together. I have no doubt he's the one, which is why I said yes when he asked me to marry him.

It was the night of my birthday. Ethan took me to the restaurant where we met and arranged for us to be seated at the same table. After dinner, the waiter brought over a chocolate torte topped with candles for my birthday. I blew out the candles and made a wish that Ethan would be my husband someday, having no idea what was about to happen. When Ethan handed me the small velvet box, I knew it was jewelry but assumed it was earrings or a necklace. I opened the box and couldn't believe what I was seeing. The ring was gorgeous. It took my breath away.

Ethan got down on one knee, took the sparkly diamond ring from the box, and held it out in front of me. Then he said the most beautiful words, about how much he loved me and treasured me and would be honored to be my husband. I couldn't speak for a moment as I took in his words and what they meant. Poor Ethan looked like he was about to be sick because I was taking so long to answer. He thought I was going to turn him down, but of course, I didn't, and now, one month after his proposal, we're getting married.

"I think we're done," Candace says, looking at my reflection in the mirror. We're in my bathroom, which is huge and has a large soaking tub, walk-in shower, two oversized sinks, and a sitting area to do my makeup. That's where I am now, sitting in front of the mirror.

"What do you think?" Candace asks. "Do you like it?"

I don't answer as my mind suddenly realizes I won't be living here after today. I'll be living with Ethan in the house we bought in Greenwich, Connecticut. It's a beautiful brick colonial on a half-acre lot with manicured grass and mature trees. It looks just like the house I imagined living in someday. The moment I saw it, I just had to have it. We made an offer on it that afternoon, and two weeks ago, we signed the paperwork to make it ours. I'm not great at decorating so I hired an interior designer to pick out the furnishings. They've all been delivered and the house is now ready for us to move in.

But I will miss my apartment. I spent years making it the way I wanted. Like this bathroom, which I had ripped down to the studs and rebuilt to my specifications. It's become my favorite room in the house. But all good things must come to an end, and I know that even better things lie ahead.

"Anna? Did you hear me?"

"Yes," I say, smiling up at Candace. "My hair looks great. Thank you."

"You're welcome," she says, unplugging the curling iron and wrapping up the cord. "You think Ethan will like it?"

"He'll love it, but he'd say I'm beautiful even if he saw me in curlers with no makeup on."

"You really found a good one."

"I did," I say, feeling extremely grateful for Ethan. I never in a million years thought I'd find a man as good as him, and then he just appeared, right before I was about to give up and accept a life of being single.

An hour later, Candace and I arrive at city hall. A month-long engagement wasn't long enough to plan a big wedding and I decided I didn't need one. My family is gone and I don't have a lot of friends, or any if I think about it. The few friends I had got married and moved to the suburbs. We lost touch, and now Candace is my only friend, but she probably shouldn't be since she's my employee.

"Now are you nervous?" Candace asks as we wait outside the room where the ceremony is being held.

"No. I'm fine."

She stands in front of me and messes with my hair. "You look amazing. I'm going to get a picture." She takes out her phone.

"Not now. Wait until after the wedding."

"C'mon, it's your last photo as a single woman."

"Okay, fine." I smile as she holds up her phone and takes some photos.

An older woman walks by and smiles at me. "Congratulations."

"Thank you," I tell her.

"I sent them to you," Candace says. "They turned out great."

"The name is Halstrom," I hear someone say. "Ethan Halstrom."

Turning back, I see Rose, Ethan's mother, talking to a security guard.

"Rose!" I wave at her.

She looks around, then back at the security guard. I don't think she saw me.

"Ma'am," the security guard says. "I think she's talking to you." He points to me.

Rose turns around, smiling when she sees me. She waves, then turns back to the security guard, patting his arm. "Thank you, young man."

She makes her way over to me, a huge smile on her pudgy face. She's wearing a pink floral dress that goes past her knees and matching pink shoes with a slight heel. I've only met Rose one time, but I immediately fell in love with her. She's barely over five feet and has a big round waist, tiny little feet, and a kind, sweet face. When she smiles, her blue eyes seem to disappear in her wrinkles. Her chubby cheeks are accented with a circle of dark pink blush that needs to be blended in, and her bright red lipstick is smudged on the top row of her teeth.

"Hello, honey," Rose says, giving me a hug. She stands back and smiles at me. "Look at you. What a beautiful bride."

"Rose, this is Candace," I say, motioning to her. "She helped me get ready today."

"You did a lovely job," Rose says to Candace.

"Thanks!" Candace turns to me. "I think she looks great."

"She looks absolutely gorgeous," a deep voice says. I know that voice.

Turning around, I see Ethan walking toward me, looking beyond handsome in his tailored black suit, white dress shirt, and gray silk tie.

"Wait!" Candace jumps in front of me. "You're not supposed to see her."

"It's fine," I tell her. "They told us we're to wait together outside the room."

"Oh." Candace steps aside as Ethan comes up to me and takes my hand.

He didn't even notice his mother, his focus completely on me.

Rose clears her throat.

Ethan looks over at her. "Mother. I'm sorry. I didn't see you."

"I can see why," she says, winking at me.

He turns to Rose and leans down to kiss her cheek. "Did you have any trouble getting here?"

"Not at all. Dorothy dropped me off at the train and agreed to pick me up."

"It's not too late to get a hotel," Ethan says. "I'd be happy to get you a room wherever you'd like."

This is another reason I love Ethan. He's so good to his mother. When he got a job here after law school, he moved his mother from Indiana to a small town in New Jersey so she'd be closer to him. I hope someday I have a son as kind and thoughtful as him.

"I don't feel safe in the city," she says. "I'd rather go home."

"If that's what you'd like," Ethan says. "But the offer still stands if you change your mind."

"We'd love to have you come see the house," I say to Rose. "Did Ethan send you pictures?"

"Yes, it's lovely," Rose says. "But I don't want to get in the way. You and Ethan need your time alone. You'll be newlyweds, after all."

"We'd still love to have you," I say. "Maybe in a few weeks, after we're settled."

Ethan smiles at me. He loves that I'm nice to his mother, but why wouldn't I be? In less than an hour, she'll be my mother as well. I'm looking forward to that. I miss my mother terribly, and although Rose can't replace her, having her in my life will be like having a mother again.

The door to the ceremony room opens and a man comes out. "Halstrom wedding?"

"That's us," Ethan says, taking my hand.

"I'm Anthony. I'll be officiating your wedding today. Once you're in the room, go ahead and step up to the podium where we'll do the ceremony."

Ethan and I walk into the room with Rose and Candace following behind. As we approach the podium, my nerves kick in. I've been fine up until now, but suddenly, out of nowhere, I'm panicking. My heart's racing and I'm feeling dizzy.

"Anna!" Ethan races to hold me up as my knees give out.

Why is this happening? It's as if my body's telling me not to do this, but that doesn't make sense. Marrying Ethan is the best decision I've ever made. He's the perfect man. Exactly what I wished for. We're going to have a wonderful life.

So why do I feel an overwhelming sense of panic and dread?

5

"Anna, what's wrong?" Ethan asks, his eyes bouncing around my face. "You're white as a ghost."

"I don't feel good."

"You want to sit down?"

"We're on a schedule here," Anthony, the wedding officiant, says. "If you need to do this another day—"

"No," Ethan blurts out. "It has to be today."

Has to be? What does he mean? Why does it have to be today? I know Ethan doesn't want to wait to get married, but the way he said that just now isn't sitting right with me.

"She's probably dehydrated," Candace says. "I'll go get some water."

Candace races off as Ethan continues to hold me up.

"Take some deep breaths," he tells me.

I try, but my heart's going so fast it's hard to get even a shallow breath in.

"I'm sure it's just nerves," Rose says, rubbing my arm. "All brides get cold feet before the ceremony."

"I think I might be sick," I say, closing my eyes.

"Anna," Ethan says, gripping my shoulders. "Look at me."

I open my eyes and see him looking back at me. It isn't the

kind, concerned look I'm used to, but more a look of annoyance.

Why is he being this way? It's not like I planned this. Does he think I *want* to feel this way? On the day I'm getting married?

"Get yourself together," he says in a curt tone. "It's a short ceremony. You can do this."

Candace appears, holding a small paper cup. "This is all I could find. It's from the drinking fountain."

I take the cup and gulp down the water. It tastes metallic and makes my stomach feel even queasier.

"Take this," I say, giving Candace the cup. "I need to sit down."

"Anna, you're fine," Ethan says. "Just take some deep breaths."

"Why don't you reschedule this for when she feels better?" Anthony says, sounding more concerned for me than Ethan does.

"She'll be okay," Rose says, rubbing my back. "It's just nerves."

"Can we do the ceremony sitting down?" Ethan asks Anthony.

"If that's what you want," he says.

"No, I'm fine," I say, holding onto Ethan's arm. "Let's just hurry up and do this."

Those aren't the words I should be saying before my wedding, especially after spending my life dreaming about this day. But the way I'm feeling, I just want it to be done so I'll stop feeling sick. I'm sure it's just nerves. I felt fine earlier. But why would I be nervous about marrying Ethan? I love him. I can't wait to start our life together.

The ceremony begins and by the time it's over, my stomach has calmed down, along with my heart. But my elegant white dress is damp with sweat, sending a chill through me. I need to get out of it.

"Congratulations!" Candace squeals as we leave the room. "You did it! You're married."

"Do you feel better now?" Rose says, rubbing my arm.

"I do, but I need to get out of this dress."

"You will," Ethan says to me, "as soon as we're done with the photos."

The photos. I almost forgot that Ethan hired a photographer to meet us at Central Park after the ceremony. It's a beautiful spring day and the flowers in the park are in full bloom. It's the perfect spot for our wedding photos, but I'm still not feeling great.

I look at Ethan. "I'd like to go to the hotel before the photos, just to rest for a few minutes."

"Anna, we don't have time. The photographer's waiting for us."

What is going on with him today? Ethan is usually caring and concerned when I'm ill, even when I only have a slight headache. But today he seems annoyed, and almost angry, that I'm feeling this way.

"Maybe you could rest in the limo," Candace offers.

"Yes, I guess I could," I say, thinking it'd feel good to lie down on the seat.

We leave city hall and I see the limo waiting for us. I feel a little better once I'm in the limo with the cool air blowing on me. Ethan puts his arm out behind me and I rest back against his chest. Rose and Candace are sitting across from us, chatting about some reality TV show they both watch. Candace is someone who can talk to anyone. Rose is the same way. I'm not like that, but I'd like to be. I'm hoping I can get a fresh start in our new neighborhood and make friends with some of the other women on our block.

"You two go ahead," Ethan says to Candace and Rose as

the limo pulls up next to the park. "We'll be there in a minute."

They get out of the limo, leaving Ethan and me alone.

"How are you feeling?" Ethan asks, running his hand up and down my arm.

"Better." I take a breath. "I don't know what happened. I felt fine when I was getting ready this morning."

He turns to me. "I'm sorry I got upset with you. I didn't mean to. I just didn't want us having to postpone the wedding. I've been looking forward to this day since we got engaged."

I smile at him. "Me too."

He cups the side of my face and looks into my eyes. "I love you, sweetheart. I'm so happy to finally be able to call you my wife." He leans down and kisses me and I feel relief wash over me as my dear, sweet Ethan returns. His harsh treatment of me at the wedding wasn't him. It was just his nerves reacting when he thought we might not get married today. But he's apologized and is back to being the Ethan I know and love.

"Do you need some more time?" he asks.

"Maybe another minute or two." I take a deep breath. "I haven't had a panic attack like that in years."

Ethan's brows draw together. "Are you saying this has happened before?"

I nod. "It started when I was a teenager. I went to a private prep school that was very competitive. The classes were extremely challenging. I could barely keep up. That's when the panic attacks began, usually before a big test or if I had to give a speech."

"Why didn't you ever tell me this?"

"Because it's not an issue anymore. Like I said, this hasn't happened in years."

"But it happened today."

"Yes, because I was nervous." I place my hand on his chest and smile at him. "I'm fine now. I promise."

Ethan doesn't smile back. "Is there anything else you haven't told me?"

"No. Of course not. We talk about everything."

"Except you having panic attacks. Do you have other mental health issues?"

"I have anxiety, but who doesn't?"

"Are you taking medication for it?"

"I was, but I'm not now. Well, unless I really need it, but I rarely do. Not anymore."

"Anna, how could you not tell me this?"

"Because like I said, it's no longer an issue. And honestly, you could be a little more understanding. You're acting like I'm damaged or crazy, and I really don't like it."

He sighs. "You're right. I'm sorry." He holds my hand. "It's just that you're my wife now, my whole life, and I worry about you."

"I know you do, but you don't need to. I'm fine. Now can we go enjoy our wedding day?"

"You know you can tell me anything," he says, rubbing his thumb over my hand. "I love you. I always will, no matter what."

I smile at him. "I love you too."

We kiss, then get out of the limo and meet Candace and Rose by the photographer.

I'm feeling much better, both physically and emotionally. I was concerned by the way Ethan was acting before the wedding, and again when I mentioned my anxiety and panic attacks, but we talked it out and everything's back to normal.

This is why I know Ethan and I will last. If something is bothering us, we talk it out. If we lash out at each other, we apologize. And most importantly, we trust each other. We don't keep secrets. Okay, maybe I have one or two, but it's nothing Ethan needs to know about.

6

"Good morning, Mrs. Halstrom," Ethan says, turning toward me in the bed and softly kissing my cheek.

"Good morning," I say, smiling as I gaze at my very handsome husband. It's really not fair that he looks this good first thing in the morning when I look like a mess, but I'm not complaining. I love waking up next to him.

We've been married for a week now and Ethan always wakes me up the same way, by calling me Mrs. Halstrom and giving me a kiss. I didn't take Ethan's last name, but he likes pretending I did so I don't correct him.

"It's Saturday," he says, tucking my hair behind my ear. "What would my lovely wife like to do today?"

"Hmm." I lay on my back, close my eyes, and stretch my arms above my head. "Staying in bed all day sounds appealing."

I hear him laugh. "You're insatiable, which is another thing I love about you."

My eyes open to look at him. "I'm not sure what you mean. I was just thinking we'd watch television."

"We haven't watched television once since we moved in." He kisses my neck as his hand moves under the sheet, over my bare skin.

Ethan and I took the week off from work and have spent most of it here, in our new king-sized bed that has a top-of-the-line mattress and the softest, most luxurious sheets money can buy. I've been wealthy for most of my life, but I never enjoyed the money as much as I do now. Buying things for the house, for my future life with Ethan, brings me more joy than I ever felt buying things just for myself. And what's even better is that Ethan doesn't care that I have more money than him. In fact, he's never even brought it up.

After we make love, Ethan insists on making me breakfast. Did I mention he's an excellent cook? The man's talents are endless. Some days I have to pinch myself to believe this is real and I'm not dreaming.

"What about Fiji?" Ethan says as we sit next to each other at the kitchen island, eating the ham and cheese omelets he made. I don't know how he gets the eggs so light and fluffy. It's like he whips air into them.

"Fiji?" I look at him. "What are you talking about?"

"For our honeymoon. You said you wanted to go to a place that was warm and tropical. We could stay at one of those little places that are right over the water."

"I thought we were going to wait and go on a honeymoon in the fall."

"I don't think we should wait." He smiles a little. "By the fall, it might not just be the two of us."

"What do you mean?"

"There's a good chance you'll be pregnant by then." He glances at my stomach. "Maybe you already are."

"I don't think so, but I suppose it's possible I could be by the fall. I wasn't thinking about that, but maybe you're right. Maybe we should plan the honeymoon for sometime next month."

"I could call my travel agent. Have her give us some options."

That's another thing I love about my husband. He doesn't expect me to do everything. When we moved in and there was a problem with the internet hookup, Ethan called and took care of it. When the garage door kept getting stuck, he had it fixed. And when we're out of something in the fridge, he runs to the store and picks it up.

He may not be like this forever. I'm sure after a while he'll slack off and we'll be like every other couple, arguing over who does what, but for now, I'm enjoying my perfect husband and perfect life. And hearing him talk about me being pregnant fills me with so much joy I can barely contain it.

Pushing my plate aside, I get up and tug apart the tie on my silk robe.

"I'm going to go take a shower," I say in my sexiest voice. "Perhaps you'd like to join me?"

Ethan slowly smiles as his gaze drops to my body. He gets up and yanks me into his arms. He kisses me, hard, as he rips off my robe. He turns me around, grabs my hips, and shoves me against the granite counter. He's never been this rough with me, but I like it. It shows his hunger for me, his raw desire. It's another thing about him I'm sure won't last, so I'm going to enjoy every second of it while I can.

In the afternoon, Ethan and I venture outside, strolling hand-in-hand down the sidewalk in our neighborhood. The houses are beautiful and every lawn is pristine, each blade of grass the exact same height.

"Hello!" someone yells.

I look to my right and see a woman in bright pink yoga pants and a fitted white tank top waving at us from the door of a large, two-story gray house with black shutters. She scurries down the narrow paved path leading from her house to the sidewalk where Ethan and I are standing.

"Are you the new neighbors?" the woman asks, smiling wide and showing off her bright white teeth.

"We are," Ethan says. "I'm Ethan, and this is my wife, Anna."

"Welcome!" She shakes our hands. "I'm Kelsie. I'm considered by some to be the unofficial welcome committee." She laughs. "I saw you two move in last week and was going to stop over but wasn't sure if you'd gone somewhere. I didn't see anyone coming or going and the drapes were closed."

Why was she watching our house like that? Ethan warned me that nosy neighbors were common in neighborhoods like this, but I didn't believe him. Growing up in the city, I'm used to everyone minding their own business, but living here, it sounds like I'll have to get used to people watching everything I do.

"We just got married," Ethan says, putting his arm around me. "We've been spending a lot of time at home."

"Oh, how adorable," Kelsie says, and I swear I hear a hint of jealousy. "My husband Mark and I were the same way after we got married." She twirls her long blond hair around her finger and laughs. "But three kids later and now we don't even have time to look at each other."

She has three kids? She's so tiny and skinny, I don't know how three kids could possibly come out of her.

"How old are your kids?" I ask.

"Paul is seven, Piper is five, and Poppy is three." She smiles at us. "Do you two have any children?"

"Not yet," Ethan says, smiling at me. "But we're working on it."

"You better get your name on a list now. The preschools around here are nearly impossible to get into. I signed up all three of my kids before I was even pregnant and still had trouble getting them a spot."

"Yes, I've heard they can be quite competitive," Ethan says. "It's the same for preschools in the city, at least the good ones."

How does Ethan know about preschools? We've never talked about it.

"So you two are from the city?" Kelsie asks.

"I was born and raised there," I say. "Ethan moved there after college."

"This will be quite a change for you," Kelsie says to me. "Are you sure you can handle it?" She laughs. "It's very quiet. No beeping trucks. No sirens going off."

"She'll be fine," Ethan says, answering for me.

"Do you have any plans for tonight?" Kelsie asks. "Because we're having a little neighborhood cookout at seven. I'd love to have you join us. It'd be a great way for you to meet some of the neighbors."

"Tonight's not good," I tell her. "Maybe some other time."

"Honey, are you sure?" Ethan says to me. "Like she said, it'd be a good way to meet the neighbors."

Why is he doing this? He's basically forcing me to say yes, knowing I don't want to go. We made plans to order takeout tonight and watch a movie in bed. I was looking forward to it.

"Sure," I say, plastering on a big, friendly smile. "We'll be there."

"Great!" Kelsie says, clapping her hands. "Oh, and you don't need to bring anything. Just show up here at seven." She waves and I notice her pink fingernails exactly match her pink pants. "See you then!"

As she heads back to her house, I glance at Ethan and notice his eyes following Kelsie. It's the first time I've seen him look at another woman, at least in the way he's looking at Kelsie.

"Like what you see?" I say, in a kidding tone.

Ethan's eyes snap back to me. "What do you mean?"

"Forget it." I take his hand. "Let's keep walking."

We're both silent as we continue down the street. When we reach the end, Ethan says, "Are you mad at me?"

"For what?"

"Agreeing to go tonight."

"Maybe a little."

He steps in front of me. "I didn't mean to speak for you. I just think it'd be good for you to meet the neighbors."

"*Me?* Why is it only good for *me* to meet the neighbors?"

"It's good for both of us, but you know how women are. They're more social than men. If you get to know these women, they'll invite you to things."

"What things?"

"Yoga. Book club. Whatever they're into."

"I don't do yoga, and I tried a book club and didn't like it."

Ethan puts his hand on my shoulder and leans down to me. "Didn't you just tell me you wanted a fresh start? That you wanted to meet people? Make some friends?"

"Yes," I say with a sigh. "But I don't see myself being friends with someone like Kelsie. She looks like a grown-up Barbie doll."

He laughs and takes my hand and we walk back down the sidewalk toward our house.

"You need to let go of that New York cynicism," Ethan says, "and be open to people who are friendly and don't wear black all the time."

"That's going to take awhile. I've been in New York my entire life."

"But you married a boy from Indiana, which shows you can adapt to people who aren't from the city."

"Yes, I know. I need to be more open-minded."

"Let's go get the car and find a store around here that sells wine."

"Because telling us not to bring anything is code for you better bring something or you'll be ostracized from the neighborhood."

"Exactly."

I laugh. "At least *that* isn't different than the city. No matter what the host says, never show up to a party empty-handed."

"Watch out!" a kid yells as a soccer ball flies toward us.

Ethan catches it, then walks over to the little boy who kicked it. He's probably around seven, with bright blond hair and big blue eyes.

"Here you go," Ethan says, handing him the ball. "I'm Ethan. I live in the house at the end of the street."

"Patrick's house," the boy says. "He was my friend, but he moved, so now we're not friends."

"Well, consider me a friend. And my wife, Anna." Ethan glances back at me on the sidewalk. "What's your name?" he asks the boy.

"Darren." He tosses the ball in the air and catches it. "Do you have any kids?"

"I'm afraid not, but we will eventually." Ethan musses his hair. "We'll see you later. Be careful with the ball. You don't want it going in the street."

Ethan walks back to me and we continue toward our house.

"You're very good with children," I say.

"I can't wait to have our own."

I love it when he says that. So many men I went out with in the past weren't ready to have children, even men who were pushing 40. I guess that makes sense since men can be fathers at any age, but as a woman, my time to become a mother is limited.

When Ethan made that comment about me already being

pregnant, I panicked a little, thinking I want more time with just Ethan and me. But thinking about it now, I'd be happy if I was pregnant. I'd still get almost a year with Ethan before the baby arrives.

Everything's coming together like I always dreamed. I have a husband who loves me. A beautiful house in the suburbs. We're planning for a baby.

Things couldn't be more perfect.

7

"Liz, come meet the new neighbors!" Kelsie says to a woman with shiny black hair styled in a sleek bob, wearing a sleeveless white dress and black sandals. Her skin is golden brown, like she just got back from a week of sunbathing somewhere tropical.

"This is Anna," Kelsie says as Liz walks up to us. "And her husband Ethan."

Liz's eyes shoot to Ethan and she smiles slightly. "It's nice to meet you," she says to him, ignoring me.

"The pleasure is all mine," he says, smiling back at her.

The way this woman is looking at my husband makes me want to slap her. He's mine. How dare she smile at him that way and pretend I'm not even here!

Ethan puts his arm around me, making Liz finally take notice of me.

She gives me an over-exaggerated smile that's clearly fake. "Welcome to the neighborhood."

"Thank you." I smile at Ethan. "We love it so far, although we haven't really left the bedroom since we moved in."

"They're newlyweds," Kelsie says with a girlish giggle.

Ethan clears his throat. "Actually, we've been doing some

renovations, starting with the bedroom. We've been painting this week."

Why is he lying? Is he embarrassed by what I said? I was just letting Liz know we're a loving couple that can't get enough of each other. What's wrong with that?

"So when did you get married?" Liz asks.

"A week ago," I say, wrapping my arm around Ethan's waist. "It was only a month after Ethan proposed, but we didn't want a long engagement. Ethan and I couldn't wait to get married."

"That's, um... unusual," Liz says, glancing at Kelsie.

"Would anyone like a drink?" Kelsie rushes to say, like she senses tension between Liz and me. I feel it too. I do not like Liz.

"I'd take a Manhattan," Ethan says.

"How appropriate," Kelsie says with a laugh. "They moved here from Manhattan," she explains to Liz.

"What do you do?" Liz asks Ethan.

"I'm a corporate attorney for Zentol. They're a—"

"Leading manufacturer of nutritional products for children."

Ethan's face lights up. "I'm impressed. Not many people know of them outside their brands."

"I used to work in marketing," Liz says. "We did a campaign for them a few years ago."

"What kind of products?" Kelsie asks Ethan. "Anything I might've tried?"

"We have a line of gummy vitamins." He rattles off the names, exciting Kelsie who claims to buy them all the time, saying how much her children love them.

I listen to them talk, feeling like I have nothing to say. This is why I don't like parties. I always feel awkward, which makes me nervous and stirs up my anxiety. I wish Ethan hadn't made us come here. I'm not ready for this. I know I said I wanted to make friends, but Liz and Kelsie aren't my type of friends. They make me very uncomfortable.

"Honey, would you like a drink?" Ethan asks me. I notice Kelsie staring at me, like she just asked me about a drink and I didn't answer. Liz is staring at me too.

"Oh, um, yes," I say. "I'll have a glass of wine."

"Red or white?" Kelsie asks.

"Red. A cab, if you have it."

She laughs. "Of course we have it. We have an entire wine cellar. Would you like to come pick something out?"

"Surprise me," I say, not wanting to leave Ethan's side. The patio is filling up with people and all the women keep looking at Ethan. What is wrong with them? They're married. They should be looking at their own husbands, not mine.

"Hi, I'm Jeremy," a guy says, going up to Ethan and shaking his hand. "Liz's husband."

"Unfortunately," she mutters.

He glances at her, then smiles at Ethan. "She's mad at me because I was late picking up our kid at soccer."

"Because he was golfing," she says, rolling her eyes. "His golf game was more important than our daughter."

"Gigi was fine," he says. "She didn't even notice I was late."

Hearing them argue is making me uncomfortable. Ethan and I will never be like that. We haven't argued once in the entire time we've been together. It's more proof that we're perfect for each other.

"How old is your daughter?" Ethan asks.

"Five," Jeremy says. "And we have a son. Gabe. He's three."

"Jeremy, this is Anna," Liz says. "Ethan's wife."

I'm surprised she introduced me, and even more surprised she remembered my name.

"Hey." Jeremy gives me a nod instead of shaking my hand, then looks back at Ethan. "You play golf?"

"I do. I'm looking forward to trying out the courses around here."

"Why don't we go tomorrow? I can get you in at the country club. Or did you already join?"

"No. I haven't been over there yet."

"You could fill out the form while we're there. You'll need a sponsor. I'd be happy to sponsor you, but we should probably play a round before I decide." He laughs. "I got a reputation to protect."

"Don't listen to him," Liz says, glaring at her husband. "He'll sponsor you."

"Yeah, I was just joking," Jeremy says. "I got a tee time tomorrow at eight. Does that work?"

"Eight is perfect," Ethan says. "I'm looking forward to it."

Why is he agreeing to this? Tomorrow is Sunday, our last day together before we return to our jobs. We were going to spend the morning in bed, then go out for a leisurely brunch. I was looking forward to it, and now it's not happening.

Kelsie returns with our drinks. A tall, muscular man with blond hair is beside her.

"This is my husband, Mark," she says, handing Ethan and me our drinks. She turns to her husband. "Honey, this is Ethan and Anna. They moved in last week."

"Good to meet you," Mark says, shaking our hands. "So you've been here a week? I'm surprised I haven't seen you before tonight."

"They haven't left the house," Kelsie says, smiling. "They just got married."

Mark nods. "Got it."

I feel Liz staring at me and when I look over at her, she says, "So do you work?"

"Yes. At Adore Fragrance."

"Oh, what fun!" Kelsie says. "I love that new one they just released! I can't remember the name."

"Be Her," I say.

"Yes! What a clever name. So what do you do there?"

Ethan answers. "Her father—"

"Used to work there too," I say, interrupting him. I don't want these people knowing I inherited my father's company and judging me for it.

"He actually started it," Ethan says.

I glare at him, anger rising up inside me. Why would he tell them that? Couldn't he figure out that I interrupted him because I didn't want them knowing this? I love Ethan, but sometimes I wonder if he's not as smart as I originally thought.

"So was it nepotism or did you actually have to work to get the job?" Liz says with a laugh, but she's not joking. That smile on her face is hiding something. Jealousy. Anger. Judgment. This is why I didn't want people knowing my father started Adorc.

"I began working there after my father died," I say. "I'm continuing his legacy."

"How kind of you," Liz says in a sarcastic tone.

"So does that mean you own the company?" Kelsie asks. "Or did it go to your mother?"

"My mother passed a few years ago. I inherited it after that."

"How fun to own a perfume company!" Kelsie says. "Oh! Sharon's here!" Kelsie waves at a woman walking toward us. She's short and curvy, with a tiny waist, full hips and very large breasts that are barely contained in her floral-patterned wrap dress. Her hair is strawberry-blond and styled in soft waves that end at her shoulders.

"What a gorgeous evening," Sharon says to Kelsie. "You always get the best weather for your parties."

Kelsie laughs. "What can I say? I have a gift for controlling the weather." She motions to Ethan and me. "These are our new neighbors. Ethan and Anna."

"Welcome to the neighborhood," she says. A tall, thin, bald man comes up beside her. "This is my husband, Kirk."

We all shake hands.

"What's your last name?" Kelsie asks me. "I forgot to even ask."

"Halstrom," Ethan answers at the same time I say 'Montgomery'.

Everyone laughs.

"Which one is it?" Liz asks. "Halstrom of Montgomery?"

"It's Halstrom," Ethan says. "Anna's maiden name is Montgomery. She just got confused for a moment."

What is he talking about? My last name is Montgomery. Ethan and I discussed this and we agreed I'd keep my name.

"We just learned that Anna owns the Adore Fragrance company," Kelsie tells Sharon. "I'm hoping that means we'll all be getting perfume for Christmas."

"I'll pass," Mark jokes.

Kelsie nudges him. "Hush." She looks up at him and he gives her a peck on the mouth. "Why don't you take the boys over to the bar so us girls can talk?"

No! Ethan can't leave me. He made me come to this party. He can't leave my side. He wouldn't, not when he can see that I clearly don't like these women and don't want to be left alone with them.

"I'll let you have some girl time," Ethan says, leaning down and dropping a kiss on my head.

He takes off with Mark, Kirk, and Jeremy, heading to the bar set up on the other end of the patio. How could he do this to me? He knows my anxiety acts up when I'm nervous, and these women definitely make me nervous.

"You have such a wonderful husband," Kelsie says to me. "He's so attentive. The way he looks at you, listens to you, puts his arm around you. Mark's never been like that, even when we were dating."

"And he's not bad to look at," Liz comments, glancing over at Ethan.

"Are you kidding? He's gorgeous," Kelsie gushes. "Anna, how did you get so lucky?"

Before I can answer, Liz says, "How did you meet him?"

"Through a mutual friend," I say, not wanting to tell her the real story. She doesn't need to know. I don't trust her. I don't want her knowing anything about me. Or Ethan.

"How long did you two go out?" she asks.

Why is she asking me all these questions? Why does she care?

"We dated for about a year," I lie.

"And then got engaged and married within a month?" Liz says. "Why the rush?"

"I already told you," I say, with a tight smile. "Ethan and I didn't want to wait to get married."

"I just find it odd that you'd be in such a hurry," Liz says. "I mean, how could you possibly plan a wedding that fast?"

"I'm sure she hired a wedding planner," Sharon says. "But it must've cost a fortune to find someone willing to put a wedding together that fast."

"Who did you use?" Kelsie asks me. "Was it that Delia woman? I can't remember her last name, but she's the best in Manhattan, or so I've heard."

Kelsie, Liz, and Sharon are all staring at me, waiting for me to tell them about my wedding. My heart's thumping hard and fast in my chest. I feel my face getting hot and sweat dampening the armpits of my blue cotton dress.

I want out of here. Now. But Ethan is in no hurry to leave. Looking over at the bar, I see him holding his drink, laughing at whatever one of the guys said.

"Anna?" Kelsie says. "Was it Delia? Is that who you used?"

"Yes," I blurt out. Then, before I can stop myself, lies tumble from my mouth. "She did a wonderful job. It was a very small wedding. Just a few family members and friends. At The Plaza Hotel."

Kelsie gasps. "I love The Plaza!"

"What kind of flowers?" Sharon asks.

"A mix of white gardenias and blush-colored roses," I say, the lies flowing easier now.

"Who was the caterer?" Liz asks.

"The hotel catered it," I say, finally telling the truth, or part of it. The wedding dinner *was* at a hotel and they *did* cater it. It just wasn't at The Plaza.

"Do you have pictures?" Kelsie asks. "I'd love to see them!"

"Maybe some other time," I say. "Why don't we talk about something else? I feel like all we're doing is talking about me." I turn to Liz. "You said you did marketing. So where do you work?"

"I don't." She stands up straighter. "Not since having children. They're my priority now."

"Same for Sharon and me," Kelsie says. "We all quit our jobs when we had children. I assume you'll do the same?"

"I haven't decided," I tell her.

The truth is, I'd always planned to stop working at Adore once I had children, but that was when I was single and dreaming of a life I didn't think I'd ever have. Now that I'm married and Ethan and I are trying to have children, I'm not sure sitting at home all day is what I want. What if I get bored? What if I miss the city?

"You really can't work and have kids," Kelsie says. "I know people say you can, but those people don't have a choice. They *have* to work. But for people who can afford it, staying home is the only option that makes sense. I mean, just think of all their activities. Driving them there, picking them up. That alone takes up half your day."

What activities? And why would I spend half my day driving to these activities? How many could there possibly be? When I was a child, I took ballet lessons, and then later, I took violin lessons. That was it, and my mother hired a driver to take me there.

"She'll see once she has children," Sharon says to Kelsie. "It's hard to remember how much free time I had before the twins were born." Sharon looks over at me. "Do you plan to start a family soon?"

"They've already started," Kelsie says, winking at me. "They spent all week in bed."

"According to Ethan, they were painting," Liz says.

"The answer is yes," I say to Sharon, ignoring Liz's comment. "We're hoping to have our first child this year."

"Ethan will be a wonderful father," Kelsie says, looking over at him. "Just look at him with Poppy."

My eyes go to my husband, who is holding a little girl with blond hair that's the same color as Kelsie's and Mark's. Ethan's lifting her in the air and twirling her around while she smiles and laughs.

"He's so good with her," Kelsie says. "Poppy is usually scared of strangers. She screams if they pick her up, but she seems to love Ethan."

Ethan sets her down and we all watch as Poppy runs over to Kelsie, stopping in front of her and holding up a lollipop.

"Mommy! Look what Ethan gave me! Can I have it?"

Kelsie takes the lollipop, reads the wrapper, and smiles. "Yes, you can have it." She pulls the wrapper off and hands it to Poppy. "But don't run with it in your mouth."

She nods and heads over to some little girls doing cartwheels on the grass.

"It's one of those vitamin C lollipops," Kelsie says to Sharon. "From the company where Ethan works. He's an attorney there."

"They make those new protein cookies for kids," Liz says. "I should ask Ethan where to buy them. I've searched the stores and can't find them anywhere."

They continue to talk about the protein cookies and vitamin lollipops while I stare at my husband, wondering why he brought children's lollipops with him to a party we assumed was for adults. He glances my way and mouths the words 'love you'.

"Aww, did you see that?" Kelsie says.

"See what?" Liz asks.

"Ethan just said I love you to Anna from across the patio. And the way he looked at her..." Kelsie sighs. "I wish Mark was romantic like that. Anna, you really do have the perfect husband."

"Yes." I force out a smile. "He's quite the catch."

But at the moment, I want to strangle him.

8

Just before midnight, Ethan and I leave the party and walk down to our house. I say nothing, wanting to wait until we're alone before I go off on him about his behavior tonight. I don't want to fight with him. I hate fighting and try to avoid it at all costs, but my temper is at a boiling point and if I don't say what's on my mind, I'm going to explode.

We go into the house and I shut the door. "Would you like to explain yourself?"

Ethan walks to the kitchen, acting as though he didn't hear me.

I follow him, stopping beside the granite counter where just this morning we made love. That feels like weeks ago now.

"Ethan," I say.

He opens the fridge. "Yes?"

"We need to talk."

He closes the fridge and turns to me. "About what?"

"The party tonight."

"What about it?"

"It was a disaster."

"I don't know what you mean. I thought it went quite well."

I walk up to him. "You lied to those people about us doing renovations. And you told them I own Adore, which you knew was something I didn't want them to know. Then you went off with the men, leaving me all alone. And what was with the lollipops? Who brings lollipops to a party?"

"Anna, you're not making any sense. Perhaps you had too much to drink. Let me get you some water." He takes a glass from the cupboard.

"I don't need water," I say, snatching the glass from him and slamming it on the counter. "What I need is for you to explain yourself."

"Regarding what, exactly?"

"What I just said!" I throw my hands up. "Why did you tell them my father started Adore?"

"Because he did."

"Yes, but telling them that makes them see me differently, like I don't really do anything and am just living off my father's success."

"Nobody thinks that. That's your own insecurities rising up. You made it clear that you work there."

"Yes, and then Liz accused me of nepotism."

"She was joking. She laughed when she said it."

"She was being sarcastic. She absolutely believes nepotism is what got me the job."

"Why do you care? You don't even know this woman."

It's no use trying to convince Ethan that what he did was wrong. He clearly doesn't see it as a problem, despite my anger.

"Are we done here?" he asks, going past me. "I'd like to get to bed so I'm up in time for my golf game."

"Oh, that's the other thing," I say, following him up the stairs. "Why did you agree to golf with Jeremy?"

"Why wouldn't I? We're new here. We need to get to know

our neighbors. And Jeremy seems like a nice guy. I could see us being friends."

We go into the bedroom.

"Are you kidding me?" I storm up behind Ethan as he goes into the walk-in closet. "The man barely acknowledged me when we were introduced. And his wife is horrible. I can't stand her."

Ethan turns to me. "I think you need some rest. Or maybe a warm bath would help you calm down. Would you like me to get the water going?"

"I don't want a bath. I want you to tell me why you didn't even talk to me before agreeing to go golfing with Jeremy?"

"Anna, I'm not a child. I don't need your permission to golf."

"Yes, but we had plans. We were going to spend the morning in bed, then go out for brunch."

"We can go to brunch next Sunday," he says, unbuttoning his shirt. "The country club Jeremy belongs to is very exclusive. My ability to become a member is dependent on having at least one current member putting my name in for consideration. And even then, it may not happen."

"Why do you want to join a country club? You said those places were pretentious and a waste of money."

"I never said that," he says, tossing his shirt in the hamper. "You must be thinking of someone else."

"No, you said it. I remember. It was on our second date. I told you my father belonged to a country club and never had time to use it, and then you made a comment about country clubs being pretentious and a waste of money."

"I don't recall ever saying that. I think a membership would be worth the money, especially if it will help get our child accepted into a good preschool." He takes his pants off and adds them to the hamper.

"We don't even have a child," I say, following him to the bathroom.

"We will soon, and I want our child to have the very best education." He picks up his electric toothbrush and takes the toothpaste from the drawer. "Mark said it's nearly impossible to get your child accepted into a proper preschool unless you know the right people. Joining the country club will give me access to those people."

It's clear I'm not going to change Ethan's mind on this topic so there's no use continuing this argument. Besides, he might be right. All the moms at the party kept telling me how hard it is to get your child accepted into the best preschool, so maybe having Ethan mingle with the right people at the country club would be beneficial.

"What about the lollipops?" I ask as Ethan brushes his teeth. "Why did you bring lollipops to the party?"

Ethan rinses his mouth and sets his toothbrush back on the charger. "Honestly, Anna, this is one of the most ridiculous conversations I've ever had." He turns to me. "What is wrong with you tonight? Are you going through some kind of hormonal changes?"

His comment infuriates me. "Just answer the damn question."

"Children like lollipops. I knew there would be children there and I was being nice. Bringing them a treat I knew their parents would approve of."

"We talked about the party before we left. I specifically asked you if you thought it'd be adults only and you said yes."

"I did not say that. Of course, there would be children there. It was a backyard cookout, not a wine tasting. And it's summer. The children don't have school. I knew it'd be a family event."

My head is hurting from Ethan denying things I know he said. Did he just forget he said them?

"I'm going to bed," he says, leaving the bathroom.

I walk behind him as he goes over to the bed and tosses the decorative pillows aside.

"Why did you tell people I'm changing my name?" I ask.

"Because you are."

"No. I'm not. I told you that. We agreed."

He turns to me, concern on his face. "Anna, what is going on?"

"You're lying to me. That's what's going on. And I don't like it. I don't like it one bit."

He steps closer to me. "You decided to change your name weeks ago. I told you you didn't have to, but you insisted."

I laugh. "Is this some kind of joke? Because I never said that. We agreed I wasn't changing my name."

He stares at me, looking even more concerned, then takes my hand.

"I'll show you," he says, pulling on me to go with him.

"Show me what?" I ask, as he leads me down the hall to the room we're using as an office. It's not quite done yet. There's a desk set up and a chair, but most of our files are still in boxes. "Over here."

Ethan brings me to the desk and picks up a large white envelope. He hands it to me. "Look inside."

I open the top flap and take out some sheets of paper. It's an application to change my last name. It's all filled out, and at the bottom, I've signed my name.

"I don't understand," I say, my heart pounding. "I didn't do this. I wouldn't have. I told you I didn't want to change my name."

"Anna, look at this." He points to my signature. "You signed it. You were about to send it in."

I shake my head. "That doesn't make sense. I wouldn't do that."

"But you did." He takes the papers from me and slides

them back into the envelope. He takes my hand. "Let's go to bed. I'm sure things will seem clearer in the morning."

I hope so, because nothing that happened tonight makes sense.

9

When I wake up Sunday morning, Ethan is gone. There's no sweet note telling me he loves me. No scent of coffee brewing. My robe isn't waiting for me at the end of the bed. Those were all things Ethan did when we were dating, when he'd spend the night at my place and have to leave early the next morning for work. I'd wake up to find he'd done all these sweet and thoughtful things. But we're married now and I suppose I can't expect him to continue doing those things forever, although just one of them would've been nice.

Throwing back the covers, I get out of bed and go into the bathroom. I'm taken aback by the mess Ethan made. There's shaving cream splattered on the mirror, his beard shavings in the sink, and his towel is on the floor. He's always cleaned up after himself. He doesn't like a mess. It's one of the many ways we're alike.

He probably overslept and didn't have time to clean up before he left. I pick up his towel from the floor and hang it on the rack. I'll clean the rest up later, or just leave it and make Ethan do it when he gets home.

After I'm done in the bathroom, I go to the closet and put on my robe, then leave the bedroom to go downstairs. I stop in the hallway and look down at the office, remembering that envelope Ethan showed me last night. The one with the paperwork to change my name. That didn't really happen. I must've dreamed it. But just to be sure, I walk down to the office and go over to the desk.

I let out a sigh of relief when I see there's no envelope sitting there. It was just a dream. But does that mean Ethan didn't actually tell people I'm changing my name? Was that also a dream?

My anxiety rises as I think about that, so I put it out of my head, leave the office, and make my way downstairs. Going into the kitchen, I get the coffee grounds from the cabinet and bring them over to the coffeemaker. It's after nine, but I'm still really groggy. Sleeping in all week has my body confused. It thinks I should still be in bed, cuddled up next to my husband. I wish that were the case. I really wanted one last day with him before we go back to our normal lives.

The doorbell rings, startling me so much that I spill the coffee grounds I was about to pour into the filter. Who would be ringing my door at this hour on a Sunday? It rings again, then I hear knocking.

"Yoo-hoo!" I hear Kelsie yell in her high-pitched voice. "Anyone home?"

"What does she want?" I mutter as I leave the kitchen. I stop halfway through the living room, thinking maybe she'll go away if I don't answer.

"Anna, I know you're in there," I hear her say. "Open up! I brought presents!"

Presents? For what?

I go to the front door and open it just a crack. Kelsie is standing there holding a white wicker basket with a pink-and-white plaid napkin covering the top, a huge smile on her heavily made-up face.

"Good morning!" she says, so loud it hurts my ears. "I brought breakfast!"

"Yes, um, thanks, but I'm really tired. I was just about to go back to bed."

"Don't be silly. It's after nine. Nobody sleeps this late." She turns to the side and uses her skinny elbow to push on the door.

I hold it in place. "Really, this isn't a good time."

"Ethan warned us you'd say that," Sharon says, appearing next to Kelsie.

Sharon's here too? Why? What are they doing here?

"Ethan said you're not a morning person," Liz says, coming up behind Sharon.

No. Not Liz too. I can't stand her, and I'm pretty sure she feels the same way about me.

"Did Ethan tell you to come over?" I ask Kelsie.

"Yes," she says with a dreamy sigh. "He's such a considerate man. He said he felt bad leaving you all alone while he plays golf so he asked if we'd stop over."

"Kirk would never even consider me," Sharon says with disgust. "The jerk doesn't even tell me goodbye when he leaves. I think he forgets I even live there."

"Jeremy's the same way," Liz says. "When he took off this morning, he left behind a trail of dirty socks, then I went down to the kitchen and found his sports drink spilled all over the counter." She rolls her eyes. "He's worse than our three-year-old."

"Can we come in?" Kelsie asks. "This basket is kind of heavy."

I want them to leave, but I feel like I can't turn them away. If I do, they'll tell everyone on the block how rude and unfriendly I was for not accepting their neighborly hospitality.

Opening the door all the way, I step aside to let them in. They immediately scan the room, assessing the drapes, the furniture, the trinkets on the shelves and tables. I'm glad I hired a decorator. The place would look terrible if I'd picked everything out.

"It looks so much different than when Jane and Ron lived here," Sharon says.

"They were kind of what you'd call pack rats," Kelsie says to me. She nods at the basket. "Where can I put this?"

"Anywhere in the kitchen is fine."

She hurries off to the kitchen.

"Are you a fan of Hopper?" Liz asks me. "Or does that belong to Ethan?"

"I'm not sure what you're referring to."

"Edward Hopper. The artist?" She points to the framed print above the sofa. Since I didn't pick it out, I didn't even notice who the artist was, and didn't care. I've never been that interested in art.

"Oh, yes, that's Ethan's."

She smiles. "He has good taste."

There she goes again, making comments about my husband that make me think she'd like him for herself. She better back off. He's mine, and I don't give up what's mine.

"Girls, come to the kitchen," Kelsie says in a tone that sounds like she's calling her kids to dinner. "I've got everything set up."

We meet her by the long, granite island where muffins, scones, and other pastries are displayed on trays. Next to them are pink paper plates with a scalloped edge and a stack of square white napkins.

"Are you gluten-free?" Kelsie asks.

"No, I eat gluten."

"Lucky you," she says, handing me a plate. "I blow up like a balloon if I have it. Same with dairy." She points to the muffins. "These are all gluten and dairy free. Oh, and nothing has nuts, if that's an issue."

"It's not," I tell her. "I can have nuts."

"My littlest, Gabe, has a horrible nut allergy," Liz says. "Just one bite and he goes into shock."

"We all keep epi-pens at the house just in case," Sharon says. "So many children these days have nut allergies, you have to be prepared."

Kelsie turns and looks up at the cupboards. "Where do you keep the coffee cups?"

"The one to the right of the sink," I say as I take a scone from the tray.

Liz and Sharon each take a muffin.

Kelsie finds a mug and sets it on the island next to an insulated white coffee carafe that must've been in the basket she brought.

"Coffee?" she says, picking up the carafe.

"I'd love some," I say, thinking I need that whole carafe to keep up with the energy of these three, especially Kelsie. It's like she's got caffeine running through her veins.

She pours the coffee into the mug. "It's light roast. Ethan said that's your favorite. With two creams, one sugar."

"Actually, I prefer dark roast," I say, "and no cream or sugar."

She looks at me, her nose crinkled. "Are you sure? Ethan was very specific when he told me how you like your coffee. He even told me twice so I'd remember."

She must've heard him wrong. Ethan knows how I like my coffee. When he used to spend the night at my place, he'd get up early and make it for me.

"Ethan doesn't always get things right," I say, but it's not true. He's a perfectionist and has a very good memory for details. He always gets things right. Unless he's purposely trying to get them wrong.

"Aren't the rest of you having coffee?" I ask as I pick up my mug.

"We don't drink coffee," Kelsie says.

"It messes with your hormones," Liz adds. "My homeopath got me off coffee when I was trying to conceive and I got pregnant a month later."

Kelsie sidles up next to me and says just above a whisper, "You really shouldn't drink it if you're trying to get pregnant."

"I'll take that into consideration," I say, before taking a big, long sip of my coffee.

The three of them stare at me, like I'm committing some horrible crime by the mere act of consuming coffee.

"Did you bring our drinks?" Sharon asks, reaching over to uncover the basket.

"Yes, sorry," Kelsie says. She takes out three bottles of green liquid and hands one to Sharon and one to Liz, keeping one for herself.

"What's that?" I ask.

"A plant-based energy drink," Kelsie says. "You can get it at the natural pharmacy in town. It has kind of a bitter taste, but it's really good for you. It's made with matcha and leafy greens."

"Matcha is tea, right?" I ask, remembering people at the office talking about it.

"It's a type of green tea," Liz says. "It gives you sustained energy. It's safer and more natural than coffee."

"Coffee's a plant," I point out. "I'd consider a plant to be natural."

"Not all plants are safe," she shoots back. "Some are toxic."

"Some teas are toxic," I say, glaring at her.

"Let's talk about something else," Kelsie says, smiling at Liz and me. "Anna, tell us about your job. Do you get to name the perfumes?"

"I weigh in on the names, but I don't make the final decision. Our research department does focus groups to decide what names resonate best with consumers."

“That’s so interesting,” Kelsie says. “Tell us more.”

“I’d rather not. I don’t like talking about work on the weekend.” I take a bite of my scone. “These are good. Did you make them?”

The three of them laugh.

“She doesn’t bake,” Liz says. “None of us do. We go to the bakery downtown.”

“Do you bake?” Sharon asks me.

“I’ve tried, but I’m not good at it.”

“Does Ethan like sweets?” Liz says. “Or is he careful about his diet?”

“He likes sweets. He doesn’t worry about his diet. He eats what he wants.”

“And still has a body like that?” Liz glances at Sharon. “He must have good genes.”

“You two will have gorgeous kids,” Sharon says to me.

“Speaking of kids,” I say. “Who’s watching yours?”

“April,” Kelsie says. “My nanny.”

“You have a nanny?” I ask. “I thought you stayed home with your kids.”

“I do, but not all the time. Moms need time off to go out with friends, get a massage, go out for drinks. You’ll see once you have children. You can’t be with them all the time.”

“We love our kids, but sometimes we need a break,” Liz says. “We all have a nanny.”

“What about your husbands?” I ask. “Don’t they watch the kids?”

“Almost never,” Sharon says. “They get distracted and forget to watch them. Like just last week, Braden and Brock, our twins, got into the flour while I was out shopping and I came home to a huge mess. Flour everywhere. I asked Kirk why he didn’t stop them and he said he was watching a baseball game and didn’t hear them.” She rolls her eyes.

"Jeremy's the same way," Liz says. "I'd never trust him to watch the kids."

"I'd trust Ethan to watch our kids," I say.

"Well, sure," Kelsie says. "He's perfect."

I used to think he was, but now I'm not sure that it's true. The perfect husband would've spent the day with me. He wouldn't tell the neighbors to come over on a Sunday morning without even letting me know. He wouldn't say I like my coffee with cream and sugar when he knows making it that way makes me gag.

That's not the perfect husband. Not even close.

10

"Where have you been?" I ask Ethan as he walks in the door.

It's nine at night. He's been gone all day and didn't even bother to call.

"Anna?" He drops his golf bag on the floor and searches for me in the dark room.

"Over here," I say from the couch.

"What the hell? You scared the shit out of me! Why are you sitting in the dark?" He fumbles with the lamp until he finds the chain that turns it on.

"Where were you?" I ask, glaring at him.

"We went out to eat after we played golf."

"You should've been done golfing at noon. It doesn't take nine hours to eat."

"So this is it?" He throws his hands in the air. "This is how it's going to be? I have to give you a rundown of everywhere I go? Everything I do? What are you... my mother?"

"I'm your wife, and I have a right to know where you are." I get up from the couch. "You could've at least texted me or returned my calls so I knew you were okay. I thought something happened to you. You know what that does to me? With my anxiety?"

"Then take a damn pill," he says, walking away.

"We're not done here!" I yell as he goes up the stairs.

I take a breath to calm myself. I don't want to fight. I don't want to be my parents. I hated it when they fought. It scared me. I said my marriage would never be like that, and here I am, fighting with my husband.

I go up to our room and find Ethan in the bathroom, showering.

"I was worried," I say, standing outside the shower. "Why didn't you reply to any of my texts?"

He doesn't answer. Maybe he didn't hear me with the water running.

Ethan's phone is on the bathroom counter. I pick it up, knowing I shouldn't snoop, but wanting to know if there's anything on there that will give me a clue about where he was all day.

I punch in his passcode. It doesn't work. I try it again. It still doesn't work. He must've changed it. But why? Is he hiding something from me?

The shower turns off and I quickly set the phone back where it was on the counter.

Where did Ethan go today? Was he really just hanging out with the guys? If so, why doesn't he just tell me that? And why did he lock me out of his phone?

I go into the bedroom and over to the bed. I toss the decorative pillows aside and get under the covers, waiting for Ethan to be done. I hear him brushing his teeth, then going into the closet. He comes out to the bedroom in his black boxer briefs, which is all he wears to bed. My body's aroused by the sight of him, but my mind is too angry to even consider being intimate with him.

"Kelsie, Liz, and Sharon came over this morning," I say as Ethan gets into bed.

"Just to visit?"

"Yes, and they brought breakfast."

"That was nice of them." He turns on his side, his back to me. "You shouldn't be so dismissive of them. They're making a real effort to be friends with you."

"I wasn't prepared for them to come over. I'd just gotten out of bed."

"Perhaps you should've gotten up earlier. You shouldn't still be in bed at nine."

Ethan and I slept way past nine every day last week, but I decide not to point that out.

"How did you know I got up at nine?" I ask.

"You said that's when they came over."

"No. I didn't."

"You did."

"Ethan, you knew the time because you told them to come over."

"And how would I do that? I didn't even see them this morning. I left here and went straight to the country club."

"They said you told them to come over."

"Then they lied. Or they're confused. Maybe one of their husbands told them to stop over."

"They said it was you."

Ethan turns on his back and sighs. "I'm not arguing about this. I've had a long day. I'm tired. And I need to get up at the crack of dawn now that we live out here. It'll take me almost an hour to get to the office." He turns away from me again, laying on his side.

"You *wanted* to live out here, and now you're complaining about it?"

"No, *you* wanted to live out here, and it's fine. I'll deal with it."

What is he talking about? He told me on our very first date that he was tired of the city and wanted to move to the suburbs. He rushed us into buying this house, saying he couldn't wait to get some peace and quiet and have a house with a yard.

I don't know what's going on with him, but I don't like it. And I don't want to keep fighting with him. I think it's the stress of the move making us this way. We're both adjusting to a new life in a new place. Once we're settled more and get into a routine, things will get better.

IN THE MORNING, I wake up to my alarm going off at six. Ethan's not in bed, but I can smell coffee brewing downstairs. I get up and go down to the kitchen. Ethan's already dressed in a suit and tie, looking very handsome. I've always loved seeing a man in a suit. My father had his suits custom made, even when the company was still young and struggling to survive. He wanted to dress as though the company was already a success. He knew it would be. He never doubted that.

Ethan's standing by the counter, looking at his phone. He hears me walk in and looks up, a smile sliding up his freshly shaved face.

"Good morning, sweetheart," he says, putting his phone away. He comes up to me, wrapping me in his arms. "How did you sleep?"

"Not well."

"I'm sorry." He looks into my eyes. "I need to apologize for yesterday. You were right. I shouldn't have been gone all day. I know you wanted us to spend the day together. I should've been here, with you, instead of out with the guys."

"I'd like to apologize too. I shouldn't have attacked you the minute you got home last night. I just missed you and was sad that we didn't get to spend our last day together before going back to our regular lives."

"Our regular life is this. Us. We're together now. Our lives aren't separate anymore."

"I know, but what I meant is... never mind. It doesn't matter. I'm just happy we're not fighting anymore."

He kisses me, then gazes at me, the way he did when we were dating, a look of love and adoration. Seeing that, and feeling his arms around me, I know in my heart that things will be okay between us. Yesterday was just a fluke. Perhaps spending a week together, not even leaving the house, was too much for us. Ethan needed some space, and I probably did too. I'm used to living alone, and so is Ethan. It's perfectly normal for us to need some time to ourselves and a break from each other.

"When I get home tonight," he says, "I'll take you to dinner and then we'll spend the rest of the night in bed. How does that sound?"

"Wonderful." I reach up and kiss him.

"I need to get to the office," he says, letting me go. "I made you some coffee. It's all ready for you."

"Thank you." I walk over to the coffeemaker and see a mug set in front of it. It's a large, white mug with 'remember I love you' written in red letters across the front. Ethan gave it to me a month after we started dating. He'd spent the night at my apartment and when I woke up, he was gone but left the mug out next to a freshly brewed pot of coffee.

I smile as I remember that day and how my heart fell even more in love with Ethan because of that sweet gesture. He was always doing things like that, proving what a great man he was, convincing me he'd be a great husband someday. Now that day has come and I need to appreciate him instead of finding fault with him. Despite what the neighbor women say, he's not perfect, but he's a good man, and he's mine.

As I pour my coffee, Ethan comes up behind me and leans

down to kiss my cheek. "Goodbye, sweetheart. Have a good day."

"You too." I take a sip of my coffee. "Is this dark roast?" I turn and see Ethan walking away.

He turns back. "Of course. That's the only kind you drink."

"Right," I say, thinking back to yesterday and what Kelsie said Ethan told her about my coffee preferences.

"See you tonight," Ethan says as he goes out the door.

Kelsie must've been lying yesterday, but that means Liz and Sharon lied too. They all made up a story about Ethan telling them to come over. Did they think that's the only way I'd let them stop by? If my husband told them to?

It's clear they desperately wanted to see the house, to see how it was decorated, so they could gossip about us. I'm sure Liz will tell people I have artwork hanging on my wall by an artist I've never heard of. Kelsie will probably tell people I showed up at the door wearing my robe at nine o'clock in the morning, a time at which she was already showered and dressed, makeup on, hair done, with time to spare to go to the local bakery and pick up pastries to bring over.

Now that I'm thinking about it, that's got to be what happened. Ethan never talked to them. They made that up, which is why they got my coffee preferences wrong. They lied to get into my house, to find out more about me, and about Ethan. I can't trust them. I was hoping I'd make new friends here, but it's clear that's not going to happen. I'll fake getting along with them, but they will never be friends.

11

When I arrive at Adore just before nine, Candace jumps up from her chair to greet me. "You're back!" She gives me a hug. "How's married life?"

"Great!" I say, as she follows me into my office. "I couldn't be happier."

"You *look* happy. You're practically glowing!" She races up to me as I go behind my desk and whispers, "Are you pregnant?"

"No," I say with a laugh. "It's just the glow of a new bride." I pause, noticing Candace looks different today. "Did you change something with your makeup?"

"Oh. Yeah." She turns her face side-to-side. "Do you like it? It's a new foundation. I also started using a new face cream at night. It's like a hundred dollars an ounce, but it's worth it. I've been using it for a week and my skin is so much better."

"A hundred dollars for an ounce?" I say, thinking that'd be nothing for me but a lot for Candace. I pay her well, but not *that* well.

"It was a gift from Tom." She goes around my desk and sits down on the chair across from it. "The money, not the face cream. I didn't tell him that's what I bought. He wouldn't understand. You know how men are. They have no idea what it costs for us to look good."

"Was the money an anniversary gift?"

"No, that's not until next month. Tom's crew got a bonus for finishing a job early so he gave me part of his bonus and told me to buy whatever I want."

Tom works construction. Candace has been dating him for almost a year. I've never met him, but she's shown me photos of him. He's tall and very muscular, the kind of man you'd imagine doing construction.

"That was nice of him," I say, sitting down at my desk. "Do you think you two will get married?"

She shrugs. "I don't know. Maybe. Neither one of us is ready for marriage so we haven't even talked about it." She leans toward me, her face lit up. "Tell me about the house. Do you love it?"

"Yes, it's beautiful. And the back yard is huge. I'm not sure what to do with it."

"You have a bunch of kids and send them out there to play."

"I suppose that's one option," I say, smiling as I picture that in my mind. Ethan and I want two children, a boy and a girl.

"Did you meet any of the neighbors?" Candace asks.

"Yes, and I can't say I like them."

"Why? Were they rude?"

"No, just the opposite. They were friendly to the point of making me uncomfortable."

"What do you mean?"

"These three women showed up at my door at nine in the morning yesterday without even asking if they could come over. They said Ethan told them they could, but he didn't. They just made that up."

"Really?" Candace scrunches up her nose. "That's kind of crazy."

"I know. I think they did it so they could see the house. They're the type of women who want to know everything about everyone. They're probably sitting around in their yoga pants right now, drinking their matcha tea and talking about me."

"So I guess you won't be making many friends there."

"I'm afraid not. But Ethan has. He went golfing with one of the neighbor guys, the husband of one of the women who came over yesterday."

"I thought you and Ethan were spending the week together, just the two of you."

"We did, but after almost a week of spending every second together, we needed some time apart, so Ethan went golfing and I did things around the house."

Thinking about it now, I feel silly for making such a big deal over Ethan needing a day to himself. We don't need to spend every second together. It's not healthy for either of us to have no outside interests or friends.

My office phone rings and I pick it up. "Hello, this is Anna."

"You're finally back," Edward says in his usual gruff tone. "About time."

"Yes, Edward, I'm back," I say, rolling my eyes, which makes Candace laugh. "Did you need something?"

"We need to discuss this new manufacturer you brought on. They messed up the packaging again."

"To what extent?"

"I sent you an email about it. Look it over, then come down to my office."

"Yes, fine. I'll be there as soon as I can." I end the call and wake up my laptop. "I need to deal with something," I tell Candace. "Maybe we can talk later, over lunch, if I have time."

"Yes, of course." She gets up. "Oh, I have some paperwork that needs your signature. It piled up while you were gone. Do you want to sign it now or later?"

"Let's do it now," I say, searching my laptop for the email from Edward. I find it as Candace goes out to her desk. The packaging issue Edward mentioned was minor and it's already been corrected. Edward always makes things seem like a crisis when they're not. I'll just call my contact at the manufacturing plant and request a refund for the damaged goods.

Dealing with our manufacturers really shouldn't be my job, but I do it because I enjoy it. When I was a young girl, my father would take me to the factory where our fragrances were bottled and packaged, then neatly put into boxes for shipping. I loved it. I was fascinated by the assembly line and the machinery involved to make sure just the right amount of fragrance ended up in each bottle. As I got older, I'd beg my father to take me to the factory, but by then the company had taken off and he didn't have time for me. My father all but disappeared from my life when I was five, the year Adore came out and made the company a success.

"Okay, here you go," Candace says, racing back to my desk with a stack of papers. "This first one is to approve the bonuses you gave to management before you left." I grab a pen and sign it, then look back at my laptop, noticing the hundreds of emails waiting to be read.

Candace takes another piece of paper from the stack and hands it to me. "This one is urgent. They can't get started until you sign off on it."

I quickly glance over the document, which is about our upcoming ad campaign, and sign my name.

Candace takes the paper from me and hands me another. "This one is for—"

"Just give me the whole stack."

She places it in front of me as Edward calls again.

I pick up the phone, cradling it between my neck and shoulder as I sign the stack of paperwork. “I need a few more minutes.”

“Hurry up! I’ve got a meeting at ten!” He slams the phone down.

I finish up with the paperwork and hand it back to Candace.

“I need to go deal with Edward,” I say, getting up from my desk.

I’ve been here less than an hour and I’m already exhausted. When I was home last week, I thought about quitting my job. It’s not like I need the money. But not being here feels wrong, like I’m betraying who I am. My father built this company and it became a success due to a perfume inspired by my mother. So even though the company ended up destroying our family, it’s part of us. Part of me. And I feel the need to protect it. I may have hated my father, but I still respect the work he did and the company he created.

Now he’s gone and Adore is mine. All mine. And after what I did to get it, I’m not just giving it up.

12

When I get to Edward's office, he's yelling at someone on the phone.

"I don't care if you don't have it!" He sees me and motions me to come into his office. "Get it done today or you're not getting paid!" He slams the phone down.

"What was that about?" I ask, sitting across from him.

"I've got a leak in my apartment and the damn plumber keeps giving me excuses for why he can't fix it. Now he's saying he can't find the part." Edward huffs. "Why are people so damn incompetent these days?"

"So about the packaging," I say, not wanting to hear him go on and on about how much worse things are now than when he was younger. It's one of his favorite topics. He could talk about it for hours.

"Forget the packaging," he says. "I trust you'll get our money back for the damaged goods?"

"Of course. I'll call as soon as we're done here."

"Good. Very good."

I've proven myself to Edward in regard to managing the manufacturers. He trusts me to handle any issues and even negotiate pricing. He knows I love that side of the business, which is why I'm good at it. When people ask me what I do here, they always assume it's something on the creative side, like helping create the fragrances or design the packaging. They assume that's what a woman would do and that manufacturing is for men. So I just let them think that. It's not worth my time to convince them their beliefs are sexist and outdated. And it's not as though I'm not involved in the creation of new products. I just find the manufacturing side of the business more interesting.

"If this isn't about the packaging," I say. "Then why did you want to meet?"

He reaches under his desk and picks up a square package wrapped in silver paper with a white bow on top. He sets it down in front of me.

"What's this?" I ask.

"Open it up and see."

"I mean, what's it for?"

"You got married, didn't you?" he asks in his deep, gravely voice.

I smile a little. "You got me a wedding gift?"

"Don't be getting all mushy about it. I kind of had to, given that... well, you know why." He leans back, folding his hands and resting them over his belt. "Go ahead and open it."

"What if someone sees?" I ask, glancing back at the door. It's closed, but his secretary could walk in.

"I'm the boss. I can give my employee a wedding gift."

His employee. I'm fine being that and nothing more. And so is he.

"You gonna open it?" he says. "Or sit here all day, staring at it?"

I put the box on my lap and yank the bow off, then tear off the paper. I open the box to find two crystal champagne flutes.

"They're beautiful," I say, holding up one of the glasses. "Thank you, Edward."

"It's not much, but I figured you and this man might have reason to celebrate from time to time and I know how much you love champagne. Now you'll have something to drink it in."

I already have champagne flutes that I inherited when my mother died, but it's nice to have new ones. Ones just for Ethan and me. The ones my mother had collected dust in her china cabinet because my father never celebrated anything. He didn't even like celebrating Christmas. I should get rid of those old champagne flutes. They hold nothing but sad memories.

"So how are you liking being married?" Edward asks, picking up a pen and tapping it on his desk. He gets very uncomfortable when talking about personal matters. Tapping the pen helps distract him from those uncomfortable feelings.

"It's good," I say. "Ethan is a wonderful husband."

"I'll have to meet him someday," Edward says, his eyes on the pen as it lightly taps his desk.

"Would you? Because I would like that. For you to meet him."

"I just told you I would. Weren't you listening?"

"Yes, I'm just surprised. I didn't think you'd want to."

Edward's eyes rise to mine. "You said he accepted the prenup. Meaning he had no objections?"

I gave Ethan the prenup soon after we were engaged. He didn't have an issue with it. He understood why I wanted it. I love Ethan and believe we'll be together forever, but I'm not stupid. I know things don't always work out.

"He was fine with it," I say. "He didn't even have any questions, but being a lawyer, he understands all the legal jargon."

"How much did you tell him?"

"About what?"

Edward's eyes narrow. "You know what."

"Why would I tell him? He doesn't need to know."

Edward's gaze goes back to the tapping pen. "So now what happens? Are you going to quit here and go become one of those suburban housewives?"

"I thought about it, but I think I'd be bored. And Adore is my second home. I can't imagine not being here."

"I assumed that's what you'd decide. You're like your father. This company is a part of you. It's in your blood."

"And yet he never wanted me to work here," I say, anger boiling up inside me.

"He was stubborn and set in his ways," Edward mutters.

"He was a sexist pig," I say with disgust. "Just say it. He's dead. It's not like he's going to hear you."

"Times were different back then. You know that."

"Adore isn't that old. When it was started, lots of women were working. Some of them were running companies."

Edward stops tapping the pen and looks at me. "I thought you were over this."

"I am. I just don't like you pretending Gerald was someone he wasn't. The man made money selling products to women and yet he didn't want women working here, including me."

"Let's not talk about the past. It clearly upsets you. This was supposed to be a celebratory meeting."

"Yes. I know. And I do appreciate the gift." I get up from the chair. "I should get back to work. I have a lot to do after being gone for a week."

"It's good to have you back," he says with a slight smile. He rarely smiles so I know he means it when he says he likes having me back.

As I head down to my office, Candace stops me as I pass by her desk. "I have another thing for you to sign. Another approval for the ad campaign."

"I'll just do it here. Where is it?"

She hands it to me and I quickly read it over. As I'm

signing my name, my mind goes back to that dream I had about changing my last name. It seemed so real, like it actually happened.

"Is something wrong?" Candace asks. "With the paperwork?"

"Oh, um, no." I hand it to her. "I was just thinking about this dream I had."

"About what?"

"Ethan told the neighbors I was changing my last name to Halstrom and when we got home I asked him why he said that when he knew it wasn't true. Then he took me into our home office and showed me the paperwork that I'd apparently filled out to change my name. The dream seemed so real that I checked the office the next morning for the envelope." I laugh a little. "It wasn't there."

Candace looks at me, not saying anything.

"Isn't that strange?" I ask.

She looks down, then back up at me with concern. "Are you feeling okay?"

"Yes, I feel great. Why?"

"It's just that, um..."

"What? What is it?"

"You had me print out the paperwork before you left. The paperwork to change your name."

I laugh. "What are you talking about? I never asked you to do that."

She looks at her computer and types something. "Come look at this."

Going around her desk, I look at her computer and see an email I sent to Candace asking her to print out the paperwork I'd need to change my last name. It was sent the Thursday before my wedding.

"I don't understand," I say. "Why would I do that? I never wanted to change my name."

"I know, which is why I was surprised when you asked me to do this."

"Did we talk about it?"

"Yeah. You said you love Ethan and wanted to take his last name."

"I don't remember saying that."

"What did you do with the paperwork? Did you ever fill it out?"

"No. I mean, I did in the dream but not in real life."

"Are you sure it was a dream?" she cautiously asks, like she doesn't want to imply I'm crazy and can't tell a dream from reality, but I get the feeling that's what she's thinking.

"The envelope with the paperwork wasn't there," I tell her. "I checked the office and it wasn't there."

"Maybe Ethan mailed it for you."

"On a Sunday?"

She shrugs. "I don't know. Maybe. I'm just trying to make sense of this."

"Yeah, me too." I take a breath. "I'll be in my office."

"Can I get you anything? Water? Tea?"

"No, I just need some time to think."

"Okay, well, I'm here if you need me."

I go into my office and shut the door. I get out my phone and call Ethan.

"Hi, honey," he answers. "This is a surprise."

He says that because I don't usually call him when he's at work.

"I just wanted to ask you something."

"Go ahead."

"Do you remember seeing any paperwork at the house for changing my name?"

"It was in the office. I mailed it for you. Sorry, I should've told you. Were you looking for it?"

"Um, yes. But I don't remember filling it out."

"You filled it out last week, but didn't get around to mailing it since we spent all week in bed." He lowers his voice. "I wish we were still there. I miss you. Tonight when we get home—"

"Yeah, we can talk about that later. So you said you already mailed the paperwork?"

"On Sunday, when I was out. I added some postage and dropped it in a mailbox. I thought I was helping you out. Did I do something wrong?"

"Um, no. I just wish you'd told me before you did that."

"Sorry. I didn't even think to check with you first. I really thought I was doing the right thing, taking care of an errand."

"Yeah, okay," I say, my stomach knotting up. "I'll let you go."

"I love you, honey."

"I love you too."

"I'll see you tonight."

"Yeah. Bye."

It wasn't a dream. It was real. But why did I do it? I never once considered changing my name. I'm Anna Montgomery. That's how everyone knows me. I've established myself with that name. It's who I am.

So why did I do it? Why did I fill out paperwork to change my name?

13

It's Friday and I'm looking forward to the weekend. Getting caught up at work last week took a lot out of me, but not enough that I didn't have time for Ethan. Every night, we'd get home, drive into town for dinner, then come back to the house and make love, christening every room.

Ethan's been so wonderful this week. He's back to how he was when we were dating. Every morning, he makes me coffee and leaves love notes on my nightstand so I'll see them when I wake up. This weekend he was invited to play golf again with Jeremy, but he turned him down, telling him we had plans.

We don't really have plans, other than to spend time together, but I'm pleased Ethan chose me over golf. Tomorrow morning, Ethan's taking me for brunch since we didn't get to go last Sunday. After that, we'll do some grocery shopping, then pick up our clothes at the dry cleaner. The day's events won't be very exciting, but doing those mundane things with Ethan makes me feel like we're a regular married couple doing regular things.

My parents never had that. My father was always at work while my mother waited for him to come home. My father didn't want my mother doing chores or running errands because he didn't want people thinking he didn't have the money to hire those things out. My father was very concerned about what people thought of him. So my mother hired people to do everything, except the cooking. She loved to cook, and since nobody saw who was making our meals, my father allowed her to do it herself rather than hire it out.

As I go into the house at six, I find that Ethan's already home. He usually gets home after me.

"You're home early," I say, going up to him.

"I was done with meetings at four so I left." He gives me a kiss. "How was your day?"

"Long. I'm looking forward to a relaxing weekend." I smile at him. "Maybe we could get some champagne and try out the glasses Edward gave us."

"It's already chilling in the fridge. Should we open it now or later?"

"Later. But thank you for getting it. You must've read my mind. I was thinking on the train ride home how much I'd love a glass of champagne."

"Where would you like to go to dinner tonight?"

"The Italian place. We keep saying we should try it."

"Sounds perfect. Why don't you go upstairs and change?"

Ethan's already changed out of his suit and has on dark gray pants and a light blue polo shirt. He rarely wears jeans. He doesn't like the feel of denim.

As I'm going up to our room, I hear Ethan's phone ring. I hope it's not his office calling. Since I met him, he's never gone into the office on weekends. He said he's had to in the past, but it doesn't happen very often.

I take my work clothes off and put on a red-and-white floral sundress. It's June now and the weather has become warm and humid. I'm most comfortable wearing lightweight dresses in this type of weather and Ethan seems to like them, given how he looks at me when I wear them and how quickly he takes them off when we get home.

Coming back downstairs, I see Ethan sitting on the couch, looking at his phone.

"I'm ready," I tell him.

He gets up, smiling when he sees me in the dress. "You look beautiful, as always."

"Thank you." I walk over to him in a slow, sexy way. "I thought you'd like it."

He puts his hands on my waist and leans down to kiss the side of my neck. "You smell wonderful. Is that the new fragrance?"

"Yes. It's not out yet, but it tested very well. I think it'll be a huge success."

"I'm sure it will be." He smiles at me. "You ready to go?"

"Yes, I'm starving, and pasta sounds delicious." I go to the chair to pick up my purse.

"About that. Change of plans."

I turn to Ethan. "What do you mean?"

"Jeremy called. He wants us to meet them at the country club for dinner."

"And you agreed to it?" I ask, my heart beating faster. "Without talking to me?"

"I assumed you'd want to go. The restaurant there is quite good. I ate there last week. Their chef has won many awards."

I walk up to Ethan. "We agreed this weekend would just be the two of us."

"And it will be. But today is Friday, which is technically not the weekend." He puts his hand on my shoulder. "Why are you getting worked up about this? We haven't seen the neighbors all week. They're going to think we're avoiding them."

"I don't care what they think. And you know I don't like Liz. The last thing I want is to spend Friday night having dinner with her."

"You need to give her another chance. I'm not saying you have to be best friends with her, but you could at least be cordial."

"*Me?* What about *her*? She's the one who needs to be cordial."

"Well, if it helps, Kelsie and Mark will be there too. You like Kelsie, right?"

"She's better than Liz, but I still don't want to do this."

"It's one dinner. We're not spending the weekend with them. And part of living in the suburbs involves getting to know your neighbors."

"I suppose," I say with a sigh.

He gives me a peck on the lips. "Let's go. And when we get home, it'll just be the two of us for the entire weekend."

"You promise? You're not going to let Jeremy talk you into another golf game, are you?"

"I already told him no." Ethan walks to the counter to get his keys. "Everyone's already there. We need to go."

As we're driving to the country club, I remember something I should've told Ethan.

"If anyone asks how long we dated," I say, "tell them it was a year."

He glances at me. "A year? We met last March."

"Yes, but I told Kelsie, Liz, and Sharon that we dated for a year."

"Why did you lie?"

"Because Liz is very judgmental and I didn't want her knowing we only dated for three months and then having her tell me that's not long enough to know someone and that our marriage won't last."

"Didn't you just tell me you don't care what people think?"

"Yes, but she kept firing questions at me at Kelsie's party and I just blurted it out. I know I should've just told them the truth, but I didn't, so now I need you to go along with this. I doubt anyone will ask, but just in case."

"Are there any other lies you told about us that I should be aware of?" he says, in a condescending tone.

"Don't act like that."

"Like what?"

"Like you're better than me." I look at him. "It's not like you haven't lied to them."

"I haven't."

"You have. More than once."

"What did I lie about?"

I take a moment to think, but can't come up with anything. I was going to bring up when he told the neighbors I was changing my name, but that turned out to be true. I still don't remember deciding to do that, but I clearly did.

"Can't come up with anything?" Ethan asks, a smug grin on his facc.

I know he lied about something. Why can't I remember what he said?

"It doesn't matter," I say. "The point is, I told them we dated for a year so we need to stick with that story."

We get to the country club and find Matt waiting for us outside the entrance doors. Since we're not yet members, he has to escort us inside.

"Good to see you two again," he says, a big grin on his face. I'm not sure what I think of Matt yet, but I definitely like him better than Jeremy.

"Thanks for inviting us," Ethan says.

"Come inside. We just ordered some drinks."

The restaurant is much fancier than I imagined. I feel like I should've worn a nicer dress.

Kelsie jumps up from the table when she sees me. "I'm so glad you could make it!" She gives me a quick hug, then steps back to look at me. "That dress is adorable! I love the print."

"Thanks," I say, glancing over at Liz. "Hi, Liz."

"Hello, Anna," she says with a smirk. Ethan would say it's a smile, but I'd definitely call it a smirk. He doesn't see her like I do, probably because she's always disgustingly sweet to him and constantly complimenting him.

Ethan and I sit down at the large, round table. A waiter stops by to take our drink order. I get a martini instead of my usual wine, deciding I need hard liquor to make it through this dinner.

An hour passes before we finally order our food. I was hoping we'd be done with dinner by now, but Mark said he's taking advantage of a night without the kids, meaning he plans to drag this dinner out for hours.

"How's life for the newlyweds?" Mark asks, before finishing off his Manhattan. He's on his third one.

"Wonderful," Ethan says, putting his arm around me.

"I still find it surprising you got married so soon after getting engaged," Liz says. "I made Jeremy wait two years."

"It was almost two for us," Kelsie says, glancing at Mark.

Ethan smiles at me. "I didn't want to wait. I knew I wanted to marry Anna soon after we met. And three and a half months later, here we are."

I look at Ethan, wondering if he realizes what he said. We just talked about this in the car. Did he have some kind of memory lapse?

"Wait," Liz says. "Are you saying you only dated for three months?"

This is Ethan's chance to correct himself and tell them he got confused and misspoke.

"Three months is all I needed to know she was the one," Ethan says.

"Anna said you two dated for a year," Liz says.

"No, I didn't," I say, deciding I have no choice but to deny ever telling her that. "I said it was three months."

Kelsie shakes her head. "No, you definitely said a year. I was there when you said it. It was at my party. We all heard you say a year."

"You must've misheard me." I pick up my martini and gulp it down.

Liz and Kelsie exchange glances. I'm sure they'll talk about this later, saying I lied to them, but I don't care. I already know they don't like me.

The waiter stops by our table. "Would anyone like another drink?"

"Yes, please," I say, holding up my martini glass.

"Nothing for me," Ethan says.

Nobody else at the table orders another drink, not even Mark, making me feel like a drunk for getting another martini. It's only my third, and I'm not driving, so I don't know why everyone's looking at me like I was wrong to order another drink.

At ten o'clock, we're done with dinner and the bill's been paid, but we're all still sitting at the table. The men are talking about golf and Liz and Kelsie are discussing their kids, trying to decide who should host the next play date. I'm beyond bored and desperate to go home. I keep nudging Ethan's leg under the table as a sign that I want to leave, but he keeps talking, like he's in no hurry to get out of here.

When there's a break in the men's conversation, I turn to Ethan. "We should get going. It's getting late."

"Yeah, let's get out of here," Jeremy says, and for the first time, I actually like him, but only because he agreed that we should leave. "We'll meet up at the house for drinks."

"Sounds good," Ethan says.

Wait—what? We're not going to Jeremy's house for drinks. I've had enough of these people. I can't take another second of them.

"Maybe some other time," I say to Jeremy. "Ethan and I have a busy day tomorrow. We need to get home."

Ethan looks at me, laughing a little. "We don't have a busy day. We're just running some errands. C'mon, honey. It's only ten. We can go over there for an hour or two."

Everyone's staring at me, waiting for me to agree to this, like there's something wrong with me if I don't.

"Um, sure, I guess we could go," I say, faking a smile.

"Great!" Jeremy nudges Liz. "Text the nanny. Tell her we're heading home."

She gets her phone out as Ethan takes his out and checks it. They're both discreet about it since the restaurant asks that phones be put away and the ringer silenced while in the dining room.

"What's this about?" Ethan asks.

"What?"

He turns his phone so I can see it. "I have three missed calls from the same number."

"It's probably scammers."

"I have two voicemails too." He puts the phone to his ear and listens to the voicemails, his expression growing grim.

"What's going on?"

He listens a second more, then says, "My mother's in the hospital. She fell down some stairs and a neighbor found her on the floor."

"Oh my God, is she okay?" Kelsie asks, before I can.

"I don't know," Ethan says. "The nurse at the hospital left me a couple voicemails, but wasn't clear about my mother's condition." He gets up, so I do as well. "I'm sorry, but we'll have to cut the evening short."

"Does your mother live around here?" Liz asks.

"No, she's in New Jersey," Ethan says. "We'll have to drive there tonight."

"Do you need us to do anything while you're gone?" Matt asks. "Check on the house? Get the mail?"

"I'll see how she's doing and let you know," Ethan says.

"We're happy to help," Liz says. "Whatever you need."

"Thank you." Ethan looks at her, then at everyone at the table. "You're all so kind. We're fortunate to have such good neighbors."

"We should go," I say to Ethan.

We finally leave and Ethan speeds all the way home. I almost tell him to slow down but decide not to, thinking he probably wouldn't listen. He's terribly worried about his mother and desperate to get to her.

"Are we leaving now?" I ask when we get home.

"As soon as we're done packing. Go upstairs and get started. I'm going to try to reach someone at the hospital."

I race upstairs to pack a bag. I hope Rose is okay. She's such a sweet lady, and the only family Ethan has left.

Spending our time at a hospital in New Jersey won't be the romantic weekend we were planning on, but it'll be good for our marriage. Ethan will see what a kind and supportive wife I am. It'll bring us closer, and make him love me even more.

14

"Mother, you need to rest," Ethan says to Rose as she turns on the TV in her hospital room.

"I can rest and watch the Wheel," she says. "I've never missed an episode."

Ethan quietly sighs while I stifle a laugh. Watching those two together the past couple days has been quite entertaining. They're different and yet the same. Perhaps that doesn't make sense, but it's the best way I know to describe them.

"Have you ever watched this?" I ask Ethan, referring to the game show.

"Yes." He glances at the TV. "Unfortunately."

"We used to watch it during dinner," Rose says. "It's the reason my son is such a good speller."

"That's not the reason," he mutters.

"I didn't watch this until college," I say, walking up to Rose's bed. "My parents didn't let me watch much TV growing up, so when I got to college I watched everything I could."

"What about now?" she asks, her eyes on the TV.

"Now I don't have much time for TV, and since Ethan doesn't really like it, we rarely have it on."

The nurse comes into the room, going up to Rose. "Time for your meds."

Rose holds out her hand for the pills. "World's largest lake."

"What are you talking about?" Ethan says to Rose.

"The answer to the puzzle." She pops the pills in her mouth and swallows them down with some water.

"What's the world's largest lake?" I ask Ethan. "Do you know?"

"The Caspian Sea."

"That's not a lake."

"It is. Look it up."

I get out my phone and sure enough, he's right.

The nurse goes up to Ethan. "Are you still planning to leave tomorrow?"

"We haven't decided. Why do you ask?"

She glances at Rose, then back at Ethan. "Let's go out in the hall."

He follows her out there and comes back a few minutes later. He walks over to his mother. "Anna and I are going to go to the cafeteria and get something to eat. Do you need anything?"

"No." She shoos him away. "Go. I can't hear my show."

Ethan comes over to me and takes my hand, leading me out of the room.

"What's going on?" I ask as we walk to the elevator.

"I spoke with the doctor. He'd like to release her tomorrow but said she can't go home alone. He's worried she'll fall again and hurt herself even more."

"So we're staying here?" I ask, as we get on the elevator.

"We can't. I have a big meeting next week at work with all the executives. I can't miss it."

We get off the elevator on the main floor and head to the cafeteria.

"Could we hire someone to care for her?" I ask.

"We could, but I'd rather not. If I'm not here to check that she's getting the proper care, all I'll do is worry. Do you know how many lawsuits involve abuse by home health care workers?"

"No."

"It happens more than you think. Even if I did trust someone to care for her, it wouldn't work for her to be at home. Her balance isn't good enough to use crutches so she'll have to be in a wheelchair. Her house is far too small for a wheelchair to fit. She wouldn't be able to get around."

"So what do you want to do?"

He pulls me over to a bench outside the cafeteria and we sit down.

"I know this is a lot to ask," he says. "But would you consider letting her stay with us?"

"Yes, of course," I tell him, knowing I really can't say no. She's his mother and she needs his help. And it wouldn't be forever. Just until her leg heals.

When Rose fell, she bruised her knee and fractured her ankle, but it's a small fracture that the doctor said would heal quickly. Luckily, Rose only fell down a few steps, not the entire staircase, making her injuries less serious than they could've been. Ethan said her walking has been getting more unstable the past couple years. I didn't notice that when I met her, but I also wasn't looking for it.

"You're really okay with this?" Ethan asks.

"She's your mother. Of course I'm okay with it."

He hugs me. "Thank you. This means the world to me."

"So are you going to stay home with her?"

He pulls back. "I can't. I just told you, I have that big meeting."

"But that's just one day. What about the rest of the week?"

"I'll need time to prepare for the meeting, and when it's over, I'll need to take action on whatever they decide to do."

"So what are you saying? That you want *me* to stay home with her?"

"It's our only option. And besides, you own the company. It's not like you'll get fired for not showing up."

"But people count on me to be there."

"I'm sure someone else could do your job."

I feel my anger rising, but try to remain calm. "Do you even know what I do there?"

"Of course I do."

"I don't think so, because if you did, you'd know I'm the only one who can do my job. Like signing off on things. A lot of projects need my approval before they can move forward."

"You can still work. Just do it remotely. Mother doesn't need constant care. She'll only need assistance in getting around and maybe some help getting dressed."

"How long would I need to be home with her?"

"Until she's well enough to live on her own again."

"Meaning what? A few weeks?"

"It could be a month. Maybe two. It'll depend on how she's healing."

"Two months? Ethan, that's the whole summer."

"Honey, I know I'm asking a lot here. I'm sorry to have to put you in this situation. It's not what I wanted."

I shouldn't argue with Ethan about this. He's worried about his mother and he's asking me to help out. And given that I wasn't able to help my own mother, I need to do this.

"It's fine. I understand. I'll stay home."

"I'm so lucky to have you," he says. "You're a wonderful wife."

I smile at him. "I'd like to think so."

He laughs and stands up. "Would you like something to eat?"

"I would, but not here. The cafeteria food is horrible."

"Visiting hours end soon. Let's go tell Mother we're taking her home tomorrow, then go find a place for dinner."

We're taking Rose home with us. To our house. Where we've only lived for a couple weeks. My dream of spending time with my new husband, just the two of us, isn't going to happen, or at least not anytime soon. It sounds like Rose will be with us for most of the summer. Ethan and I talked about spending the next few months going to the beach, taking weekend trips to Vermont and New Hampshire, staying in cute B&Bs. But none of that will happen now.

"Mother, we have good news to share," Ethan says when we go back to her room.

"In a minute. It's the final puzzle."

Ethan puts his arm around me and whispers in my ear, "Sorry. She can be a handful. It's not too late to back out."

"It's fine," I whisper back.

"You're amazing." He kisses the top of my head. "I love you."

"Be careful what you wish for," Rose says.

"What was that?" Ethan asks.

"The puzzle." She points to the TV. "That idiot couldn't guess it. I'm twice his age and got it right away."

"You're very smart, Mother," Ethan says.

"Damn straight." She taps her head. "I may be old, but my mind's sharp as a tack."

Ethan takes my hand and walks us over to her bed. "Mother, we need to talk."

She finally looks away from the TV. "What is it?" She narrows her eyes at him. "You're not putting me in a home, are you?"

"No, but I spoke with the doctor and he doesn't want you living on your own while you're recovering. So Anna and I decided to take you home with us."

"To Connecticut? But my home is here. In New Jersey. I

have friends. A house."

"Yes, and you'll come back to all that when you're better. But for now, you'll be living with us."

"It's a beautiful house," I say, trying to sell her on the idea, even though I'm still not sold on it myself. "And a very nice neighborhood."

"We've met some of the neighbors," Ethan adds. "They're very kind. They've been extremely welcoming to us since we moved in."

More like nosy, wanting to know everything about us. I don't trust the neighbors, not a single one of them. They're the type of people who pretend to be your friend but would turn on you in an instant.

"What do you think?" Ethan asks Rose.

"Sounds like I don't have a choice," she grumbles.

Ethan laughs a little. "You'll love it. I promise. And this will be a chance for you and Anna to get to know each other better. She'll be the one staying home with you and caring for you while I'm at work."

"You quit your job?" Rose asks me.

"No, I'll just be working from home while you're staying with us."

"We've got it all worked out, Mother," Ethan says. "Don't you worry about a thing. Anna will take good care of you."

But I don't want to take care of her. I have a job. A new husband. New house. And plans for the summer, ones that didn't involve Ethan's mother.

It's only for a couple months, maybe not even that. And I'm doing this for Ethan, the man I love, and for myself. Maybe caring for Rose will help relieve my guilt for not caring for my mother during the final part of her life.

I can do this. It's just for a short time. And Rose is my family now. She has her quirks, but overall, she's a sweet, little old lady. I'm sure we'll get along great.

15

"What do you mean you're not coming back?" Edward barks at me over the phone when I tell him about Rose.

"I'm coming back, just not for a few weeks," I say, knowing it'll probably be longer, but Edward doesn't need to know that. I'll give him that news later, when I have a better idea of how long Rose will be staying with us.

We arrived back in Connecticut last night. Rose got settled in the guest room and fell asleep right away, which gave Ethan and me time to move things around in the house to make it as fall-proof as possible. Fortunately, the guest room is on the main level. I wanted that room to be the office, but Ethan insisted it be the guest room, saying he didn't want guests staying on the same floor as our bedroom. I went along with his request, and now I'm thankful I did because there's no way I could lift Rose up the stairs. Even if she held onto the railing and I only had to support part of her weight, I couldn't do it. She's at least fifty pounds heavier than me.

"I'll still get my work done," I assure Edward. "I'll just be doing it from home. Candace is setting everything up so I can work remotely."

"And why again are you doing this?"

I've already told him, but I explain it again, emphasizing that it's only temporary and that I'll be back as soon as Rose is able to live on her own.

"Why isn't her son taking care of her?" Edward asks.

"He has a lot going on at work right now. They expect him to be there."

"And I expect you to be here. Why don't you hire one of those home nurses to take care of her?"

"Ethan doesn't trust them. He's read too many court cases where home care workers abused their patients. Edward, please, don't make this difficult for me. I need to do this. I wasn't there for Mom and I always regretted it."

"Your mother was too far gone," he says in a somber tone. "You wouldn't have been able to care for her. Even the care center had to restrain her."

I don't like thinking about that. Imagining my mother strapped to a bed pains my heart. When a nurse called to tell me my mother was about to die and I needed to hurry and get there, I requested they take off the restraints. I didn't want to see her that way, and by then she was too weak to hurt anyone, or herself.

"Still, this is a chance for me to do the right thing," I say. "Rose is my family now. The least I can do is help her while she recovers."

"Fine," he says with a huff. "But I expect you to check in with me weekly, or more than that if need be."

"Yes. Of course."

"You're a good girl, Anna," Edward says. "Not many people would do something like this. Good luck to you, kid. We'll talk soon."

He ends the call just as I hear Rose calling for me.

"I'm coming!" I say, going to her room.

She's sitting on the side of the bed, reaching for her walker.

"Rose, don't!" I race over to her. "You're not supposed to get up."

"I can't stay in bed all day. I'll get bedsores. You know what those are?"

"Yes," I say, remembering my mother had them. "But you've only been in bed a few days. I doubt you have bedsores."

"Even so, I can't stay in this room. You've got nothing to look at in here. Would it hurt you to hang some pictures? And I need a TV. I can't be in here without a TV."

"I talked to Ethan about the TV. He'll go shopping after work and get you one."

"I can't wait that long. I'll miss my programs."

"You can watch the TV in the living room."

"Then hurry up and help me out of this bed. My program starts in a few minutes."

I go over and get her wheelchair. The doctor said she's not ready to use the walker, but to try it in a couple weeks, when her ankle has had more time to heal.

Once I've got Rose set up in the living room, the TV on and turned to her favorite program, I go to the kitchen where my laptop is set up. I already missed a meeting this morning and am about to miss another if I don't hurry up.

"Anna!" Rose yells.

"Yes? What do you need?"

"You didn't give me my blood pressure pills!"

She's right. I forgot. I'm starting to get an idea of what it'd be like to have children. Rose is constantly needing things from me. I feel like I haven't had a moment to myself since she got here.

"Here you go," I say, shaking a pill from the bottle and handing it to her.

"I have to take this at the same time every day," she says.

"Yes, I know."

"Then why did you forget?"

"I just have a lot on my mind. And I'm tired. I didn't sleep well last night. Rose, I can't talk right now. I have a meeting for work."

"I can't take my pill without water."

"I'll go get you some." I run to the kitchen, fill a glass with water, and bring it to her. "The meeting should be less than an hour. I'll check on you when it's done."

I race back to the kitchen. By the time I log into the meeting, it's already started.

"I'm here," I say, announcing myself and seeing the members of our ad team seated around the table in the conference room.

"Anna," James says. He's our director of advertising. "There's an issue with the ad that was supposed to be shooting today. The model we chose is no longer available."

"What? No. We have to use her. She's perfect for the brand and she tested well in the focus groups."

"Yes, but unfortunately, she overdosed last weekend and was put into a rehab facility."

"Have you talked to the ad agency? Maybe they could find someone who looks similar to the original model."

"Anna!" Rose yells.

I cringe, then realize I'm on camera and force out a smile. "Excuse me. As you all know, I'm caring for my mother-in-law and she's calling for me."

"Anna, did you hear me?" Rose yells.

"Yes, what do you need?"

"I need to use the bathroom! Now!"

I'm sure everyone in the meeting heard that. Rose is very loud.

"I'm sorry, but I need to go take care of something," I say.

"This can't wait," James says. "The ad agency needs a decision on what to do."

"I'll have to call you back," I say. "I'm sorry, James. I'll call you as soon as I can."

I hurry back to the living room and find Rose laughing at something on the TV. She doesn't look like someone who desperately needs to use the bathroom.

"Okay, I'm here," I say, moving her wheelchair next to the couch.

"Just a minute. I want to see the end of my program."

"Rose, I left a meeting for this. C'mon. Let's get you to the bathroom."

She ignores me, her eyes on the TV, then says, "Okay, we can go."

I help her into the wheelchair, then down to the bathroom. She insists on using it alone, which is fine with me, but I don't know how she manages to go on her own. She'd have to lift herself out of the wheelchair and balance on her good leg to get herself to the toilet.

"I'm done!" I hear Rose say as I stand outside the bathroom.

Opening the door, I see her back in the chair, waiting for me to wheel her out.

"False alarm," she says.

"You didn't go?"

"That's what false alarm means, dear. I thought I had to go, but I didn't. Now hurry up and wheel me back. I'm missing my show."

It's been less than a day and Rose is driving me crazy, pushing my patience to the absolute limit. She's constantly calling for me and making me do things for her. How am I going to get any work done when she won't leave me alone for more than a few minutes?

At eleven, Ethan calls to check in.

"How's everything going?" he asks.

I pause to consider how to answer that. I don't want to say

unkind things about his mother, so instead I say, "We're adjusting."

"Meaning what?" he asks, sensing from my tone that things aren't going as well as he'd hoped. I'm surprised he noticed. He usually doesn't pick up on things like that.

"Caring for her is more work than I expected," I say, keeping my voice down as I hurry up the stairs. I don't want Rose hearing me, although I doubt she would with the TV as loud as she keeps it.

"How is it more work?" Ethan says. "What has she done?"

"I can't get a moment alone. I've missed two meetings and had to leave the other one early to take Rose to the bathroom. And then it turned out she didn't have to go."

"I'm sorry, honey. Maybe you could try talking to her, explaining that you need time to work."

"I already told her, but it doesn't seem to matter. Maybe you could try talking to her."

"Yes, of course. When I get home."

"You won't be late tonight, will you?"

"I'm afraid so. I have to prepare for that meeting tomorrow. But I'll come home as soon as I can."

"I told Rose you'd get her a TV tonight, but I suppose you won't have time."

"No, but you could give her the one in the living room for now."

"She insists on watching that one during the day. She said she can't be in the bedroom all day and night so she insisted I take her to the living room."

"It's not good for her to watch that much TV. Why don't you take her outside this afternoon? It's a beautiful day and it'd be good for both of you to get out of the house and get some sun and fresh air."

"I have meetings this afternoon."

"Yes, well, maybe after they're done."

"I'm not sure I'm ready to deal with the neighbors. If they see me with Rose, they'll run out of their houses and bombard me with questions."

"Everyone already knows she's staying with us and they've offered to help. Perhaps you should take them up on the offer. Maybe then you wouldn't feel so overwhelmed."

"What do you mean? How does everyone know she's here? We just got home last night."

"I spoke with Liz and Kelsie. They were checking in with me all weekend, asking how Mother was doing."

"Why didn't you tell me that? And why did they call you and not me?"

"Sweetheart, you've made it quite clear you don't like them. They're afraid to reach out to you. And Rose is *my* mother, not yours. It makes sense they would call me."

No. It doesn't. Women call other women. They don't call another woman's husband. It's inappropriate, especially given the way Liz looks at Ethan. I've noticed Kelsie looking at him that way too.

"Anna!" Rose yells from the living room. "Where are you?"

"Upstairs!" I yell back.

"I'll let you go," Ethan says. "You're doing a great job, sweetheart. I love you."

"I love you too." I end the call.

"Anna, get down here!" Rose yells.

Her panicked tone worries me and I race down the stairs, hoping she didn't fall.

But when I reach the living room, I see her on the couch, holding the glass of orange juice I gave her.

"What is it? What do you need?"

"I don't want this," she says, holding out the glass of orange juice. "It's too acidic. What brand is this?"

"I don't know, but I could check."

"Don't bother. Just don't buy it again."

"Is that why you called me down here? To talk about orange juice?"

"And to tell you I need to eat. I have lunch at eleven and it's already past that."

I grit my teeth, willing myself to remain calm. She's an old lady, and old ladies can be very rigid and set in their ways. If Rose wants lunch at eleven, I can make that work. It's not a big deal.

"What would you like for lunch?" I ask.

"A Reuben sandwich with extra dressing."

"I'm sorry, but I don't have the ingredients for a Reuben sandwich."

"Can't you go to the store?"

"Yes, but I'm supposed to be here watching you. And by the time I went to the store and back, it'd be way past your eleven o'clock lunch time."

She huffs. "Fine, then I'll have turkey on rye with lots of mayonnaise."

"I don't have turkey. Or rye bread, but I think I have whole wheat."

"Wheat bread hurts my stomach. What else you got?"

"I don't know. I'd have to check."

"How could you not know what you have for food? What kind of wife are you? Are you starving my son?"

"Ethan and I go out a lot. We don't have time to cook."

"You do now. I suggest you put on an apron and spend some time in that fancy kitchen of yours. Figure out how to use a stove."

Remain calm, I tell myself. *Don't get upset. She's from a different generation. She doesn't know that women have progressed beyond the traditional roles she's accustomed to.*

"What are you standing there for?" Rose says. "Get in the kitchen and find me something to eat."

I go to the kitchen and try to remember the techniques my

therapist taught me to calm myself down. It's been years since I've seen her, but the tips she gave me did help relieve my anxiety and stress, both of which I'm experiencing a great deal of right now. I squeeze my hands into tight fists, then release them and do it again, remembering how that used to help relax my muscles. I keep it up and add some deep breaths. I'm almost back to a semi-calm state when Rose yells at me again.

"Well? Did you find anything? I'm starving!"

I take another deep breath. It's only day one. Rose and I are still adjusting to each other. Things will get better. They have to.

16

All I'm able to find for lunch is some cheese and the wheat bread Rose said would hurt her stomach. I told her I'd order whatever she'd like and have it delivered, but she refused, saying she doesn't trust food that's been sitting in someone's car. It might not be kept at the proper temperature, resulting in food poisoning.

I offer to make her a grilled cheese sandwich, but told her it'd have to be with the wheat bread. After a lot of complaining, she finally agreed to eat the sandwich, saying it was better to have stomach pains than starve to death.

There's almost no food in the house. I really need to get groceries, but I don't know when I'll have time. Maybe I could leave Rose alone for an hour. As long as she stays put on the couch, she's not going to fall and hurt herself.

Just after one, I'm trying to answer emails when someone knocks on the door.

"Yoo hoo!" a woman says in an overly cheery tone. "Anyone home?"

It's Kelsie. Ethan probably told her to stop over. I'm still irritated with him for talking to her without telling me. And talking to Liz, who I swear is out to steal Ethan from me. I wonder if last weekend was the first time she called him or if they'd been talking before that?

The doorbell rings.

"I'm coming!" I yell, running to the door. I open it and see Kelsie standing there in white shorts and a tiny pink t-shirt with the word 'love' bedazzled on it. Is bedazzling still a thing? Maybe it's called something else now. It must be in style because Kelsie only wears whatever's trending at the moment.

"Hi, Anna!" she says in her usual chipper tone. "I brought you this!" She picks a basket up from the porch and shoves it at me. "A little something for your mother-in-law." She frowns. "Ethan told me she was in a lot of pain. Is she resting?"

"No, she's right here." I glance at the couch. "Watching TV."

"Oh! Can I meet her?" Kelsie pops her head in the house and sees Rose. "Hi, Mrs. Halstrom! I'm Kelsie, from down the street."

Rose's face lights up. "Come on in! Ethan told me all about you."

He did? When? And why was he telling Rose about Kelsie?

"Let me just grab the kids," Kelsie says, turning to get the stroller I didn't even notice was behind her. She rolls it into the house and I see Poppy asleep in the top part of the stroller and Piper sitting in the lower part.

"Oh, my, they're adorable," Rose gushes, looking at the kids.

"Thank you!" Kelsie says. "Poppy is three and Piper is five."

Piper waves her tiny hand at Rose. "Hi!"

"Hi, sweetie," Rose says. "Would you like to come sit with me?"

"It's okay, honey," Kelsie says to Piper. "You can sit with her."

Piper gets out of the stroller and goes over next to Rose, smiling at her.

"Aren't you just the sweetest little thing," Rose says.

"We have an older child too," Kelsie says. "Paul is seven. He's with the nanny. She took him to soccer practice while I stayed home with the girls. It's such a gorgeous day. If you're up for it, you might want to get outside for a little while."

"I wanted to," Rose says, "but Anna said it was too much trouble to take me out."

Wait—what? I offered to take her outside after lunch, but she told me it was too sunny and would hurt her eyes.

"Rose, I told you we could—"

"She has to work, you know," Rose says to Kelsie. "Her job is very important to her. I really can't expect her to take me outside when she's so busy with meetings and such."

"I'd be happy to take you," Kelsie says. "Would you like to go right now?"

"I'd love to!" Rose says. "But I don't think you'll be able to push the wheelchair and the stroller at the same time."

"Piper can push the stroller," Kelsie says. "She does it all the time, don't you, sweetie?"

She nods really fast.

"Piper, come over by Mommy," Kelsie says. "Give Mrs. Halstrom room to get up."

"I'll help her," I say, setting the basket down and going over to Rose. I take her arm and assist her into the wheelchair. "Do you need to use the bathroom before you go?"

"No, but I might have to later. My stomach's really hurting after that lunch."

"What did you have?" Kelsie asks.

"Grilled cheese," Rose says. "With wheat bread. My stomach can't handle wheat."

Kelsie shoots me an angry look. "Why would you give her wheat bread if she's gluten intolerant?"

"She's not. And it's all we had. I need to go to the store."

"I told her I'm gluten intolerant," Rose says to Kelsie. "But she said a little wouldn't hurt me."

Kelsie walks up to me, her hands on her hips. "Gluten intolerance is a serious medical condition. If I have even a small amount, my stomach cramps up and I get a horrible migraine."

"She never told me she—"

"Good thing I came over," Kelsie says, interrupting me. She picks up the basket she brought and brings it over to Rose, uncovering it to reveal a loaf of bread and some muffins. "These are gluten and dairy free. They shouldn't cause you any problems."

"Bless you," Rose says, putting her hand on Kelsie's arm. "You are such a dear. Ethan told me what wonderful neighbors he has, but I never imagined they'd be as wonderful as you."

"Aww, thank you," Kelsie says, tilting her head to the side.

"I like this one," Piper says to Rose, pointing to a blueberry muffin in the basket.

"Should I have a taste?" Rose asks.

Piper nods and Rose picks up the muffin, tearing off a bite and tasting it. "Oh, my, it's delicious."

"Oh, and none of the baked goods have nuts," Kelsie says. "A lot of the neighborhood kids have nut allergies so all us moms make sure our kitchens are nut-free, along with anything we bring into the house." She smiles. "Well, should we go?"

"How long will you be gone?" I ask.

"As long as Rose would like," Kelsie says.

"Anna would like it to be as long as possible," Rose says with a laugh. "She's already sick of me."

"I'm sure that's not true," Kelsie says, shooting me a dirty look.

"Not at all," I say, but Kelsie doesn't look like she believes me.

"Piper, honey, you go first with Poppy," Kelsie says, going behind Rose's wheelchair and pushing it behind the stroller.

I get the door for them and watch as they leave. Then I shut the door and collapse on the couch. It hasn't even been one day and I'm already fed up with Rose. All she's done is criticize me and order me around. And then Kelsie shows up and suddenly Rose is a sweet, old lady again, the way she was at my wedding.

My phone rings and I see it's Candace calling.

"Hey, what's up?" I say, answering the call. "Did I miss a meeting?"

"No, I just wanted to check in. How's everything going with your mother-in-law?"

"Not great. She won't let me get a minute to myself. Even when I'm in the bathroom she's yelling at me to do something."

"It's probably because she's in pain. People get cranky when they're in pain."

"I don't think she's in pain. She's taking pain pills and the fracture in her ankle is very small. The doctor didn't even seem that concerned about it. He was more concerned about her living alone and falling again."

"So what does that mean? That she'll be staying there indefinitely?"

"No. Absolutely not. This arrangement is only temporary. Until she's healed."

"But if you're saying she can't live alone..."

"Ethan will have to figure something out for her. Maybe a retirement home."

"Where is she now? Taking a nap?"

"No, Kelsie, one of my neighbors, took her for a walk. Well, she's pushing her in the wheelchair."

"That was nice of her. I thought you said the neighbors were awful."

"I don't know if awful is the right word. More like fake. They're the type of people who pretend to be nice to your face and then stab you in the back."

"Yeah, I know people like that."

"I should probably try to get some work done while Rose is gone."

"Okay, well, I hope things get better with her. I'm sure they will once she's been there longer."

"I hope so."

But I have a feeling things will only get worse.

17

With Rose gone, I try to get through all my emails. I'm almost finished when I hear the doorbell ring. It must be Kelsie bringing Rose home. I open the door and see Kelsie there, but not Rose or the kids.

"Where's Rose?" I ask, glancing behind Kelsie.

"The kids were having so much fun with her that I wanted to see if she could stay longer."

"Stay where?"

"At the house. She's out back, watching Gigi and Piper run through the sprinkler." Kelsie laughs. "This was after they did a ballet performance for her. The girls love having an audience."

"Gigi's there?"

"And Gabe. Liz brought them over. I called and told her about Rose and she just had to meet her. Then, of course, Sharon had to meet her too so she stopped by with the twins."

Why do they all want to meet Ethan's mother? She's only going to be living here for a short time.

"Rose is okay staying there?" I ask.

"It was her idea. And we love having her! She's such a delight!"

Delight? That's not how I'd describe Rose, not after this

morning. But maybe Candace is right and Rose was cranky because she wasn't feeling well this morning.

"So it's okay if she stays?" Kelsie asks. "She doesn't need to be back at a certain time, does she?"

"No," I say, relieved to have a break. "In fact, if she could stay until maybe three or four, that would give me time to get to the store. I'm completely out of groceries."

Kelsie gives me a funny look. "It's almost four now."

"Oh." I check the clock on the wall. "I was busy with work and didn't realize it was so late."

"You know, you might want to consider taking some time off while Rose is here," Kelsie says. "I mean, she *is* your family."

She's actually Ethan's family. I just met the woman. I know she's my mother-in-law, but I barely know her. I'm doing this for Ethan, and because of the guilt I feel over having to put my mother in a home.

"I have a lot of responsibilities at work," I tell Kelsie. "Things I can't just hand off to someone else. And it's not like I'm in the office. I've got everything set up so I can work from home."

"Yes, but..." She pauses. "It's just that Rose feels like you don't have time for her, like she's in the way. She doesn't think you want her here. She thinks you only agreed to it because of Ethan."

"She said that?"

"Those weren't her exact words, but that's clearly what she meant."

"Well, I'm sorry if she feels that way. That certainly wasn't my intention. I'll talk to her when she's home later."

"I should get back to the house." Kelsie turns to leave, then turns back. "If you don't have time to make dinner, Rose could stay and have dinner with us. You could come too, if you want."

"Um, maybe."

"If you decide to join us, we'll be eating around six."

"Okay, I'll leave for the store right now. I'll try not to take too long."

"No rush." She gives me a wave. "Bye!"

It sounds like Rose has found a new family, one she likes better than her own. I feel bad that Rose thinks I don't want her here. I guess I *was* rather impatient with her this morning. I'm just not used to someone needing that much attention and care, but I guess it's good practice for having a child.

I'll have to work on being more patient with Rose, but it wouldn't hurt her to stop being so demanding. It's a two-way street and I shouldn't be the only one who has to change.

When I get to the grocery store, I feel too tired to shop. I didn't sleep much last night and I've been living on coffee all day. Dealing with Rose and all the problems that came up at work, I didn't have time to eat anything.

"Can I help you find something?" a woman asks as I stand in the cereal aisle. She's wearing a red shirt with the store logo on it.

"Um, no, I can find what I need," I tell her.

"Just wanted to check." She smiles and continues down the aisle.

I stare at the shelves of cereal, then realize Ethan and I don't even eat cereal, and I'm sure Rose doesn't since most cereals contain wheat. Rose never told me she was gluten intolerant and she didn't once complain about stomach pains after eating that grilled cheese sandwich. It wasn't until Kelsie got there that Rose suddenly felt ill.

Still standing in the cereal aisle, I call Rose, hoping she has her cell phone turned on.

"Hello?" she answers, like she doesn't know who this is, even though I put my name and number in her contacts list.

"Rose, it's Anna. I'm at the grocery store. I wanted to ask what you'd like me to get for your meals this week."

"Yes, sweetie, I'll be right in," she says, in a tone you'd use with a child. "Tell your mom I just need a few minutes."

"Who are you talking to?" I ask.

"Braden. Sharon's little boy. He's the cutest thing, and his brother, Brock, looks just like him."

"Yes, they're twins," I mutter. "So anyway, what would you like?" I ask, pulling up the notes app on my phone.

"Let me think a minute." She pauses, then says, "Get me some cans of tuna, the kind in oil, not water. Oh, and canned soup. Lots of canned soup. And raspberry jam. Now that Kelsie got me bread I can actually eat, I can have my toast in the morning."

I grit my teeth, reminding myself to be patient. "Anything else? What about foods for dinner?"

"Pot roast. And a big bag of potatoes."

I'm supposed to cook pot roast? I've never made a roast. I don't even know how to buy one.

"And some chicken," Rose says. "A whole chicken, not those cut-up pieces. And you'll need carrots and onions too."

What am I going to do with a whole chicken? Is she planning to teach me to cook? Because I don't know the first thing about cooking. That grilled cheese sandwich I made was basically the extent of my cooking skills.

"That's enough for now," I tell her. "I better get back to shopping."

"That's only enough for a few days," she says.

"Then I'll come back later this week. I don't want to be gone too long. Ethan will be home soon."

He won't, but I tell her that to get her off the phone so I can finish up at the store. I don't enjoy grocery shopping. When I lived alone, I never went to the store. I went out to eat or had food delivered.

"Kelsie invited me for dinner," Rose says.

"Yes, she told me. Just call when you're done and I'll come get you."

"That's okay. Kelsie or one of the other girls will take me home."

"Okay, Rose. Bye." I end the call and close my eyes, taking a calming breath.

When I open my eyes I see a woman coming toward me with her cart. She looks like Kelsie, a young petite blonde wearing black yoga pants and a pink cropped hoodie.

"I'm fine," I say, noticing she's looking at me like there's something wrong with me.

Why can't the people here mind their own business? I feel like they're watching everything I do. In Manhattan, nobody cares what other people are doing. I once saw a guy in a deli doing yoga poses while he waited for his order. The place was full of people, but I was the only one who even noticed him. But here, I shut my eyes for a moment and some woman looks at me like I'm crazy.

An hour later, I'm back home with the groceries and the sushi I picked up for dinner. There was no way I was going to show up at Kelsie's house, watching everyone fawn over Rose and look at me like I'm a terrible daughter-in-law. I'm sure Rose told everyone I yelled at her earlier when I was on a work call. I wasn't actually yelling, but I did sound angry. It's because Rose turned the TV up so loud I couldn't hear the people on the call so I told her to turn it down.

After the groceries are put away, I enjoy my sushi with a glass of white wine, feeling relaxed for the first time today. Honestly, I haven't felt relaxed since last Friday, before that horrible dinner at the country club that ended with the call about Ethan's mother. From then until now, everything's been about Rose. It's nice to finally get some time to myself.

Around seven, I'm pouring myself another glass of wine when the doorbell rings. It can't be Kelsie. I told her to text me before she brought Rose back. The doorbell rings again and I hear Rose say, "She probably went out."

Going to the door, I open it and see Rose in her wheelchair, and right behind her is Liz. My least favorite person. She already thinks I'm a terrible wife and now probably believes I'm a terrible daughter-in-law too. So much for feeling relaxed.

18

"Liz." I smile at her. "I wasn't expecting you."

"Kelsie had to get the kids ready for bed so I offered to take Rose home." She wheels Rose into the house.

"I would've been happy to get her myself. I'm sure you need to get your own children ready for bed."

"I already did. Rose helped. The children love her. We all do."

"Sounds like you had a good time," I say to Rose.

"From the looks of it, you did too," she says, noticing the bottle of wine on the coffee table. "That bottle's almost empty."

"Yes, well, it wasn't full to begin with," I rush to say, noticing the look of disapproval on Liz's face.

She walks in front of Rose and kneels down to her. "Do you need me to stay?"

Stay? Why would she stay? Does she think I'm not capable of caring for Rose because I had a few glasses of wine?

"Thank you, dear," Rose says, "but I'll be fine. I've had a long day. I'm just going to go to bed."

"Okay, but call if you need anything." Liz rises to standing.

"I will, dear. Be sure to give those little ones of yours a kiss from me."

"I sure will. Goodnight, Rose." Liz takes off, not even acknowledging me.

"Did you hear from Ethan?" Rose asks, rolling herself toward the kitchen. This morning she said she didn't have the strength to do that, but now suddenly she does?

"No, I thought he'd call, but he hasn't." I meet up with Rose in the kitchen.

"I spoke to him. He said he'd be home just after seven." She checks her watch. "So I guess any minute now."

Ethan called Rose but not me? Maybe I missed his call. I check my phone but don't see any missed calls or even a text from Ethan.

"When did he call you?" I ask Rose.

"Right after you called from the store, so what was that... around four?" She gives me a smug smile, gloating over the fact that Ethan called her and not me. "Ethan's a good son. Some would say a bit of a mama's boy. Always has been. But I'm sure you knew that when you married him."

I clear my throat, feeling uncomfortable with this conversation. "What can I get you? I assume you came to the kitchen because you need something."

"Some water. I need to take my pill."

Her pills are lined up on the counter. I don't know what they're all for, but there's a lot of them. I fill a glass with water and hand it to her.

"Which pill do you take?" I ask.

"Just slide them over. I'll figure it out."

I hear the garage door open as Rose takes her pill. Moments later, Ethan comes through the door to the kitchen.

"Hello, sweetheart," he says, walking up to me and giving me a kiss. I'm pleased he greeted me before his mother. I glance at Rose and see her examining one of her pill bottles, not paying attention to Ethan and me.

"Hello, Mother," he says. "Did you have a good day?"

She sets her pill bottle down. "It was wonderful. That sweet neighbor girl, Kelsie, took me out for a nice walk, then invited me to her home for dinner." Rose looks at me. "Since your wife didn't have time to cook."

"I didn't have time because I have a job," I say, my anger rising. "Kelsie has all day to prepare dinner."

"She also has three children to care for," Rose says. "If you were a mother, you'd know that caring for children takes far more effort than sitting behind a computer all day."

Ethan goes over to the fridge, completely unaware of the tension between his mother and me, or just choosing to ignore it.

"Speaking of dinner," he says, opening the fridge. "I need somcthing to cat."

"I just went to the store," I tell him. "There's some deli meat and I got that mustard you like. You could make a sandwich."

"A cold sandwich for dinner?" Rose scoffs. "Ethan, honey, help me over to the stove and I'll make you something."

"You need to rest," he says, going over to her and leaning down to kiss her cheek. "A cold sandwich is fine."

"We have soup," I say, opening the cabinet to show Ethan. "I got all different varieties at the store today."

Ethan's brows draw together. "Why did you buy that?"

"For your mother."

"My mother can't have canned soup. It has far too much sodium. You know Mother has high blood pressure. She's on medication for it."

"Yes, I know, but she asked me to buy it. I called her from the store. Tell him, Rose."

"I don't know what she's talking about," Rose says to

Ethan. "She called me to ask if I was having dinner at Kelsie's. She never asked me about groceries. If she had, I wouldn't have told her to buy canned soup. If I want soup, I make it homemade."

I laugh, thinking Rose must be playing some kind of prank on me. "She's kidding," I say to Ethan. "She gave me a list of things to get at the store. Canned soup. Tuna." I open a cabinet and take out a can of tuna. "I made sure to get the kind in oil, not water." I put the tuna back. "Oh, and raspberry jam for her toast." I smile at Ethan, knowing he'll be pleased that I went to all that effort for his mother. Ethan knows how much I dislike grocery shopping, unless I'm going with him, in which case I don't mind it.

Ethan clears his throat. "Honey, can I talk to you a minute?"

He isn't smiling. He doesn't seem pleased.

"Why?" I ask. "Is something wrong?"

"I'm missing my program," Rose says. "Ethan, dear, would you wheel me to the living room?"

"Of course," he says, going behind her and wheeling her out of the kitchen. Rose wheeled herself in here, but now she can't wheel herself out?

The TV blares from the other room. Ethan can't stand it when I have the TV too loud, and I've never had it anywhere near as loud as it is now, yet somehow he's okay with his mother having it at that volume.

He returns to the kitchen, walking up to me. "What's going on?"

"What do you mean?"

"Are you and my mother not getting along?"

"We're getting along fine. Why do you ask?"

"You got her foods she can't eat, and then you send her away for the afternoon?"

"What? No! I didn't send her away. Kelsie offered to take

her outside and then brought her to her house. Rose was the one who wanted to stay. I had nothing to do with it."

"That's not what Mother said."

"Why? What did she tell you?"

"It doesn't matter." He pulls me into his arms. "I'm sure you two just need more time to adjust to each other."

"Ethan, no." I push away from him. "Whatever she told you is a lie. I never sent her away."

"You didn't ask Kelsie to watch her so you could have time to yourself?"

How did he know that? Did he talk to Kelsie?

"Okay, yes, I asked Kelsie if Rose could stay with her, but it was so I could get groceries, not have time to myself."

"Mother said you were invited to join them all for dinner but instead you chose to stay here, by yourself, and have a bottle of wine."

I feel my face heating up as my anger rises. "I was tired," I say, doing my best to remain calm. "I didn't feel like going to Kelsie's house for dinner. And yes, I had some wine, but since when is that a crime? Before Rose got here, you and I shared a bottle of wine several nights a week."

"Yes, you and I, not just you." He sets his hands on my shoulders and leans down to me. "Anna, do you have a problem you neglected to tell me about?"

"Are you kidding me?" I huff. "You think I'm an alcoholic because I drank some wine?"

"I'm concerned because you chose to stay home and drink rather than join my mother and our friends for dinner."

I yank away from him and take a step back. "First of all, those people are *not* our friends. We just met them, and you know I don't like being around them. I've told you that more than once."

"You just need to give them more time."

"Ethan, you're not listening. I don't feel comfortable

around them. Kelsie, Liz, and Sharon all act like they're better than me just because they're mothers, like having a child somehow makes them superior."

"Anna, that's not what they're doing. You're letting your own insecurities get the best of you."

"No! I'm not. You don't notice how they talk to me or the looks they give me. Men don't notice those things, but I'm telling you, those women don't like me. They may smile and pretend to be friendly, but I swear to you, they'd be the first in line to stab me in the back."

Ethan walks up to me. "Let's talk about something else. I didn't mean to upset you. I was just concerned."

"If you want to be concerned about someone, you should be concerned about your mother. She's clearly having memory issues. She didn't even remember me calling her about the groceries."

Ethan doesn't say anything. He's just staring at me with a concerned look.

"Wait," I say. "You don't actually believe her, do you?"

"It's just that..." He sighs and shakes his head.

"Ethan, why would I lie about calling your mother to ask what she'd like at the grocery store? That's completely ridiculous. She's clearly showing signs of dementia. You just don't want to see it because you're her son."

He opens the cupboard and takes out a can of tuna. "My mother hates tuna. Always has. You know that."

"And how would I know that when she specifically told me to buy it for her?"

"She told you the story." Ethan sets the can of tuna down. "On the ride here from New Jersey, Mother told us stories from her childhood, about how her family was very poor and had to take whatever food donations they could get from the church. People always donated canned goods, like canned tuna and canned soup, so that's all my mother ever ate. She got so sick of it that to this day, just the sight of those foods makes her ill."

What is Ethan talking about? I don't recall Rose saying any of that on our trip home. I was tired, so it's possible I didn't hear her, but even so, if that story's true, why would Rose tell me to buy those things?

"Ethan, do you see what's happening?" I say, finally making sense of it. "Your mother told me to buy the foods she ate as a child. She's reverting to the past. She can't remember recent events, but is able to recall memories from many years ago. It's a classic sign of dementia."

"My mother does not have dementia. She's sharp as a tack."

"Then how do you explain this?" I ask, holding up the can of tuna.

"Perhaps you misheard her when she was telling us those stories." He steps up to the counter and picks up the mail, sorting through it. "I would hope it's not something more sinister than that."

"Sinister?" I say, beyond shocked that he would even imply my motives were sinister. "What exactly do you mean by that?"

He looks over at me. "When Mother told you those stories from her childhood, you could see how just recalling them upset her. There were days when the only thing she had to eat was a can of tuna or a can of watered down tomato soup. And here you are buying her those exact things."

My jaw drops, then snaps shut as I storm up to him. "I can't believe you're accusing me of trying to traumatize your mother. What about the jam? Was I trying to torture her with that as well?"

He sets the mail down. "Mother's not allowed to have jam with seeds in it. It lodges in her dental work and causes her extreme pain."

"And how would I possibly know that?" I ask.

"It's on the list I left you of Mother's medical issues and

things to avoid." He pulls open a drawer, takes out a piece of paper, and hands it to me. "Perhaps you should review it again."

"I've never seen this," I say, looking at the list and seeing the seeded jam listed under 'things to avoid'. "You never gave this to me."

"I gave it to you this morning," he says. "You must've forgotten."

I slam the list down on the counter. "What the hell is going on here?"

"I don't know what you mean," he innocently says.

"You and your mother. You're both playing some kind of trick on me and I don't like it. I need you to stop."

"Trick?" Ethan's brows rise. "Sweetheart, I think you might've had too much wine. Why don't you go upstairs and rest? Or maybe just go to bed. It's getting late and I can tell you're tired."

He's talking to me like a child, which infuriates me to the point I can't be around him.

"Goodnight, Ethan," I say, storming out of the kitchen.

"I need some water," Rose says as I pass by her on my way to the stairs.

"Ask Ethan," I tell her. "I'm going to bed."

"What do you need, Mother?" I hear Ethan say, in the kind, caring tone he used to use with me.

I go up to the bedroom and try to figure out what is happening. Ethan was acting very strange tonight. And I didn't like the way he was accusing me of things I didn't do and acting like I was the one with memory issues when it's clearly his mother. Why is he taking her side over mine? Believing her over me?

19

The next morning, I pretend to be asleep when Ethan gets up for work. I'm still too angry to talk to him. I was up all night, replaying what happened yesterday and the day before, trying to figure out if anything Ethan or Rose said was true. Did Rose really tell us those stories from her childhood? And if so, how is it possible I didn't hear her? Even if my mind wandered a bit, I would have heard at least part of what she said, but I didn't, which means Ethan was lying. But why would he lie about that? It doesn't make sense.

And I know Rose told me to buy those things at the store. I still have them listed in the notes app on my phone, although showing that to Ethan wouldn't prove the list came from his mother. But does he really believe I'd purposely buy his mother foods that bring up bad memories from her past or get her a type of jam that would cause her pain? Why would he think such horrible things about me?

At one point in the night, I found myself wondering if everything Ethan and Rose said was true. I began to question my own sanity, wondering if maybe what happened to my mother was happening to me. She was much older than me when she was diagnosed with dementia, but what if the signs were there earlier than that and nobody noticed?

What if I'm showing those signs and don't even realize it? Like that form I filled out for changing my name. How could I not remember that? I don't even remember making the decision or how I came to that decision.

Those thoughts had me panicking to the point I felt like I couldn't breathe. Just after midnight, I got up and went into the bathroom, hoping Ethan wouldn't hear me. I didn't want him seeing me that way. I assured him my panic attacks weren't an issue anymore, and they weren't, until just recently. I splashed cold water on my face, then sat on the floor, hugging my knees to my chest and rocking back and forth. If anyone saw me, they'd probably say I was crazy, but what I did worked and a half hour later, I was able to go back to bed.

Ethan got up at six and I heard him leave the house at seven. Now it's eight and I need to get up and deal with Rose. I should be logged into the office by now, but I'm going to be late today. Helping Rose get ready and making her breakfast will take at least an hour.

I put on my robe and as I'm heading downstairs, I hear the TV in the living room turn on. Rose must already be up, but how did she get out of bed?

"Rose." I stop when I see her on the couch, already dressed for the day and her makeup on. "What are you doing up already?"

"Already? It's after eight," she says, staring at the TV as she flips through the channels.

"How did you get out of bed?"

"My son helped me." Her eyes shoot to mine. "He's a very good boy. Very loyal. Always has been."

Her words and the look she's giving me send a chill through me. Why does she keep saying Ethan's a good boy, as though implying he'd do anything she says? And now she added that he's loyal. Is she trying to tell me something? If so, I wish she'd just tell me instead of being so cryptic.

"Did Ethan help you get dressed?" I ask.

"Heavens, no," she scoffs. "He's not going to dress his own mother. What kind of sick question is that?"

I walk over to her. "I don't understand. I thought you couldn't dress yourself with your injuries."

"You thought wrong."

"But the doctor said—"

"A doctor only knows what you tell him," she says with a smile that sends another chill through me. "You tell him something hurts, he has to believe you. Much like a son has to believe his mother."

That time I got the message. Rose set me up, or she's trying to. She wants me to look bad to Ethan, like she's the good one and I'm somehow bad. But why? Does she not want me to be his wife? She seemed happy about it at our wedding, so what changed?

"Rose, we need to talk," I say, sitting beside her.

"I need to eat. I have to take my pills and they must be taken with food."

"This won't take long." I take the remote from her and shut off the TV.

"Hey! My show is on!"

I turn to her. "Rose, do you not like me?"

"I like you just fine," she says, staring at the TV, even though it's not on.

"Then why are you trying to sabotage me?"

She looks at me and laughs. "Honey, nobody is trying to sabotage you. Ethan warned me you have an active imagination and the past couple days I've seen that he's right. You seem to think everyone's against you, even those sweet neighbors of yours."

"Rose, you know what you did. You specifically told me to

get those things at the grocery store, then denied it when Ethan got home."

Her expression turns angry. "Why would I tell you to buy things that bring up horrible memories for me? I told you all those stories about my childhood, about never having enough food and having to take whatever my mother could get from the church donations." She shudders. "Just the sight of a can of tuna makes my stomach sick. And then you go out and buy enough to fill a cupboard."

So she really did tell me those stories from her childhood. Why don't I remember? I know she told me to buy tuna, but she denies doing it. Did I make it up in my head? Am I having delusions, like the kind my mother used to have? Is that an early sign of dementia?

No. I'm only 35. People my age don't have dementia. Rose has to be lying. She's trying to make me doubt myself. I don't know why, but I'm not playing this game. I'm just going to go on as though it never happened.

I set the TV remote down and get up from the couch. "What would you like for breakfast?"

"Some of that bread that Kelsie brought over."

"With raspberry jam?" I ask, to see what she'll say.

"Just butter," she says, ignoring my jam comment as she turns the TV on. "And I'd like two eggs, scrambled."

"Of course," I say, in my most pleasant tone.

As I go into the kitchen and get the coffee going, I remind myself this situation is only temporary. If Rose was able to dress herself this morning, it means she's recovering faster than the doctor anticipated. But did she lie to the doctor? She made that comment about the doctor having to believe what she said. Does that mean she's not as injured as she claims to be?

"How much longer?" Rose yells from the living room. "I have to take my pills."

"Just a few more minutes," I yell back, getting the eggs from the fridge. I take a skillet out and crack two eggs into it, mixing them with a fork. I put it on the stove, then go to make the toast. I've never made this elaborate of a breakfast for myself, or Ethan. I guess it's not really elaborate, but for someone who doesn't cook, it's a lot of effort and Rose doesn't even appreciate it.

After her breakfast is made, I bring it to her on a tray so she doesn't miss her program and so I can be alone in the kitchen and try to get some work done. I'd rather work upstairs in the office, but Rose insists I stay on the main floor in case she needs me.

My phone rings as I'm sipping my coffee and reading through emails. I see it's James calling and answer.

"Hi, James," I say, scrolling down to his email from this morning. "I saw that the photo shoot for the ad was postponed."

"Yes, that's why I'm calling. I need to meet with you before I reschedule it with the ad agency."

"Can we talk through it over the phone? I'm kind of stuck here. I can't leave."

"This really needs to be done in person. I've got a stack of headshots for you to look at and I want to show you video of some of the models."

"When does this need to be done?"

"Today, if possible."

"I can't get to the office today," I say, but then wonder if maybe I could. "Actually, let me see what I can do and I'll call you back."

"Sounds good. Hey, how's everything going? I heard about Ethan's mom. Is she okay?"

"She's better than she was a few days ago. She's already getting her strength back."

"Then maybe she'd be okay alone for a few hours."

She would be, but Ethan insists she not be left alone. He's afraid she'll fall again, but I think he's being overly cautious. And I'm starting to wonder if Rose is only pretending to be weak and exaggerating her pain so she can stay here longer.

I end the call with James and go out to the living room.

"How was breakfast?" I ask Rose.

"The eggs were overcooked."

I force out a smile as I take her tray. "I'll try to do better tomorrow."

"I'd like something else tomorrow. Maybe French toast."

"Sure! Whatever you'd like. So anyway, I noticed it's going to be another beautiful day outside. I was thinking maybe you'd like to spend some time at Kelsie's house again, on her patio. You could watch the children play."

"Why?" Rose eyes me with suspicion. "Are you trying to get rid of me?"

"No, I just thought you might enjoy it. And it sounds like the children enjoyed having you there."

"Just tell me the truth. Why do you want me gone?"

I sigh, knowing she'll find out eventually. "James called. He manages our ad campaigns. A problem came up and he needs to meet with me right away. In person. He was hoping I could come into the office for a few hours."

"Today?"

"Yes." I set the tray on the coffee table and sit next to her. "Rose, this has nothing to do with you. I'd love to stay here with you, but I need to get this ad campaign back on track so we don't lose time and money. This is a very important campaign. It's for the launch of our new fragrance. A delay with the ad could affect the launch."

"Was your father like this? Obsessed with his work?"

I sit up straighter. "I suppose he was, but that's to be expected when building a company. It consumes your life."

"He must've wanted the same for you. Leaving you the company and all."

"He didn't—" I stop, before I tell her more than I should. "So you're okay if I call Kelsie?"

"Yes. Fine. So what were you saying about your father?"

I pause as I think of what to tell her. "My father didn't leave me the company. He left it to my mother, with the condition that Edward become the CEO. Edward and my father were close friends."

"And when your mother died, the company went to you?"

"The majority of it, yes. Edward also owns some shares."

"It seems unusual that your mother would leave you with such a burden."

"Adore isn't a burden. I'm honored to continue my father's legacy. And I'm not responsible for running the company like my father was. Edward's the one in charge. He has to oversee everything. I pick and choose what I want to do."

"You're putting a lot of trust into this man. Do you think that's wise?"

"I've known Edward my entire life. He's like family. I absolutely trust him."

"You should never give someone that much trust. They'll take advantage of it and turn on you."

"Are you speaking from experience?"

She smiles and pats my hand. "I'm just giving you some motherly advice. Now you go ahead and find me a babysitter for today."

"That's not what I'm—" I decide to keep quiet rather than argue over her babysitter comment. I pick up her tray and bring it to the kitchen, then get my phone and find Kelsie's number.

I can't believe I'm doing this. Kelsie is the last person I want to ask for a favor, but I really need to go into the office, not just for work purposes but for my own sanity. I'm going crazy sitting around the house all day. And I miss the city. For years, I dreamed of leaving it behind for a life in the suburbs, but now that I'm here, I'm finding I don't like it.

"Anna?" Kelsie says, answering my call. She said my name like she thinks I must have called her by mistake.

"Yes, it's me. Do you have a minute?"

"Of course. Is something wrong? Is Rose okay?"

"She's fine. Actually, she's the reason I'm calling. She had such a great time with you and the kids yesterday that I was wondering if she could go over there again today?"

"You're asking me to watch Rose for you?"

"I'm not asking you to watch her," I say, although that's exactly what I'm asking her to do. "I just think she'll have a better time there than here. But if it doesn't work for you, I understand."

"No, I'd be happy to have her come over. What time?"

"Would after lunch work? Around one?"

"Why doesn't she come over at noon? She could join us for lunch."

"Great! I'll bring her over at noon."

"I'll just come get her. The kids like to walk beside her wheelchair."

"Okay, I'll tell her you'll be by at noon. Thanks, Kelsie."

"Anytime! We all just love Rose! You're so lucky to have her for a mother-in-law."

"I sure am," I say, rolling my eyes. "See you soon." I end the call and go to the living room to tell Rose, but she's not there. I go down the hall and hear her in the bathroom. But her wheelchair is still in the living room.

I wait outside the door. When it opens, I see Rose holding onto her walker.

"Well, look at you," I say. "Already able to use the walker. Guess you'll be going home sooner than planned."

"Don't you wish," she says with a smirk. "Could you get out of the way, dear?"

I step aside and watch as she makes her way to the living room, putting weight on her ankle that just a couple days ago she claimed was causing her terrible pain. It doesn't look that painful now. It has a small brace over it, which really isn't necessary for a minor fracture, but due to her age and brittle bones, the doctor was being extra cautious.

"Did you find me a babysitter?" Rose asks, gripping the walker as she lowers herself to the couch.

"Kelsie said she'd love to have you come over. She invited you to lunch, if you're up for it."

"It's better than eating here," Rose mutters.

I ignore her comment. "Kelsie will stop by around noon. She didn't say how long you could stay, but I'll ask her when she gets here."

"You might as well leave me there until Ethan gets home. We both know you'd rather stay at work than be stuck here with me."

I grit my teeth and tell myself not to respond. I walk away and return to the kitchen where my laptop is set up.

The morning goes by quickly and before I know it, it's just before noon. I'm supposed to be at the office at one and I haven't even showered. I tell Rose I'll be upstairs getting ready, then unlock the front door in case Kelsie arrives before I'm done.

After a quick shower, I go to the closet to find something to wear. It's going to be ninety degrees today so I put on a light, summery dress, then go over to my dresser to get my jewelry. As I'm putting my earrings on, I notice my wedding ring is missing. Every night, I take it off and place it in a small marble bowl on top of the dresser. But it's not there. I get down on the floor and search for it, but don't see it. I search the bathroom, then the closet, but it's nowhere to be found.

Where could it be? I remember taking it off last night and placing it in the marble bowl. So why isn't it there? It couldn't have just disappeared.

20

"Rose, have you seen my wedding ring?" I ask, racing down the stairs.

"No. Why isn't it on your finger?"

"I take it off at night." I look around the living room, checking the floor, then the tables. "I always put it on my dresser but it's not there. I don't know what happened to it."

"I'm sure it'll show up," she says as the doorbell rings.

"That must be Kelsie." I hurry to the door and see Paul, Kelsie's oldest son, standing there holding a bouquet of flowers. Kelsie's behind him with the stroller.

"What pretty flowers," I say to Paul. "Are those for me?"

He shakes his head. "Grandma Rose."

He's calling her 'grandma'? Why? Did she tell him to?

"Is that little Paul I hear?" Rose says in a sickeningly sweet voice. She used that voice with me the day of my wedding, but hasn't since. Now she only uses it when the neighbors are around.

"Grandma Rose!" Paul yells, running into the house and over to Rose. "These are for you! To make you feel better. I helped pick them out!"

"Oh, aren't you a sweetie." She hugs him and kisses his

cheek. "Could you take these to the kitchen so Anna can put them in some water?"

He nods and runs off to the kitchen.

"Hi, Kelsie," I say as she pushes the stroller into the house.

She gives me an uncomfortable smile, then looks over at Rose. "Hi, Rose! We're so thrilled we get another afternoon with you!"

Piper jumps out of the stroller and runs over to Rose. "Hi, Grandma Rose!"

"Hi, sweetie." Rose leans down to hug her.

Paul returns, running over to Rose and sitting beside her on the couch.

This whole scene is making me ill. Rose was rude to me all morning, then Kelsie and the kids show up and it's like Rose turns back into a sweet old lady.

"Could I talk to you a minute?" I say to Kelsie. "In the kitchen?"

"Um, sure," she says, like she really doesn't want to. "Kids, I'll be right back."

Kelsie follows me into the kitchen.

"Thanks for doing this," I tell her. "I really appreciate it."

"Honestly, Anna, I don't understand you," she says.

"What do you mean?"

"You act like having Rose around is some kind of punishment when she's the absolute sweetest, kindest person I know."

"This isn't about my feelings for Rose. I just need to go into the office for—"

"I'd love to have her as a mother-in-law," Kelsie says, interrupting me as she opens my cupboards. "Mark's mother is okay, but she's very reserved and uptight. She doesn't even allow the children to sit on her lap, saying it wrinkles her clothes." She glances at me. "Don't you have a vase?"

"Here." I reach under the center island and pull one out.

She takes it from me and goes over to the sink.

"Why are your kids calling Rose grandma?"

Kelsie smiles. "They did it without even thinking, I guess because Rose seems so much like a grandma in the way she looks and how she interacts with them." Kelsie fills the vase with water. "When I pointed out that she wasn't really their grandmother, Rose insisted they call her that." She takes the flowers from the cellophane. "Do you have something to cut the stems?"

I open a drawer and hand her some scissors. "I'm not sure how late I'll be at the office, but I'll try to leave there at five."

"You don't have to rush home," she says, snipping the flower stems. "We'd love to have Rose stay for dinner. She gave me her recipe for pot roast and I'm making it tonight so it'd actually be nice if she stayed."

"Well, if she'd like to, then maybe I'll stay later at the office and catch up on some things. I haven't been able to work much from home and I'm way behind."

The vase is filled with flowers now and Kelsie lifts it from the sink and sets it on the kitchen island. "You really should think about quitting. I mean, if you're unable to work and care for Rose, you definitely won't be able to work when you have children. They take up every second of your time."

I'm starting to wonder if I'm not cut out to be a mother. It's what I always dreamed of, but that was before I spent any time around children. Being around the neighbor kids, I'm realizing how noisy children are and how they're always running around and bumping into things. It makes me very anxious and uncomfortable. But maybe that's because they're someone else's children and not mine.

"Mommy, let's go!" Piper yells, running up to Kelsie.

"Yes, honey, I'm coming," she says.

Piper jumps up and down. "Mommy, can we go to the park?"

Her little girl voice is so high and shrill it hurts my ears. And why is she jumping like that? Why can't she stand still?

"Not today," Kelsie says. "We already have lots of other fun activities planned with Grandma Rose."

"We're gonna make cookies," Piper says to me, still jumping around.

"Gluten-free, of course," Kelsie adds.

"That sounds fun," I say. "Well, I need to get going so..."

"Yes, we're leaving," Kelsie says, taking Piper's hand as we all return to the living room.

"Ready to go?" Kelsie says, smiling at Rose.

"Yes." Rose looks over at me. "Could you help me into the chair?"

I laugh a little. "Rose, you don't need the wheelchair. You've been using the walker all morning."

"No, I haven't," she says in a harsh tone. "You tried forcing me to use it, but I couldn't do it. I don't have the strength. I almost fell just trying."

Kelsie shoots an angry look my way. "How could you do that to her? She was in the hospital just last weekend and you're already forcing her to use the walker?"

"I didn't force her. She did it herself. I swear. She used the walker to get to the bathroom this morning."

"I wish that were true," Rose says with a sigh. "I desperately want to stop using the wheelchair, but sadly, I'm just not healed enough yet."

"Of course you're not," Kelsie says, going over to Rose. "Here. Let me help you." She takes Rose's arm and helps her into the wheelchair, then wheels her toward the front door. "Paul, can you get the door for me?"

"I'll do it," I say, but Paul beats me to it, opening the door for Kelsie. She pushes the wheelchair outside while Paul waits behind the stroller as his sister gets in her seat. The younger one, Poppy, is asleep, a blanket over her. I don't know how she can sleep through all the noise and commotion her siblings make. Paul pushes the stroller outside and follows his mom down the path leading away from the house.

None of them even told me goodbye. Rose has them convinced I'm a terrible person. Like saying I made her use the walker? Rose clearly wanted to make me look bad to Kelsie, who she knows will blab that story to the entire neighborhood. Why is Rose doing this? Why is she trying to turn everyone against me?

Even though they're gone, I'm still feeling on edge. I open the drawer where I keep my anxiety meds and take out the bottle. I've been trying to wean myself off my meds, but today I need them to calm down so I can think straight at work. I take a pill, then call Ethan, realizing I need to tell him I'm going into the office.

"Hi, honey," he answers. "Everything okay?"

"Yes, I just wanted to let you know I'm going into the office this afternoon."

"What about Mother?" he asks, sounding alarmed, like I'm leaving her all alone.

"She went to Kelsie's house for the afternoon. She's having lunch there and probably dinner too."

"Why? Did you and Mother have an argument?"

"No, it's nothing like that. I just need to go into the office. This new ad campaign has turned into a huge mess now that the model we wanted isn't available."

"And Mother's okay with you leaving?"

Who cares if she's okay with it? I don't need her approval. I think that, but don't say it.

"She was happy about it," I say. "She loves spending time with Kelsie's children."

"I can't wait to have our own," Ethan says. "Mother will be so happy. She's been wanting this for years."

But do I want it? I'm not so sure anymore. Ethan definitely

wants children, so I guess I don't have a choice in the matter. Telling Ethan I've changed my mind about children would probably lead to him divorcing me.

"What time will you be home tonight?" I ask Ethan.

"I'm not sure. I have a meeting that might run late."

"Then I might work late too. I have so much to catch up on." I check the time. "I need to get going. I was hoping to be in the office by one."

"Yes, goodbye, honey. I love you."

"I love you too." I end the call and race out the door, locking it behind me.

On the short drive to the train, I feel an overwhelming sense of freedom, like a teenager who cut class and got away with it. I shouldn't feel this way. I'm an adult. I should be able to come and go as I please, but I feel like my freedom's been taken away from me since Ethan's mother moved in. Taking care of Rose, I feel like I'm stuck in that house and have to beg for permission to leave.

I wish I'd never agreed to let her live with us, but I have a feeling that even if I hadn't agreed to it, she'd be living with us anyway. Ethan's far more attached to his mother than he led me to believe. He would've never stuck her in a home, even for just a few weeks while she recovers. Even if I'd told him no, he would've insisted she stay with us.

Sometimes I wonder if Ethan loves his mother more than he loves me.

21

When I get to the city, it instantly feels like home. The crowds, the noise, the smells, were all things that used to bother me, but now I miss those things. Suburban life isn't giving me the peace and happiness I thought it would. I love living with Ethan, but I wish we'd chosen to live here rather than the suburbs.

"Anna!" Candace squeals, running up to me as I get off the elevator. "Why didn't you tell me you were coming in today?"

"I wanted it to be a surprise." I smile at her, realizing how much I missed her, and missed being here at the office. I'm quickly learning I'm not the stay-at-home type, which makes me question if I should be a mother. Sure, I could get a nanny for when I'm at work, but Ethan doesn't want that. He's already told me he wants me to stay home with our children, at least until they start school.

"Do you want me to get you some coffee?" Candace asks. "From that place you like down the street?"

"That would be wonderful," I tell her, realizing how I used to take for granted that someone got my coffee each morning. Now I have to make my own. Ethan used to make it before he left for work, but now he won't, worrying that the noise in the kitchen might wake his mother. Since she moved in, our entire life revolves around her and I'm getting tired of it.

"Anna," James says, catching me before I go into my office. "I need to move our meeting to later this afternoon. You're not leaving early, are you?"

"I was actually planning to stay late. A neighbor is watching Rose so I don't need to rush home."

"Great! So maybe meet around four?"

"Yes, see you then."

James races off as I go into my office. I stop in front of the floor-to-ceiling windows and gaze out at the city. I miss it so much. What was I thinking moving to the suburbs? That's not me. I'm a city girl. Born and raised in Manhattan. Why did I ever believe I'd want to live anywhere else?

I know the reason, but I don't like thinking about it because it brings up painful memories from my childhood. Memories of my father leaving for work before sunrise and returning hours after the sun went down. When he'd finally get home, he'd go into his study and drink. I rarely saw him, and when I did, all he wanted to talk about was work. He had no interest in what I did at school that day or how my violin lessons were going or anything related to my life. The only real time I spent with him was when he'd take me to our factories and show me around. I treasured those times, which is why I'm so enamored with the manufacturing side of the business. It's a connection to my father, and one of the few memories I have of us doing something together.

Growing up, I dreamed of having the family you see on TV, the kind that ate dinner together every night and did things together on the weekends. I wanted to live in a big house with a yard in a neighborhood with trees and perfect lawns, because that's what the families on TV had. I wanted a handsome husband who had a good job but always made time for his family.

I held on to that fantasy into adulthood, believing it was not only possible, but something I really wanted. Now I'm not so sure. A few weeks into my so-called perfect life isn't proving to be the dream I had hoped for. And with Rose living with us, it's more like a nightmare.

Sitting down at my desk, I start up my laptop and look through the files stacked up next to it. I'm going through them when Candace returns with my coffee.

"Here you go," she says, handing me the cup, along with a small paper sack. "I got you a blueberry scone too. I know they're your favorite."

I sip the coffee and relax back into my very expensive chair. It's another thing I miss. Working in my kitchen and sitting on an uncomfortable stool all day has left me with a big knot in my back.

"This is heaven," I say, taking another sip of my coffee.

Candace laughs. "What do you mean?"

"Being here. Back at work, in this comfortable chair, having my coffee, looking out at the city."

"I thought you liked living in Connecticut."

"Not really," I say, being honest. Candace is one of the few people I feel I can be totally honest with, knowing she won't judge me. "The neighbors don't like me and now, with Rose there, they pretty much hate me."

"Why?" Candace asks, sitting down across from me.

"Rose is trying to turn them against me by telling them I don't want her there. She's making me sound like a terrible person." I pause. "Maybe I am." I look at Candace. "I hate to say this, but I wish Rose had never moved in. Does that make me a bad person?"

"No! Not at all," Candace says, like I'm crazy to even think that. "You and Ethan are newlyweds. You're supposed to be enjoying this time as a couple and now you can't because his mother is living there. Ethan's a great guy, but I think it's wrong of him to make you take care of her. I mean, it's his mother. Why isn't *he* the one who has to work from home and take care of her?"

"Exactly," I say, pleased to finally have someone take my side on this. "Ethan thinks since Adore is my company that I can just take time off whenever I want. He doesn't seem to understand that people depend on me to be here. I don't think he even knows what I do here. When I try to tell him, it's almost like he doesn't believe me, like he thinks I'm just delegating the work, not actually doing it."

"So what are you going to do?"

"Nothing. I just have to adjust to this new life and hope it gets better."

"I'm sorry things aren't going well." Candace frowns. "You seem really sad, almost depressed."

"I *am* depressed, but only because I didn't think it would be like this. I imagined my life with Ethan looking totally different than how it turned out."

"You've only been married a few weeks. Maybe just give it some time. I'm sure things will get better. And Rose won't be there forever."

"I'm not so sure about that," I say, taking the scone from the sack.

"What do you mean?"

"She made some comment about not being able to live alone, like she was going to make sure she never went back to her house." I take a bite of the scone, certain they must have changed the recipe because it tastes even better than I remember. Being back in the city, everything seems better than I remember.

"Ethan would have to agree to that," Candace says. "Do you think he would?"

"Yes. Especially if Rose puts on the helpless old lady act. I think she's lying about what she can do. She makes Ethan and everyone else think she needs the wheelchair, but this morning she went to the bathroom by herself using her walker. Then the neighbor came to get Rose for the afternoon and when I told her Rose no longer needs the wheelchair, Rose acted like I was crazy."

Candace sighs. "I wish I had some advice, but I don't know what to tell you."

"There's really nothing I can do. She's Ethan's mother. I can't just kick her out on the street." I take another sip of coffee. "It's gotten so bad that I had to take my anxiety meds today. I've been off them for months, but with everything that's happened, my anxiety feels out of control."

"Is it better now?"

"Yes, but I don't know if it's because of the pills or because I'm finally away from Rose and the house and the neighborhood I'm starting to hate."

"Maybe I shouldn't ask this, but... do you regret marrying Ethan?"

"No. Absolutely not. I love Ethan. I just don't like living so far from the city and having nosy neighbors who watch everything I do."

"Then move back here."

"I don't think Ethan would agree to it. He loves it out there. He loves the house, the yard, the neighbors. I can't see him ever moving back." I lean back in the chair. "I feel trapped. Like I'm stuck there forever, living a life that isn't me. But it's what I chose. I can't get out of it now." My office phone rings and I pick it up. "This is Anna."

"I heard a rumor you were here," Edward says in his deep, gravelly voice. "Come down to my office. We have a lot to go over, including this ad campaign delay I keep hearing about."

"Yes, okay. I'll be there in a minute." I end the call and get up from my desk. "I need to go talk to Edward."

"Go ahead. Is there anything you need me to do?"

"Just make sure my calendar is up to date. James changed our meeting to four."

"I'll get right on it," she says, hurrying back to her desk.

Going to Edward's office, I realize I've missed him too. He's harsh and demanding and sets unreasonably high expectations, but I still missed the old man, which just shows how much I took my old life for granted.

"Mrs. Halstrom," Edward says as I go into his office. I look behind me for Rose, then realize Edward meant me. *I'm* Mrs. Halstrom. "Welcome back."

"Thank you, but it's just for the afternoon." I sit down across from him. "How did you know I changed my name?"

"I saw it on one of the company memos." He folds his hands, resting them on his desk. "I thought you'd decided to keep your maiden name."

"I thought so too."

He chuckles. "Is that supposed to be a joke?"

"No. I don't know what happened, but for some reason I can't remember deciding to change my name or filling out the paperwork."

His brows draw together, concern filling his wrinkled face. "What do you mean, you don't remember?"

"I just don't. I saw the email I sent, telling Candace to print out the paperwork, but I don't remember sending it."

"I see," he says in a serious tone. I know what he's thinking but it can't be. I'm only 35.

"I had a lot going on before the wedding," I say, trying to explain my memory lapse. "I was so busy trying to get everything done that I must've just forgot about the name change."

"Seems like a rather major thing to forget."

I look down. "Yes. It does."

The room is silent. I feel a lump in my throat and my heart going faster.

My eyes rise to Edward's. "You don't think..." I wait for him to finish the thought.

"No! Absolutely not. You're far too young. Your mother was much older before she started showing signs."

"Yes, but it can happen when you're younger. I looked it up online. It's called early-onset dementia and it can happen in your thirties."

"Listen to me!" he says, slamming his hand on the desk and leaning toward me. "You are young and healthy. You do not have dementia simply because you forgot you'd sent an email."

"Yes, but like you said, this is something major. It wasn't an email about rescheduling a meeting or what day to have the company picnic. It was about changing my name, something I never intended to do. How could I forget that?"

"I don't know, but it isn't because of what you're thinking."

I let out a heavy sigh. "It's not just that. It's other things. Things Ethan claims I said that I don't remember saying. Or the whole grocery list thing with Rose."

"What grocery list?"

"I went to the grocery store and got all these things Rose said she wanted, but when I got home, she claimed she never asked for those things. They were all foods she doesn't even like."

"Maybe your mother-in-law is the one with the memory issues. It's possible she told you to get those things and then forgot."

"I told Ethan that, but he doesn't believe me."

"Because he doesn't want it to be true. It's just like you and your mother. Remember how you kept denying she was having issues?"

"Yes. I denied it even when I knew it was true."

"Exactly. Ethan may be doing that as well. Has his mother shown other signs of forgetfulness or confusion?"

"She often forgets to take her pills, and the other day she

asked me to get her slippers when they were already on her feet."

"Well, there you have it. It's her who's getting things mixed up, not you."

"But that doesn't explain me forgetting about changing my name."

"It's probably like you said. You were busy with things here at work along with the wedding preparations and simply forgot you'd sent that email. Perhaps you and Ethan had discussed the name change and he convinced you to at least consider it, which explains why you printed out the paperwork. It doesn't matter. The point is, you do not have what your mother had. You need to put that out of your head."

"Thank you, Edward. That makes me feel a lot better." I laugh a little. "I was honestly starting to wonder if I was going crazy."

He looks at me, cocking his head slightly. "I think it might be time I meet this new family of yours."

"Yes. Definitely. Maybe next week. Would you mind going to the house? I'd love for you to see it."

"I'll need to check my schedule, but sometime next week should work." He wakes up his computer. "Enough personal talk. Tell me what's happening with this ad campaign."

I go over it with him, feeling so much better now that he's convinced me it's Rose that has memory issues, not me. She's at the right age for this to be a problem. Even older people without dementia can get confused or struggle to remember things. Sometimes it's a side effect of their medication and Rose takes a lot of pills.

I'm so glad I came into the office today. Seeing everyone again. Talking to Edward. Being in the hustle and bustle of the city. It's just what I needed.

22

"I'm glad we decided to do this," I say as the waiter clears our plates. "I miss all the great restaurants here."

My meeting with James got pushed to five so we decided to go to a restaurant and discuss things over dinner. It was my idea. I don't mind being in the office, but I wanted to go out tonight. Being back here, I'm appreciating the city and all there is to do here, in a way I never have before. I can't believe I used to hide in my apartment every night and never go out. If I lived here now, I'd be out all the time.

James chuckles. "You've mentioned that several times tonight. All the things you miss about the city. Have you considered moving back?"

"I can't. Ethan and I have a house now, and he loves it there. He loves the town and our neighborhood. He's already made several friends and they were able to get him accepted for membership at the country club. Soon I'll officially be a golf widow." I laugh, but it actually makes me sad. I didn't want Ethan joining the country club. I worried he'd spend his weekends there instead of with me, and sure enough, that's what's happening. He's already reserved tee times for both

Saturday and Sunday, which means I'll be stuck at home, caring for Rose.

"But what about you?" James asks. "Are you happy there?"

I shrug. "I'm sure I will be after I've been there longer. Being there is a huge change after living in the city my whole life. It's taking time to adjust."

He nods. "I get that."

I pick up my glass of wine and finish what's left of it. I ordered a bottle and drank almost all of it. James just had a glass. It was an excellent wine. I splurged on a very expensive bottle. Since this was a work meeting, I'm charging the meal to Adore. Ethan will never see the bill, not that I care if he did. There's nothing wrong with me going out for dinner or letting it drag out for two hours. Why should I have to rush home to care for Rose? Ethan can do it. He needs to be helping out more instead of making me do everything.

"You okay?" James asks.

"Yes." I smile at him. "Why do you ask?"

"Your face. You looked angry all of a sudden. Was it something I said?"

"No. It has nothing to do with you. It's the situation at home. I'm feeling overwhelmed having to care for my mother-in-law. But that's none of your concern. I shouldn't even be talking about it."

"You can if you want." He smiles. "I'm a good listener."

James is a very nice man. I've always liked him. I hired him after only one interview, impressed with his knowledge of the ad industry and his drive and dedication to his career. He was married in his twenties, but it didn't work out. Now he's almost forty and not seeing anyone as far as I know. Not that I'm interested in him. I'm a married woman.

In a way, James reminds me of Ethan, or how he used to be before we got married. Back then, Ethan listened to me and was very attentive to my needs. Now he doesn't pay attention to my needs and barely notices when I'm talking. And yet all the women who meet him gush about how wonderful he is and how lucky I am to have him. "He's such a good husband," they say, as if they know what he's like when we're alone.

I really shouldn't complain. Ethan *is* a good husband. He's just not the same man he was before we got married. He used to act as though I was the most special person in the world to him, the love of his life, something to be treasured. Now he takes me for granted, expecting me to care for his mother just because I'm his wife.

"Anna." I hear Ethan's voice and think I must be imagining it, until I see him coming up to the table.

"Ethan," I say, my heart racing, my throat going dry. I need to calm down. I didn't do anything wrong. I'm just having dinner. A work dinner. With an employee. "What are you doing here?"

"I thought we could take the train home together. I went to your office looking for you, but Candace said you were here."

"Candace is still at the office?" I check the time. "It's after seven."

"She's probably getting things ready for the presentation tomorrow," James says. "Jill asked her to help out because her assistant went home sick. It sounded like they'd have to stay late to get everything done."

Ethan clears his throat. "I'm Ethan Halstrom," he says to James.

"Sorry, I should've introduced you," I rush to say. "Ethan, this is James. James, this is Ethan."

"Anna's *husband*," Ethan says, glaring at James.

Is Ethan jealous I'm here with James? That's ridiculous. He knows I'd never cheat on him. I just wanted a night out in the city. I'd rather be here with Ethan, but he doesn't seem to have time for me anymore.

"It's nice to meet you," James says. He backs his chair out. "I should go," he says to me. "I didn't realize it was this late."

It's not late. James is only saying that because he senses Ethan is angry at him for being out with me.

"Let me know if the ad agency can get the model we chose in time for the shoot," I tell him.

"Yes, I'll be in touch." He glances at Ethan. "Hope to see you again sometime."

As he leaves, Ethan sits down in the chair next to mine. "This is certainly a surprise. We've only been married a few weeks and I already find you with another man?"

"Ethan, it was a business meeting. James is my employee. We were just having dinner."

"At a very nice restaurant." Ethan glances at the empty wine bottle. "Having a very expensive bottle of wine. I'd like to believe you, Anna, but I don't think you'd be too happy if the roles were reversed."

"Ethan, please, don't be like this." I put my hand over his. "You know I love you. You know I'd never be with another man."

"And yet you were."

"For a work meeting. That's all it was."

He glances down at my hand. "Why aren't you wearing your ring?"

My ring! I forget I wasn't wearing it.

"I couldn't find it," I say. "I left it on the dresser last night and when I went to put it on this morning, it was gone."

"Your ring just disappeared? You really expect me to believe that?"

"Yes, because it's true. I searched our entire bedroom for it, then the bathroom, the closet. I couldn't find it anywhere."

"And what do you suppose happened to it? We're the only people there and I certainly didn't take it."

"I don't know how to explain it. I just know it wasn't there."

The waiter stops at our table and says to Ethan, "Can I get you anything?"

"No, we're leaving. We'll take the bill."

"It's already been paid." The waiter smiles at us. "Have a good evening."

Ethan waits for the guy to leave, then says, "Let's go."

We get up and Ethan grasps my arm and marches us out of the restaurant.

"Ethan, I swear, nothing happened," I say as we head to the train station.

"I don't want you going there again." He's walking fast, so fast I'm finding it hard to keep up.

"Going where?"

"To the office. You can work from home, which is what you should've been doing today instead of having a romantic dinner with another man and calling it work."

"You're being ridiculous. It was just dinner. There was nothing romantic about it. Nothing happened with James, and nothing will ever happen with him. And as for going into the office, I will do so if I please."

He glances at me with dark, angry eyes. "We'll talk about this when we get home."

Ethan and I are silent on the train ride back to Connecticut. When I check my phone, I see a text message from Candace, saying Ethan came by the office and asked where I was, then another message asking if I'm mad at her for telling him. I text her back that I'm not angry with her and that Ethan met up with me at the restaurant and we're on our way home.

What's strange is that Ethan never tried to contact me. If he wanted to meet up with me, why didn't he just call or text me?

We're home just before eight. Rose is in the living room, watching one of her shows.

"Mother, what are you doing here alone?" Ethan asks, racing up to her.

"Kelsie had to get the children to bed. I didn't want to be in her way so I asked her to take me back to the house. I told her you'd be home soon."

"How are you feeling?"

"Tired," she says with an exaggerated sigh. "I should probably get to bed."

"Anna, would you help her?" Ethan asks.

"Can't *you*?" I shoot back.

Maybe I'm imagining it, but I swear I see Rose's lips turn up just slightly. She knows Ethan and I are fighting. The tension between us is impossible not to notice.

"Anna, let's go upstairs and let Mother finish her program," Ethan says, then he says to Rose, "One of us will be down shortly to help get you ready for bed."

I follow Ethan upstairs to our room and shut the door.

"Doesn't seem to be missing now," Ethan says, standing by the dresser.

"What do you mean?" I walk over to him.

He points to the small marble bowl on the dresser. And there, in the center of the bowl, is my wedding ring.

23

"I don't understand." I turn to Ethan. "I swear to you, my ring wasn't here this morning. I searched this entire room and it wasn't here."

"Do you really expect me to believe that? Why don't you just tell me the truth?"

"I did!" I say, raising my voice. "I'm telling you, it wasn't here."

He folds his arms over his chest. "So you're saying it disappeared into thin air sometime this morning, then reappeared tonight?"

"Obviously it didn't disappear," I snap. "Someone had to have taken it."

"Who? I certainly didn't. So who else could it be?"

I hesitate, then say, "Your mother."

Ethan laughs. "You think my mother did this? She can't even walk on her own, and you think she somehow made it up a flight of stairs?"

"Maybe. She's not as weak and feeble as you think. This morning I found her using her walker to get to the bathroom."

"Anna, she could've fallen! Why weren't you watching her?"

"I was in the kitchen. I didn't see her get up. Ethan, you're missing the point, which is that Rose had enough strength to get to the bathroom on her own using the walker. She doesn't need the wheelchair. She's just pretending she does."

"Pretending?" He shakes his head in disbelief. "Are you seriously accusing my mother of *pretending* to need a wheelchair?"

"How else do you explain it? If she was able to use the walker, why would she keep using the wheelchair?"

"I don't know, Anna," he says sarcastically. "Why don't you tell me, since you seem to be the expert on my mother."

"Just forget it," I say, walking away. "I can't talk to you when you're like this." I turn back to him. "Oh, and I'm off duty for the night. You'll have to care for your mother yourself."

I go into the bathroom and shut the door, hearing Ethan's footsteps as he leaves to go be with Rose. I fall to the floor and silently cry, wondering how we ended up here. Just a few weeks ago, everything was perfect. Now it feels like it's all falling apart.

Rose had to be the one who took my ring, but I don't know how she did it. Did Kelsie help her? What if Rose convinced Kelsie I'm a horrible wife and that her dear son Ethan deserves someone better? I could see her doing that, and I could see Kelsie going along with it, and the two of them hatching a plan to make Ethan think I'm cheating on him so he'll divorce me.

But how was Kelsie able to hide my ring? Her only opportunity to do so would've been when I was in the shower. But that means Rose would've had to call Kelsie and get her to race down here and sneak up to my room before I got out of the shower. It's certainly possible, but how did they know to do it today? They didn't know I was going to have dinner with James and that Ethan would show up at the restaurant and find us together.

When I get into bed, Ethan is still downstairs, making me

wonder if he's going to sleep down there. I don't care if he does. I really don't want to be around him right now. I'm his wife. He should believe me when I tell him something, not accuse me of making things up.

Just after midnight, Ethan comes back to the bedroom and gets into bed. He doesn't say anything and doesn't kiss me goodnight. He doesn't even get near me. He turns so his back is to me and stays on his side of the bed.

When I wake up in the morning, Ethan is gone. I get up and check for my ring and see it's still sitting in the bowl. During the night, I thought more about my theory and decided it was far-fetched and a little ridiculous. Kelsie and Rose wouldn't come up with some elaborate plan like that, especially since they had no idea I was going to have dinner with James. I still can't explain what happened to my ring, but it's back now and my focus needs to be on fixing things with Ethan.

"Good morning, Rose," I say, seeing her on the couch as I come down the stairs. As usual, the TV is blaring with whatever show she's watching. "Did Ethan help you get ready this morning?"

"No." Her eyes dart to mine and a slight smile appears on her pudgy face. "Liz did."

"Liz?" I stop as I reach the second to last stair. "Did Ethan call her?"

"Yes, and she was more than happy to help out. She gets up early, you know, to go to the gym." Rose glances at my body. "Maybe you should join her. Ethan's always preferred women who are fit and trim."

I ignore her comment and continue to the kitchen, but part of me is wondering if maybe I *should* go to the gym. I'm not fat, but I'm certainly not in shape, especially compared to

Liz and Kelsie. Those two could be fitness models. Liz is always wearing sleeveless shirts to show off her arms, which I have to admit are impressive. She must work out constantly to have arms like that. I'm sure Ethan's noticed them, along with the rest of her perfect body. Is that why he had her come over this morning? To make me think there's something going on with him and Liz? To get back at me for being out with James?

I have to get my marriage back on track. I'm angry with Ethan, but I still love him and want to be with him. Maybe I could do something special for him, like make him a special dinner. One that takes time and effort and shows how much I care about him and our relationship. But how can I have a romantic dinner with Ethan with his mother here?

"Anna!" Rose yells from the living room. "I need to eat and take my pills!"

"I'm coming." I go over to her. "What would you like today?"

"Two poached eggs and toast."

"I don't know how to make poached eggs."

She sighs in annoyance. "Take me to the kitchen. It's about time you start learning to cook."

I help her into the wheelchair. "Speaking of that, could you teach me how to cook that roast you had me buy?" I wheel her into the kitchen. "I don't know what to do with it."

"I'd teach you tonight, but I won't be here."

"Why? Where are you going?"

"Piper and Gigi are putting on a little show for me tonight." She smiles. "They're calling it a dance recital. It's a practice run for the actual recital, which is this weekend."

"So you're going to Kelsie's house tonight?"

"No, Liz's place. She's making dinner. I haven't been to her house yet, but Ethan has. He said it's quite nice."

"Ethan's been to Liz's house?" I ask, my stomach knotting up.

"Get the eggs out. We need to hurry this up. I'm starving."

I'm not going to worry about Ethan being at Liz's house. I'm sure he was there to see Jeremy. The two of them are becoming good friends, which is unfortunate because I really don't like Jeremy.

Rose instructs me how to make the poached eggs and is surprisingly nice about it. She doesn't criticize me once, even when I drop an egg on the floor. I make four eggs total so I have two for myself.

Rose and I eat our breakfast at the counter and it's actually pleasant. Why can't Rose be like this all the time? Why is she always antagonizing me?

"Since you'll be gone tonight," I say, "I think I'll make dinner for Ethan. Something he'll really like. Do you have any suggestions?"

She pauses a moment to think. "He likes those fancy raviolis."

"What do you mean by fancy?"

"The kind with lobster inside. I don't know where you get that, but I know he really likes it."

"I'm sure they sell it at the store. What kind of sauce would you use?"

"Something with butter and garlic. I'm sure there's recipes on that computer of yours."

"Do you think I could make it or would it be too hard?"

"Cooking isn't hard. All you have to do is follow instructions."

I get up and take our plates to the sink. "If I'm doing this, I'll need to get to the store. I'm not sure I'll have time."

"Go right now."

I look at Rose. "And leave you here?"

"I'll be fine. Just don't be gone too long."

Is this a trick? Is she going to call Ethan the minute I leave and tell him I left her alone?

"What are you waiting for?" Rose says.

"Are you sure you're okay with this?" I walk up to her. "You're not going to tell Ethan, are you?"

"For heaven's sake, you're so paranoid. Always thinking everyone's out to get you."

"I'm not paranoid. But we both know Ethan doesn't want me leaving you alone and if he finds out—"

"He's fine with it. I talked to him this morning, told him I don't need so much supervision. I feel like I'm suffocating with you two always watching me. I'm used to living alone, having time to myself."

I grab my keys from the counter. "Okay, I'm going. I won't be gone long. Do you want me to take you back to the living room?"

"No, I'll stay here until you get back. I need a change of scenery."

"You're just going to sit here with nothing to do?"

"I'll figure out something. Now stop asking so many questions and get out of here."

As I'm driving to the store, I wonder if I can trust that Rose was telling me the truth. She better not be calling Ethan right now, tattling on me for leaving her alone. If she does, Ethan and I will be having another fight tonight instead of a romantic dinner.

24

"Welcome home," I say to Ethan when he walks through the door. I go up to him, wrap my arms around him, and give him a kiss.

"That's quite the greeting," he says with a cautious smile. "What's going on?"

"We're having a romantic dinner." I take his hand and bring him to the kitchen. "I've got the pasta cooking, the sauce simmering, and the salad chilling in the fridge."

"What's the occasion?"

"There's no occasion. I just want to end this fight we're having. I want us to go back to how things were."

"I couldn't agree more." He gives me a kiss. "I love you, sweetheart. I hope you know how much."

"I do," I say, although I was starting to doubt his love for me last night.

"I'll go up and change," he says. "How soon is dinner?"

"In a few minutes. I was just about to open a bottle of wine."

"I'll be down shortly." He walks off, then comes back. "Where's Mother?"

"At Liz's house. Rose was invited to have dinner there and then Piper and Gigi are going to put on a little recital for her."

Ethan smiles. "It's funny how much the children have taken to her. They're even calling her Grandma Rose." He undoes his tie. "Whatever you're making smells delicious. I can't wait to try it." He leaves and goes upstairs to our room.

This dinner is just what Ethan and I needed. Just the two of us, enjoying a romantic dinner without any interruptions from Rose. Then after dinner, I'm hoping we'll go up to our room and finally be intimate again. We haven't made love since Rose moved in. Before that, we were intimate daily, sometimes more than that. I understand Ethan's libido suffered when he was worried about his mother's health, but she's better now and we need to get that part of our relationship back.

When Ethan comes back downstairs, dressed in casual pants and a black polo shirt, I notice how handsome he is and feel my desire for him return. Last night, his refusal to believe me made me not even want to kiss him, but I'm over it now. I have to be if I want to save my marriage.

"Are you hungry?" I ask, in a seductive way.

"More than you know." His eyes move down my body, which is barely covered by the short and revealing dress I have on. It's red and clings to me in all the right places and has a low neckline that shows off some cleavage. Ethan comes up to me, his hands wrapping around my hips as he leans down to kiss my neck. "Why don't we move dinner to later and start with something else?"

"I would, but I've already got everything ready and I'm really excited for you to try it." I give him a sexy smile. "But we'll have time for other things later."

He looks at me with lust in his eyes. "Let's hurry up and get this dinner started."

Ethan and I are back. I can already feel it. We're back to how we were, reeling with desire for each other, our hearts overflowing with the love we felt on our wedding day. This past week was just a bump in the road, one of many we'll experience in the years ahead, but our love will get us through them.

"This looks wonderful," Ethan says as we take our seats across from each other at the dining room table. We've only used this table once since moving into the house, mainly because we always went out to eat. It's nice to use the table. We should do it more often.

I pick up my wine glass. "To us."

Ethan raises his glass to mine. "To us."

We clink our glasses and our eyes meet across the table. I can feel our desire for each other bubbling up, heating up the space between us. I almost want to skip dinner and get to the next part of our evening, but after all the time I spent making this meal, we should probably eat it.

"What do you think?" I ask as Ethan tries the salad.

"It's excellent. What's the dressing?"

"An herb vinaigrette made with champagne vinegar. I didn't know that was a thing until I found a recipe that called for it. I had to ask someone at the store where to find it."

"When were you able to go to the store?"

"This morning."

"You left Mother alone?"

"I wasn't gone long. And Rose said you two spoke this morning and agreed she doesn't need to be watched all the time."

"Yes, we did talk about that, but I'd like to be informed when she's left alone so I can check in with her and make sure she's okay."

"Of course. That's not a problem, and I can certainly check in with her as well."

This is good progress. We're having a conversation about Rose that isn't leading to an argument. When I told Ethan I'd left Rose by herself, I was prepared for him to yell at me for it, but instead, we calmly discussed it and moved on. This is how marriage should be. Two mature adults talking things out. I couldn't be happier with how this evening is turning out and it's only just begun.

"How do you like it?" I ask as Ethan takes a bite of the ravioli.

He stops chewing and looks down at his plate. "What are these filled with?"

"Lobster," I proudly say. "Your favorite."

Ethan's eyes get huge and his hand goes to his throat. He shoves away from the table and races out of the dining room.

"Ethan, what's wrong?" I yell, thinking he choked on something. I jump up from my chair and search for where he went. "Ethan?"

Going to the living room, I hear noise coming from the hall bathroom. I run down there and see the door is closed.

"Ethan!" I knock on the door, hearing the sound of the sink turning on. "Ethan, can I come in?"

He doesn't answer. Maybe he didn't hear me over the running water. I slowly open the door and see him bent over the sink, scooping water into his mouth with his hand, then spitting it out.

"What happened?" I ask, my heart pounding in my chest. "Did you choke on something?"

He shuts the water off and grabs the hand towel, drying his hands and mouth. He tosses the towel on the counter and turns to me.

"How could you?" he asks, with venom in his eyes.

"What... what do you mean?" I feel my heart going even faster. He's never looked at me this way. It's scaring me.

"You gave me lobster," he says, through gritted teeth. "Knowing I'm allergic to shellfish."

"You're..." I shake my head. "No. No, I would know if you were allergic to shellfish."

"You DO know. I told you on our first date. And there's a note in the kitchen that lists out what I'm allergic to, just in case you forget."

"What note? There's no note in the kitchen."

He grabs my wrist and drags me through the living room to the kitchen, stopping next to the cupboard that's closest to the fridge. He opens the cupboard, and taped to the door is a piece of paper. Printed on top, in big bold letters, it reads 'Ethan's Allergies', and under it is a list of foods. All shellfish. Lobster is the first one.

"Ethan, I..." My throat does dry as I stare at the list, not believing it's real. How could it be? I don't remember ever seeing it before now. And I have no memory of Ethan ever telling me he couldn't have shellfish.

"Were you trying to kill me? Is that what this dinner was for? You regret marrying me so you decided to—"

"No!" I turn to face him. "Ethan, I swear, I didn't know you were allergic to shellfish."

"Christ, not this again," he says, walking away. "It's just like last night, claiming you lost your ring when it was right there, on the dresser." He turns back to me. "Anna, what the hell is wrong with you? Do you have some kind of mental issue you neglected to tell me about? Dual personalities? Memory problems?"

My heart nearly stops when he says memory problems. Oh, God, what if it's happening? What if I really am becoming my mother, slowly losing my memory and forgetting things? Edward said I was too young, but what does he know? He's not a doctor. The articles I found online said dementia can happen as early as age 30. It's extremely rare at that age, but still possible.

"You're just lucky I didn't eat more of that," Ethan says. "If

I had, I'd be covered in hives right now. I still have a scratchy throat, but that should pass." He rubs the front of his neck and takes a deep breath.

I race up to him. "Ethan, I'm so sorry. I don't know what's wrong with me. I don't know how I could—" I stop when I realize it was Rose who told me to make the lobster ravioli. Rose did this. She set me up. Again.

"I need to go take an antihistamine," Ethan says, walking away. "Just to be safe."

"Ethan, wait!" I catch up to him, grabbing his arm and stopping him. "It was your mother. I asked her what you'd like for dinner. She's the one who told me to make the lobster ravioli."

He yanks his arm from my grasp. "You're blaming my mother for this?" He turns to me, gripping my shoulders. "Anna, do you hear yourself? Do you hear how crazy you sound?"

"Ethan, I'm telling you. She did this. She told me to make lobster ravioli. She said it was your favorite."

"Anna, listen to what you're saying. You're claiming my mother, my own flesh and blood, told you to make something that could make me, her son, very sick."

He's right. It doesn't make sense. Rose wouldn't do that. She loves Ethan more than anything in this world. But I know what she said this morning. I know she told me he likes lobster ravioli, that it was his favorite. And she knew I was going to the store to get it.

Or what if none of that really happened? What if I was the one who decided to make Ethan lobster ravioli? What if my ring was never missing? What if everything that hasn't made sense the past few weeks all leads back to me? To my mind? What if I'm becoming delusional like my mother? And forgetful? And paranoid, accusing people of turning against me?

"I don't know what to say," I mutter as I gaze at the floor.

"Perhaps you should see someone," Ethan says, his voice now soft and concerned. "Anna, I'm worried about you."

I am too. I'm worried I'm developing the same condition that took my mother from me long before she died. As her mind deteriorated, she became someone else, a hollow shell with glassy eyes that stared at blank walls, barely blinking. I'd say her name and she wouldn't respond, as if she could no longer hear me. But before that, years before she got to that point, there were signs that something was wrong. Signs I'm now seeing in myself.

Oh God, no. Please no. This can't be happening.

"Come sit down," Ethan says, taking my arm and leading me to the sofa.

"I'm so sorry," I whisper as Ethan sits beside me. "I don't know what's wrong with me."

"It's okay." He puts his arm around me. "We'll figure it out."

"I had to have known. About your allergy." A tear slides down my cheek as I realize the awful truth that I'm becoming my mother.

"It's going to be okay," Ethan says, in a calm, soothing voice.

I turn and rest my head on his chest, more tears going down my face. Despite what Ethan said, it's not going to be okay. This is just the start of what will soon by a long, painful journey. I know because I was there, for every horrible part of it. I watched my dear, sweet mother slowly lose her mind, until there was nothing left of it.

25

"I never told you about my mother," I say to Ethan, knowing he might be angry I didn't tell him this before, but I can't keep this from him. Not now.

"What about her?" he asks.

I sit up and turn to Ethan. "She wasn't well... mentally."

"What do you mean?"

"She couldn't remember things, and over time, she became paranoid and delusional. It got worse every year. In the last year of her life, she didn't even know me. She wouldn't look at me when I went to see her. It was like she was in a trance."

"Why didn't you tell me this before now?" Ethan says.

"I didn't want you to know. I thought you wouldn't marry me if you did."

"Are you saying this is hereditary?"

"The doctors say it's not, but I'm still terrified I'll get it."

Ethan holds my hand. "If the doctors say it's not hereditary, then maybe you're fine."

"I want to believe that, but Ethan, think about all that's happened. Like me forgetting I filled out the paperwork to change my name. How could I just forget that I'd done that?"

"You had a lot going on during that time. Planning our wedding. Picking out a house. Dealing with things at work."

"Those things shouldn't have caused me to forget something as important as changing my name. And what about my ring? It obviously didn't just disappear yesterday. What if I made it up in my head? I even had myself thinking Kelsie was in on it. That she and your mother were setting me up so you'd think I was cheating and want to divorce me."

Ethan doesn't say anything.

I grip his arm. "You think I'm crazy, don't you?"

"I think you're under a lot of stress. And I know you struggle with anxiety. Maybe you need to go back to taking your medication. That, and taking some time to rest, may be all you need to feel like yourself again."

"I don't think it's that easy, but I guess I could try."

"Have you considered talking to someone? I have a friend in the city who's a very good psychiatrist. Perhaps you should meet with him. Discuss your concerns. I could go, too, if you'd like."

"Maybe," I whisper, still in shock that this is happening. I hope it's not. I hope there's some other explanation, although I don't know what it would be.

Ethan gives my hand a gentle squeeze and looks into my eyes. "I'm here for you, Anna. I know you're going through something right now, but you're not going through it alone. I love you, and I want to help you in any way I can."

I softly smile. "You're such a good husband. Sometimes I'm not sure I deserve you."

"Why don't I take you to dinner? A romantic dinner at a nice restaurant, just the two of us. Would you like that?"

"Very much. I wanted to have a romantic dinner here." I look down. "But instead, I almost killed you."

He chuckles. "I'm fine. I didn't eat enough of it to cause a serious reaction. Just some discomfort from the swelling and itching."

I look up at him. "I really am sorry."

"It's all but forgotten. Now where would you like to go for dinner?"

I decide on the steakhouse we went to on the day we signed the paperwork to buy the house. It was our celebration dinner, to celebrate being home owners, our first major step as a couple. We were deliriously happy. I wish I felt the same way now, but I don't. Not when I'm consumed by thoughts that I'm going crazy.

I'm relieved Ethan was so understanding when I told him about my mother. I thought he'd be angry that I waited so long to tell him, or accuse me of being crazy like her, but instead he comforted me and offered to help. Maybe I should consider talking to that psychiatrist Ethan mentioned. I want to believe there's nothing wrong with me, but I don't, not after everything that's happened.

We get home from dinner just before eight. Rose texted Ethan that she'd be coming home at eight-thirty so we go up to our room and make use of the time we have left. But when we're done, I'm left feeling uneasy and a little concerned. I'm relieved Ethan and I were finally intimate, but there was something off about it. Ethan didn't seem as into it as before, which makes me wonder if he sees me differently after what I told him about my mother. Maybe he really does think I'm crazy but doesn't want to admit it to me.

At exactly eight-thirty, Liz brings Rose back to the house. Ethan answers the door and thanks Liz for inviting Rose over for dinner. I'm on the couch, listening to Liz talk about how wonderful Rose is and how the children love her and are already begging for her to come back. I don't get it, but if I really am crazy, then maybe I'm not seeing Rose the way everyone else does. Maybe I'm paranoid she's trying to break

Ethan and me apart so I'm making up a version of her in my head that's evil and manipulative when in reality she's like everyone describes—just a sweet old lady.

Liz leaves and Ethan closes the door. "Did you have a good time tonight, Mother?"

"I had a wonderful time." She smiles at Ethan. "Liz is a fantastic cook. That woman has so many talents. Did you know she plays classical violin?"

"I did not," Ethan says, sounding impressed. "Did she play for you?"

"No. The children were consuming our time with the little show they put on."

"How was it?" I ask.

She glances at me. "Not all that good, but they did their best. They've only taken dance lessons for a few months. They're not very coordinated yet." She laughs. "Little Piper kept tripping over her feet and getting frustrated. Kelsie promised to help her practice for the actual recital."

"Are you going to that?" Ethan asks. "Or is it only for parents?"

"It's for anyone in the family, but since the children insist on calling me grandma, Liz and Kelsie invited me to go."

"What night?" I ask, hoping this means I'll get another night alone with Ethan.

"Saturday," she says. "They're picking me up at four-thirty. The recital's at five, then we're all going to dinner."

"Can they handle getting your wheelchair into the car?" Ethan asks.

"It'll fit in Liz's minivan, but I'm hoping to be using the walker by then. I'm going to practice using it tomorrow."

"Are you sure you're ready for that?" Ethan asks with concern. "Your ankle hasn't healed. I don't think you should be putting weight on it yet."

"I'm going to try. If it gives me pain, I'll go back to using the wheelchair. It's just such a hassle getting around in it."

Ethan looks over at me. "Now that Mother has plans, you can attend the charity event with me on Saturday."

"What charity event?" I ask.

"For the children's hospital. I told you about it last week. I'm required to go for work. I didn't think you'd be able to attend because of Mother, but now it seems that you can."

"Yes, I didn't realize it was this weekend."

Ethan's company is one of the sponsors of the charity event and has several tables reserved for their senior level employees.

"That should be fun!" I say. "A night in the city."

"Unfortunately, I'll need to go into the office that day, but we can meet up later at the hotel where the event is being held."

"You're working Saturday? I thought you were golfing."

"In the morning. I'll go to the office in the afternoon."

"Why do you have to go to the office on Saturday?"

"The product team from California will be here that day to attend the event and they've asked to meet with me to go over the new legal language required on some of our packaging."

"You can't do it on Friday?"

"They're getting here late on Friday. Saturday was our only option."

"Then I guess I'll meet you at the event," I say, wondering if Ethan already told me he had to work Saturday and I forgot. I'll be questioning everything now that I think my mind is failing. What's real? What's not? What's true and what did I make up? I feel my anxiety rising and go to the kitchen to get my meds. Maybe Ethan's right and the pills will help. I doubt it, but it's worth a try.

When I return to the living room, Ethan is gone.

"He went upstairs," Rose says, noticing me looking for him.

"I told him you could help me get ready for bed. You don't mind, do you?"

"Not at all." I smile and go over to her wheelchair. "It sounds like you had a nice time tonight." I wheel her down the short hallway to her room.

"Very nice."

"Do you need to use the bathroom?" I ask, stopping next to it.

"No, just take me to my room."

We go in there and I bring her over to the dresser. She pulls open a drawer and takes out her pajamas.

"I can get dressed myself," she says as I wheel her beside the bed.

"Are you sure? I don't mind helping."

"I can do it." She reaches down and yanks off her shoes. Just this morning she couldn't reach down past her knees, and now she's able to reach her feet?

"Okay, well, I'll give you some privacy."

"How was your dinner?" Rose asks as I turn to leave.

I turn back. "We ended up going out."

"After all that trouble you went to? Making that special meal?"

My pulse races as my mind goes back to what I did. I still can't believe I made Ethan a meal that made him sick.

"The dinner I made didn't turn out," I say.

"Why?" she asks. "Did you overcook it?"

"No, I, um, made something Ethan can't have."

"Lobster?" Rose says, her red-stained lips rising just slightly.

"Ethan told you?" I ask, feeling embarrassed.

"No. I already knew."

"How?" I ask, knowing what I told Ethan about his mother suggesting I make him lobster ravioli was just a story I concocted in my delusional mind. It had to be. She wouldn't tell me to do something that would harm her precious son.

"This morning," Rose says. "You asked me what to make Ethan. What he would like."

"And? What did you say?"

"You can't remember?"

"No," I say, shaking my head.

"Come here."

I go up to her. She motions me to bend down, then whispers in my ear, "Lobster ravioli. It's his favorite."

26

I wake up, my heart racing, beads of sweat running down my chest. I bolt up in bed, searching the dark room for Rose, but she's not here. It was just a dream. A nightmare.

"Honey, are you okay?" Ethan asks. I feel his hand on my arm and the bed move as he sits up.

"It was just a bad dream," I tell him. "Go back to bed."

"What was the dream about?"

"Nothing. It was stupid. I was just late for a meeting and Edward yelled at me."

"You realize you could fire him, right? You own the company."

"I'm not firing him. He knows how to run the place. He's been there for years."

"Yes, but if he's giving you nightmares—"

"Ethan, everything's fine. Go back to bed. I need to use the bathroom."

I get up, go in the bathroom, and shut the door. I stare at myself in the mirror, noticing the dark circles under my eyes. I haven't slept well in weeks and it's been worse since Rose moved in.

I lied to Ethan just now. The dream I had was about Rose.

I was helping her get ready for bed. I was about to leave her room, but she called me back, had me lean down to her, then said, *Lobster ravioli. It's his favorite.*

The dream seemed so real, like I was actually in the room with her. I could smell her sickly sweet perfume and feel her hot breath as she talked in my ear.

It was just a dream, I tell myself as I stare at my reflection in the mirror. *You're not crazy. You're just under a lot of stress. It'll get better. You'll be okay. Ethan will help you. He loves you. He'll never leave you.*

"Anna?" I startle at the sound of Ethan's voice through the door. "Is everything okay in there?"

"Yes. I'm fine." I take a deep breath, then open the door. "Did you need to use the bathroom?"

"No, you've been in here awhile and I got worried."

"You don't have to worry. I'm fine. It was just a bad dream."

He brings me into his arms. "You know I'm here for you. You don't have to hide things from me."

"I'm not hiding anything," I lie.

"Good." He pulls back and kisses my cheek. "Let's go back to bed."

When I wake up the next morning, Ethan is gone, but he left a note on my nightstand.

My beautiful wife, Anna. I hope you feel better today. Please take some time to rest. Call if you need anything. I love you with all my heart. Ethan.

I read the note again, my heart swelling with love for my dear, sweet husband. We've had our share of spats, but we always manage to move past them and come out stronger as a couple. Sharing my fears with Ethan last night about my mother's mental struggles and how I'm worried the same will happen to me was not something I would've done a few weeks ago. I wanted to keep living the fantasy, where Ethan and I are in newlywed bliss, enjoying our shiny new marriage, unmarred by troubles and fears.

But then Rose landed herself in the hospital and our fantasy life quickly turned to reality. For the first time, I saw Ethan panicked and frightened when he'd learned his mother had been hurt. I saw the concern in his eyes when the doctor said he worried Rose might fall again if she returned to her house. Ethan let me see his fears and vulnerabilities, so when it came time to tell him mine, I wasn't afraid. I was nervous, but I wasn't afraid. And he reacted in such a kind and caring way. I feel so much closer to him now that I've opened up to him like that.

My phone rings from the nightstand. I pick it up, see Ethan's name, and answer the call.

"Good morning," I say.

"Hello, sweetheart. How are you feeling?"

"Kind of groggy. I'm not quite awake yet."

"Why don't you go back to sleep? I'm sure the office will get along fine without you for an hour or two."

"I'll be okay once I get some coffee." I shove the covers back and get up from the bed, but feel like the room's spinning and have to sit down.

"Anna? Are you still there?"

"Yes. Oh, thank you for the note. It was very sweet of you."

"I realized I hadn't given you one of those since Mother moved in."

"I've missed them," I say with a soft smile. "I love waking up to your notes."

"Then I'll have to go back to doing them. I need to get to a meeting. I just wanted to check in and see how you're feeling. You were rather upset last night."

"I feel better today. How are you feeling? I mean, after the lobster incident."

"I'm fine. I'm sorry I got so upset with you about that. I shouldn't have reacted that way. I know you didn't intentionally try to make me ill."

Then why did I do it? If I knew about his allergies, why did I give him lobster? It doesn't make sense.

"Mother is already up and dressed," Ethan says. "She insisted on doing everything herself today so I let her, but remained nearby, just in case."

"She was up that early?"

"I didn't leave until eight. My first meeting isn't until eleven."

I check the time and see it's after nine. "Ethan, I need to go. I have a meeting at ten."

"Take it easy today. And maybe... well, it's up to you, but you might want to take your pills today."

"Yes. I will. I've already started taking them." I stand up, noticing the dizziness is gone. "I'll see you tonight."

"I love you, honey."

"I love you too."

After a quick shower, I race downstairs and see Rose in her usual spot on the couch, watching one of her game shows.

"Sleeping in?" she asks.

"I didn't mean to," I say, passing her on my way to the kitchen. Now that Rose is better able to care for herself, maybe I could start working in the office upstairs. I could really use the privacy and would get more done without the constant interruptions from Rose.

When I log into my computer and check my calendar, I see the meeting at ten has been cancelled. I scan through some emails and notice I feel dizzy again. It's probably because I haven't eaten.

"Rose, did you have breakfast?" I yell, hoping she can hear me above the TV.

"An hour ago," she yells back. "You gonna clean up that mess you left in the dining room? I can smell it from here!"

Oh, no! I forgot to clear the table from last night!

I go into the dining room and see the two plates still sitting there, the food mostly untouched, other than the half-eaten piece of ravioli that remains on Ethan's fork. I gather the plates and bring them to the kitchen, scraping the food down the drain in the sink. As I run the garbage disposal, the smell of the garlic butter sauce wafts in the air, making me feel sick. It's not just the smell making me feel that way, but the memory of last night. The horror on Ethan's face when he realized what I'd served him, then watching as he clutched his throat and ran from the table.

I hold my stomach and dry heave over the sink.

"What's going on in there?" Rose yells.

I grab a glass and fill it with water, taking small sips and hoping I can keep them down. The smell of the garlic sauce still permeates the air. I move away from the sink and sit down on one of the stools near the island.

Rose appears in her wheelchair. "Are you okay?"

"No." I take another sip of water. "I feel sick to my stomach."

"Maybe you should go lay down."

"Not now. I don't want to move." I stare down at the counter, at the glass of water held between my hands, and take some deep breaths.

Rose wheels herself closer to me and rubs my back. "That's good. Just keep taking deep breaths."

Her voice is soothing, comforting, and the feel of her hand rubbing my back is somehow lessening my nausea.

"Keep going," she says. "Deep breaths."

I do as she says, focusing on my breathing as she rubs my

back. She's actually being nice to me and helping me. If this is how she is with the neighbors, I see why they love her. Why doesn't she treat me this way all the time?

A few minutes later, the nausea subsides. "Thank you, Rose. I feel better now."

She takes her hand off my back. "Drink some water. You're probably dehydrated."

I finish what's left in the glass.

"Do you think you're..."

I look over at Rose. "What?"

"Pregnant?"

The word sits in my mind a moment before I'm able to process it. What if she's right? What if I'm pregnant? I'm dizzy, nauseous, sensitive to smells, and I've been feeling like my emotions are all over the place. And my forgetfulness. I've heard women talk about pregnancy brain and how they're always forgetting things. Maybe I'm not losing my mind after all. Maybe I'm pregnant.

"I guess it's possible," I say.

"Maybe you should take a test."

"Um, yes, I suppose I should."

"Go right now and get one!" she says, unable to hide her excitement. "I might be a grandma! A real one!"

"I'm not sure I should drive right now. I might need to wait. I've been feeling dizzy and—"

"You need to eat." Rose wheels her chair around the center island. "What can you tolerate? How about some toast?"

"Yes, that would be good."

She takes the bread from the counter and brings it over to the toaster, lifting up from her chair so she can reach it. "How about some juice?"

"No, that doesn't sound good."

"Give me your glass." She reaches for it. "I'll get you more water." I hand her the glass and watch as she fills it. She hands it back to me, then wheels herself to the fridge and opens it up. "Oh, dear."

"What?"

She shuts the fridge. "Your dinner from last night is still in there, in the saucepan. And it's quite fragrant."

"Oh. Then you should probably keep the door shut. I'll deal with it later."

"You can't be cleaning that up, not feeling the way you are. I'll do it myself, when you're not around."

She's being unusually kind to me, but now that she thinks I'm having her grandchild, she probably thinks she should treat me better.

"Rose, thank you. I really appreciate it."

"Don't worry about it. I raised a son. I'm used to cleaning up messes."

I smile. "Are you saying Ethan was a messy child?"

"All boys are. Always bringing mud in the house. Staining their clothes. Getting their shoes dirty. You'll see when you have your own."

What if it's really true? What if I'm going to be a mother? I'm not sure I'm ready for that, but I might not have a choice.

I eat the toast and drink some more water. It makes me feel a little better, but I'm still extremely tired. I go up to my room and lay down while Rose deals with the food in the fridge. I'm glad she's getting rid of it. I want all memories of that dinner gone.

27

When I wake up, it's noon and I realize I forgot to tell Candace to cancel my meetings. I text her that I'm not feeling well and will be taking the rest of the day off. She immediately texts back, confirming she cancelled my meetings and telling me to get some rest.

That short nap made me feel better, but my energy level is still low. I go downstairs and find Rose asleep on the couch, her head back, mouth open. I don't know how she sleeps with the TV so loud.

The doorbell rings, waking up Rose. "What was that?"

"Someone's at the door," I say, going over to open it.

It's Kelsie and the kids. Sharon's there, too, but I don't see Liz.

"Hi!" Kelsie says. "We were just out taking a walk and the kids wanted to stop and say hi to Rose."

"Come on in." I move aside and Brock and Braden, Sharon's boys, come running into the house and over to Rose.

"I beat Braden in a race!" Brock tells Rose.

"No, he didn't!" Braden yells. "He cheated!"

"Boys!" Sharon barks like a drill sergeant. "What did I say would happen if you fight with each other?"

They both cross their arms and pout.

"Hey, there's a dog out here!" Paul says, pointing out front, causing Sharon's boys to run back outside, followed by Paul.

"They're begging us to get a dog," Sharon says.

"I want a dog!" Piper says to her mom, doing that jumping up and down thing she does.

"Honey, we talked about this," Kelsie says. "No dog until Poppy is older."

Poppy is in the stroller, stuffing her face with tiny crackers shaped like bunnies.

"Are you done working for the day?" Kelsie asks me.

"I took the day off."

"Really?" Kelsie's eyes get huge. "Then you're free to come over!"

"What? Oh, I don't think so."

"Anna, c'mon. It's Friday! Come have a glass of wine with us out on the patio. Rose, you're coming too."

"Yay!" Piper squeals. "Grandma Rose is coming!"

"Boys, stay out of the street!" Sharon yells, standing at the door. "I'll meet you there," she says to Kelsie before running outside to deal with her boys.

"Will you come?" Kelsie asks, her face begging me to say yes.

"Not today. Maybe some other time."

"She needs to go run an errand," Rose says, holding onto the arm of the couch as she moves herself into the wheelchair.

"Let me help!" Kelsie races over to her.

"I'm good," Rose says. "I've been practicing all day."

Kelsie turns back to me. "If you change your mind, just stop down at the house. We'll be out back, but if you holler, one of us will hear you."

They leave and I grab my purse and go out to the car. I drive to the closest drugstore and buy a pregnancy test. I've never taken one. Never needed to until now. I'm still not sure how I feel about this. I think I want children, but I don't feel ready for them. Just those few minutes of the neighbor kids yelling and running around and jumping up and down had me on edge. That reminds me, I didn't take my meds today. I'll take them tomorrow. I don't want to risk having them upset my stomach when it already doesn't feel well.

Back at home, I run upstairs to the bathroom and carefully follow the instructions for the test. I nervously pace the floor as I wait for the results.

"Negative," I say as I look at the stick. I toss it in the wastebasket and breathe a sigh of relief. I wasn't ready to be a mom. But being pregnant would've explained all the symptoms I've been having. Now I'm back to thinking my brain is failing me.

Feeling like I could use a glass of wine, I decide to walk down to Kelsie's house. It's Friday afternoon and I have nothing else to do. Plus, doing this will show Ethan I made an attempt to be social. He keeps telling me I need to do more with the neighbors.

"You came!" Kelsie says.

I look at the side of the house and see her picking up a ball from the yard.

"My errands didn't take as long as I thought they would."

"Come on back!"

I follow her around to the back patio where Sharon and Rose are sitting.

"You decided to come," Sharon says when she sees me, not sounding as enthusiastic as Kelsie, but nobody does. Kelsie would sound excited about a root canal. It's just how she talks.

"Got your errands done?" Rose asks, and by 'errands' I know she means the pregnancy test.

"Yes. All done." I glance at her.

"Red or white?" Kelsie asks, picking up a wine glass.

"Red," I say, feeling Rose's eyes on me.

"I have this new pinot noir you just have to try," Kelsie says, pouring me a glass.

I take the empty seat next to Rose. She nudges my arm. I look over at her and shake my head. She pats my forearm and gives me a sad smile.

"Is everything okay?" Kelsie asks, handing me the wine. She must've noticed the interaction between Rose and me.

"Anna had a rough day," Rose says.

"But I'm fine now," I add.

"The wine will fix it," Sharon says, holding up her glass. "Wine fixes everything." She takes a drink, then yells, "Braden! Stop hitting your brother!"

Rose and I stay there until five, then go back home to wait for Ethan. He's taking me to dinner. Rose decided to stay home. She said she wanted to rest and watch TV, but I think she really just wants me to have a date night with Ethan. Rose has been kind to me all day. I hope it continues. It's nice to finally get along with her.

Ethan's home at six. He changes out of his suit, then we go to dinner. He's quieter than usual but says it's because of some issues at work. Being a corporate lawyer, he's always dealing with stressful lawsuits from consumers claiming the company's products made their child sick in some way. He can't talk about the lawsuits with me, but I'm guessing that's what's making him so quiet.

"Let's stop at the store on the way home," I suggest as we leave the restaurant.

"The grocery store?"

"No, a place that sells TVs. We keep telling your mother we'll get one for her room, but we haven't done it. And it'd be nice if she wasn't always watching the TV in the living room."

"That *would* be nice. She keeps it at such a high volume." Ethan holds my hand. "It's kind of you to think of her. I'm glad you two are getting along better."

I'm not sure that we are, but I'm hoping our interactions today are a sign that things are going to improve.

We get the TV and bring it home to Rose. She's beyond thrilled and insists we set it up right away. It only takes a few minutes and by nine, Rose is happy as can be, tucked in her bed, watching her new TV.

"I can't even hear it," Ethan says as we go into our room. "That was an excellent idea."

"I wish we'd done it sooner."

Ethan goes into the bathroom. "Anna?"

"Yes?"

"Could you come in here, please?"

I go to the bathroom and see him holding the small wicker basket we use for trash.

"What is this?" He points to the pregnancy test. I should've wrapped it up so he wouldn't see it.

"I thought I might be pregnant," I say. "But I'm not."

He sets the basket down. "Why didn't you tell me?"

"I didn't see a need to since it turned out to be negative."

"Anna, that's not something you should keep from me. If you thought you were pregnant, you should've told me."

"I didn't want to get your hopes up and then have to tell you the test was negative."

He comes over to me. "Anna, please stop hiding things from me. I'm your husband. You can tell me anything, even if it might upset me." He runs his hand over my hair. "How are you feeling about this?"

"Okay. Maybe a little relieved. I wasn't quite ready to be a mother."

He backs away and looks into my eyes. "But you still want that, right? To be a mother?"

"Of course," I say, but it's not entirely true.

In fact, I'm considering going back on birth control and not telling Ethan. He's in a hurry to have children. He wouldn't understand if I told him I wanted to stop trying for a few months, or a year.

He tells me not to keep things from him, but I can't tell him everything. There are things that must stay hidden, even from my husband. Besides, I'm sure he has secrets too. They might even be worse than mine.

28

The sound of the TV wakes me up, the volume growing louder by the second. I realize my arm's on the remote, pressing on the volume button. I turn the TV down and toss the remote on the floor.

It's Saturday and Ethan's at work. Rose is with Liz and her family. As soon as she left, I decided to take a nap. I've been tired all day and I have to stay up late tonight for the charity event. Ethan said it probably won't end until midnight.

Picking up my phone from the coffee table, I see five missed calls from Ethan. I sit up and notice Ethan's name pop up on the screen. He's calling me, but I can't hear the ring.

I answer the call. "Sorry I missed your calls. I must've—"

"Anna, where the hell are you?" Ethan says.

"At home. Why?"

"You haven't left yet? You should've been here an hour ago."

I check the time. It's after eight! I'm missing the charity event! Ethan told me to meet him there at seven.

"Ethan, I'm so sorry. I fell asleep. I didn't hear my alarm. I think my phone was on silent."

"Why would you silence your phone? What if I needed to reach you?"

"I don't remember silencing it. I don't know what happened." I get up from the couch. "I'll go get ready. I can be there in an hour."

"That's too late. Just forget it."

"It's not too late. I'll be there by nine."

"There's a presentation at nine, followed by an awards ceremony. You can't be walking in during that."

I collapse back on the couch. "I don't know what to say. I don't know what happened."

"I really wanted to introduce you to people. They keep asking when they'll meet my wife, and now I have to come up with a reason to explain why you're not here."

"Tell them I wasn't feeling well. Ethan, please don't be mad. I didn't do this on purpose."

"Are you sure about that?"

"What's that supposed to mean?"

"You don't like these events. You don't like going out. Meeting people. Being social."

"That's not true."

"It is. When I met you, you never went out. You'd go to work and come home. And now we're surrounded by neighbors who want to be our friends and you keep telling them to go away. Anna, I understand these situations make you uncomfortable, but I really needed you here tonight. And you let me down."

"Ethan, I—"

"I have to go. I'll see you at home."

He ends the call. I check my phone and see that I have it silenced. And my alarm is off. Why would I do that? I knew I had to go to that event tonight. Why would I turn off my alarm?

What is wrong with me? I keep doing things that don't

make sense or that I don't remember doing. Maybe I should see a doctor.

The front door swings open and I see Liz pushing Rose's wheelchair into the house.

"Anna," Liz says, sounding surprised. She's wearing a red sundress and sandals and her dark hair is pulled back in a sleek ponytail. "What are you doing here?"

"You're supposed to be at that charity thing with Ethan," Rose says.

"I wasn't feeling well," I tell them. "I decided to stay home."

"You're sick?" Liz says. "Is it contagious? Because that means Rose could have it and then my kids—"

"It's not contagious," I say. "I'm just really tired." I get up, noticing I'm wearing sweats. I look like a mess, especially compared to Liz, who always looks perfect. "You can go," I say to Liz. "I'll take care of Rose."

"Um, yeah, okay." She leans down to Rose. "It was so nice of you to come tonight. We'll talk tomorrow."

"Give the kids a hug for me," Rose says.

"Will do." Liz smiles at Rose, then leaves.

"Bye," I mutter, closing the door.

"I had a wonderful time tonight," Rose says, her face beaming. "They took me to a very nice restaurant. What did you do for dinner?"

"Nothing." I sit down on the couch. "I slept through it." I rub my head. "I don't know what happened. For some reason, my alarm didn't go off."

"Did you talk to Ethan?"

"Yes, and he's very upset with me. He told me not to bother going there this late."

"That's a shame. He really wanted you to be there." Rose rolls her chair past me. "I'm going to my room to watch TV."

"Okay. Goodnight, Rose."

She continues to her room, then stops and turns back to look at me. "Oh, and Anna?"

"Yes?"

"You really shouldn't use your birthday as your passcode."

She winks at me, then goes into her room and shuts the door.

Wait—what is she saying? That she got into my phone and silenced it? Shut the alarm off?

I get up and race to her room, knocking on the door. "Rose!"

The TV turns on. I try the door, but she locked it.

"Rose! Open the door!"

The volume on the TV rises, drowning out my voice.

She did this. Rose purposely messed with my phone so my alarm wouldn't go off and I wouldn't hear Ethan's calls. Why would she do that? She was so nice to me yesterday. I thought we were finally getting along, and now this happens. She's back to trying to break Ethan and me apart.

I go up to my room and get into bed. I'm so tired. I've been tired all day. Maybe I'm coming down with something.

Ethan gets home just after midnight. He stumbles into the room and takes off his clothes, tossing them on the floor, then gets into bed, reeking of alcohol. Moments later, he's snoring. I was hoping we could talk, but that'll have to wait until tomorrow.

In the morning, Ethan is gone. There's a note on my nightstand that says 'golfing with Jeremy'. That's it. No 'I love you' or 'have a nice day' or any indication of when he'll be home.

It's after nine, so I get out of bed and go to the bathroom

to take a shower. I usually check on Rose first, but after what she did last night, I don't even want to see her.

After a long, hot shower, I put on shorts and a t-shirt. It's a warm, sunny day. Maybe I'll go for a walk. I'm feeling better than I did yesterday and I have more energy.

Going down the stairs, I stop when I hear Liz's voice coming from the kitchen. What is she doing here on a Sunday morning? Shouldn't she be with her family?

"She looked terrible," Liz says. "The worst I've ever seen her."

"She's probably feeling down about not being pregnant," Kelsie says.

Kelsie's here too? And how does she know I took a pregnancy test?

"She was like this even before finding out she wasn't pregnant," Rose says in a somber tone. "Ethan and I are very concerned about her."

"Why?" Liz asks, sounding eager to hear more. "What else has been happening?"

"She's forgetting things," Rose says. "Not just Ethan's event last night, but other things. Things no normal person would forget."

"Like what?" Kelsie asks.

"Don't tell her I told you this," Rose says. "I don't want her feeling worse than she already does."

"We'll keep it between us," Liz assures her. "So what is it? What did she do?"

"She made dinner for Ethan last week." Rose pauses. "And served him ravioli filled with... lobster."

I hear Liz and Kelsie gasp, as if Rose just told them I held a gun to Ethan's head and threatened to shoot him.

"Ethan's allergic to shellfish," Liz says, making me wonder why and how she knows this.

"There's a note, right there by the fridge, listing out what he's allergic to," Kelsie says, answering my question about how they knew about Ethan's allergies.

"Did he eat any of it?" Liz asks.

"Yes," Rose says, "but he stopped when he realized what was in the ravioli."

"Do you think she did it on purpose?" Liz asks.

"I don't think so," Rose says. "I think it's her condition. Her memory issues. The paranoia."

"Paranoia?" Liz says.

"Oh, yes. She thinks everyone's out to get her, even me. She blamed me for the ravioli incident. She told Ethan I was the one who told her to make it. She said I did it to make Ethan angry at her and break them up."

"That's crazy!" Kelsie says. "A mother would never do something to harm her child, especially a mother as good as you."

"Ethan knows that," Rose says, "which is why he's so concerned about her. She also accused me of taking her wedding ring."

"What?" Kelsie laughs. "Why on earth would you take her ring?"

"To make Ethan leave her, or so she claims. Apparently, she went to the city to meet up with some man and Ethan caught her with him. Not wearing her ring."

"She's cheating on Ethan?" Liz asks, sounding shocked.

"Ethan can't prove it," Rose says, "but it sure does sound like it, doesn't it?"

"Well, maybe they were just friends," Kelsie says, giving me the benefit of the doubt. Sometimes I think Kelsie's not that bad. She's definitely better than Liz.

"Then she should've told Ethan she was having dinner with this man," Rose says, "instead of trying to hide it. And then she tells Ethan she wasn't wearing her ring because I took it from her bedroom and hid it somewhere."

"That doesn't even make sense," Liz says. "You can't get up the stairs."

"Not only that, but it was never missing," Rose says. "When Ethan and Anna got home, the ring was right where she left it, sitting on the dresser. I could go on and on with stories like this. This is why Ethan and I are so concerned."

"Has she considered seeing someone?" Kelsie asks. "Like a psychiatrist?"

"Ethan brought it up, but Anna wouldn't agree to it," Rose says. "He's afraid to bring it up again because he's worried how she'll react. Given her paranoia, she'll think Ethan's out to get her instead of trying to help her."

"Poor Ethan," Liz says. "He's been so kind and patient with her."

"He's such a good husband," Kelsie says. "It's too bad he's going through this."

"This is why you shouldn't rush into marriage," Liz says. "You need time to get to know someone."

"I told him that," Rose says. "But he didn't listen. Ethan's always been someone who follows his heart. Unfortunately, his heart led him astray this time."

"It's so sad," Kelsie says. "Anna seemed so normal when we met her. I mean, she wasn't super friendly, but that's just how some people are. I didn't think anything of it."

"I always thought there was something not right about her," Liz says, which doesn't surprise me since she hasn't liked me from the moment we met, probably because she's trying to steal my husband. And that's not me being paranoid. I really think she wants Ethan.

"I thought the same thing," Rose says. "The first time I met Anna I had this feeling she wasn't quite right. I think Ethan felt it too, but married her anyway, hoping her problems would go away."

"It sounds like they've gotten worse," Liz says. "So what's he going to do?"

"He's talked about getting her help," Rose says. "He has to, especially now that he knows about her mother. He needs to get Anna help before it's too late."

"What do you mean?" Liz asks. "About her mother?"

I hear Rose let out a heavy sigh. "Anna told Ethan the other night that her mother suffered from severe mental illness. Delusions. Paranoia. Forgetfulness. All the same signs Anna is showing, only she's developing them at a much younger age than her mother did."

Ethan was never supposed to tell anyone that. It was supposed to stay between us. How could he just blab it to his mother? It's none of her business. He should've known Rose would go tell the entire neighborhood, or Liz and Kelsie, who would tell everyone else. I'm furious with Ethan for doing that. I trusted him and he betrayed me.

"That's terrible," Kelsie says. "And so sad. Poor Anna."

"Anna?" Liz says. "What about Ethan? He's the one who has to deal with having a crazy wife."

"Liz, don't be mean," Kelsie says. "Crazy is not the right term to use for someone suffering from mental illness."

"Okay, fine. She's mentally disturbed. Call it whatever you want, but the bottom line is she needs help. What if it gets worse? What if we find out she's dangerous?"

"She's not dangerous," Kelsie says.

"She almost killed Ethan!" Liz says. "She made him a dinner that could've killed him!"

"Please don't tell Anna I shared any of this with you," Rose says. "I just wanted you two to be aware of what's going on."

"We appreciate it," Liz says. "And if you ever feel uncomfortable around her, you're welcome to come stay at my house for the day, or even at night if you're feeling unsafe."

Unsafe? Is she serious? What does she think I'm going to

do? Kill Rose in her sleep? The woman broke into my phone yesterday so I'd miss the charity event. If anyone's crazy, it's her! Maybe Rose really did tell me to make the lobster for Ethan. I thought I had dreamed it, but maybe it was real.

"You're welcome to stay with me too," Kelsie says. "We don't want anything to happen to you."

"You girls are so sweet," Rose says. "I don't know what I'd do without such kind neighbors."

I've heard enough of this. I'm not letting Liz and Kelsie believe these lies about me. It's time to go in there and set things straight.

29

"Good morning, everyone," I say, smiling at Liz and Kelsie as I join them in the kitchen. They're sitting along the center island, a tray of pastries in front of them, along with bottles of their green matcha drink. Rose is between them, sipping her coffee.

"Anna," Liz says, looking surprised to see me. "We thought you were sleeping."

"Nope. Wide awake." I go to the coffeemaker and get a mug from the cupboard. I fill it with coffee, then walk over to the three women I now consider my enemies. "What are you doing here, Liz? Don't you have children to care for?" I sip my coffee.

"They're at Sharon's house this morning."

"Same with mine," Kelsie says. "We're going over there soon to pick them up."

"How are you feeling today?" Rose asks me, a smirk on her face.

"I feel great." I smile at her. "Couldn't be better."

"Oh, sweetie." Kelsie gets up and rushes over to me, hugging me and making my coffee splash over the side of my mug. "You don't have to pretend everything's fine. We know about the pregnancy test."

"I'm not upset about that," I say, pulling away from her. "I was glad it was negative. I'm not ready to have children."

"Whatever you have to tell yourself to get through it," Kelsie says, looking at me with big, sad eyes. "We totally understand."

"No, really, I'm fine." My eyes bounce between Kelsie and Liz. "So is that why you're here? To talk about my negative pregnancy test? Or to just talk about me in general? Get some juicy gossip to spread around the neighborhood?"

Kelsie gasps. "Anna, we would never do such a thing." She puts her hand on my arm. "But we *are* concerned about you. Rose said you haven't been feeling well. We wanted to check and make sure you're okay."

"Yes, I'm sure you have my best interests at heart," I say, setting my coffee down. "But I can assure you I'm fine." I look at Rose. "And I wouldn't believe everything my mother-in-law tells you. Her mind isn't always that sharp."

Liz and Kelsie give Rose a look of sympathy, like they're sorry she has to put up with someone like me—her outspoken, crazy, unstable daughter-in-law. She's got those two right where she wants them, believing everything she says. I'll never convince them Rose is the one making up stories and telling lies. It's too late.

"We should get going," Kelsie says, going back over to Rose. "Would you like to come with us? The children would love to see you."

"Maybe later," Rose says. "I'm going to go to my room and rest."

"I'll call and check on you around lunchtime," Kelsie says, leaning down to hug Rose in the wheelchair. "Would that be okay?"

"Of course, honey," Rose says. "But don't you worry about me. I'll be fine."

Liz gets up, glaring at me like she thinks I'm going to do something to Rose. She's really got everyone fooled, making them think she's some sweet old lady when she's really a conniving, manipulative psychopath.

"Call us if you need anything," Liz says to Rose.

"I will, dear," Rose says as Liz follows Kelsie to the door.

I walk to the living room and watch as they leave, then close the door.

"I'll be in my room," Rose says, and when I turn around, I see her wheeling herself toward her bedroom.

"Wait!" I race up to her wheelchair and get in front of it. "What are you doing?"

"I'm going to rest. Maybe watch some TV."

"No, I mean with Liz and Kelsie. Why are you telling them stories about me? Making up lies?"

"I don't know what you mean, dear. They were just here to drop off some pastries from that bakery I like. They're so very thoughtful."

"I heard you talking to them. I know what you said."

"It's not nice to eavesdrop, Anna. Didn't your mother teach you that?"

I lean down to her. "Why are you doing this? Why are you telling people I'm crazy?"

"Honey, you can't help how you are. It's in your genes. I want to help you, but I don't know how. I thought Liz and Kelsie might have some suggestions."

"You don't want to help me." I spit out the words, seething with anger. "You're trying to destroy me. Make everyone think I'm crazy. Make Ethan divorce me."

She frowns. "It's sad how paranoid you are. Has it been happening for long, dear, or is this something new?"

I stand up straight. "I can't talk to you. I can't even look at you right now. Just go." I move out of her way.

She remains there, a creepy smile forming on her red-stained lips. "Don't you worry, dear. It's almost over."

"What... what's almost over?" I ask as she wheels herself to her room. She reaches the door and gets up from the chair with no effort at all. She looks back at me and winks, then goes in her room and shuts the door, locking it behind her.

A chill goes through me and I shudder. I need to get out of here. I need to go talk to someone who doesn't think I'm crazy and explain what's going on. Except I have no friends, unless you count Candace, but I can't call her today. She spends weekends with her boyfriend. They're probably still in bed.

Going up to my room, I shut and lock the door, then call the one person I know will agree to see me today.

"Anna?" he answers, sounding surprised to hear from me on a Sunday.

"Yes, it's me," I say. "I need to talk to you."

"Go ahead."

"No, not over the phone. I need to talk in person. Can I come over? Are you home?"

"I am, but I was just about to go for a walk. When were you thinking of coming here?"

"Now. I mean, I'll leave now. It'll probably be an hour before I get there."

"I'll make sure I'm home. Anna, what is this about?"

"I'll tell you when I get there. I'll see you soon."

Before I go, I write Ethan a note, telling him I had to go into the city for a work emergency. There really aren't emergencies in the fragrance business, but it's the only excuse I could come up with that would justify me leaving his mother alone. He still insists I stay home with her, even though she's fine on her own. The ease with which she got out of her wheelchair earlier makes me think she's been faking her feebleness this whole time. It's just another way to convince people she's a harmless old lady.

I tape the note to the bathroom mirror so Ethan will see it. I wasn't going to risk leaving it on the kitchen counter, knowing Rose would probably throw it away before Ethan got home. I could've called Ethan to let him know I was leaving, but I didn't want to risk him telling me I couldn't go, not that I'd listen to him. I can't stay in this house and let his mother continue playing these mind games with me. This whole time I've been thinking I'm crazy, but now I think it's her making me think that. She's setting me up and it needs to stop.

"COME ON IN," Edward says as I stand at the door of his penthouse apartment.

"Thank you for seeing me," I say, walking straight to the bar that's set up in his living room. His apartment is what you'd imagine for an older, wealthy bachelor. Lots of dark mahogany wood, brown leather chairs, shelves lined with old books, and the scent of cigar smoke lingering in the air.

"Why are you being so formal?" he says. "We're not at the office."

"Yes, I forgot. I'm not feeling myself today." I pour some whiskey into a glass. I really shouldn't drink. I took one of my anxiety pills before I left and they don't mix well with alcohol, but I need something to take the edge off.

"Have a seat," Edward says, pointing to the long leather couch I used to play on when I was a child. My mother would yell at me not to jump on it, saying I'd wear out the cushions or damage the leather, but Edward didn't mind. When Mother would excuse herself to go to the kitchen or use the bathroom, Edward would tell me to jump around to my heart's content.

It hits me that perhaps that's why I don't like it when

Kelsie's child is always jumping around. Because it reminds me of being a child myself and being reprimanded by my mother.

"Is this about troubles in your marriage?" Edward asks.

"In a way, yes. This morning I caught Rose, Ethan's mother, telling lies about me to the neighbors." I swig the whiskey. "I think she's setting me up."

"For what?"

"She wants everyone to think there's something wrong with me, maybe so that they can convince Ethan to divorce me. I don't know her end game. I just know she's doing everything she can to turn people against me."

Edward's sitting across from me, his legs crossed, his arms casually resting on the arms of his leather chair. He's staring at me, not responding to what I said.

"Edward, say something. The woman is setting me up and I don't know what to do."

"And you're sure this is what's really happening?"

"Well, no. I can't prove it, but why else would she tell the neighbors stories about me and about Mother?"

His bushy gray brows draw together. "They know about your mother?"

"Ethan apparently told Rose. I'm furious about it. He was never supposed to tell her, or anyone."

"Did you tell him that?"

"No, but I shouldn't have had to. He should know I told him that in confidence."

"You can't assume anything. It's best to always make it clear not to share information if that's your wish."

"Okay, fine, but even so, Rose shouldn't be discussing Mother's mental health issues with the neighbors. And she only did it to convince them I'm the same way. She told them I'm delusional and paranoid and that I can't remember things."

He rubs his wrinkled hand along his jaw. "And you think she's doing this to make Ethan divorce you?"

"I don't know why else she'd be doing it." I finish the whiskey and set the glass down. "There have been other things. Strange things happening that I can't explain."

"Like what?"

I tell him about the lobster ravioli, the missing ring, and whatever else I can think of that's happened since Rose moved in.

"I was thinking I was going crazy," I say. "But now I think it all leads back to Rose. That she's doing these things to make me look bad."

"If your assumptions are correct, she's going to great lengths to get Ethan to divorce you." He pauses. "Do you think her efforts are working? Has Ethan been treating you differently?"

"Not really. I mean, we have more arguments now than before Rose came to live with us, but Ethan still tells me he loves me. And he was very understanding when I told him about Mother. He didn't seem scared off by it. In fact, he made sure to tell me he was there for me, that he wasn't leaving."

"So do you think Rose might be doing this for some other reason?"

"I don't know what it would be."

"And it's just her doing this? Or has Ethan done it too?"

I pause a moment before answering. "I guess if I think back, Ethan has made me second-guess myself on a few occasions, but I don't think he did it intentionally."

"Why else would he do it?" Edward asks.

"What are you implying? That Ethan's part of this?" I laugh a little, finding the very of idea of that ridiculous. "No. This is about Rose, not Ethan."

Edward shrugs. "Anything's possible."

I shake my head. "Ethan would never do anything to harm me, or my reputation. I'm his wife. He loves me."

"And yet he told his mother a secret you didn't want her knowing."

"Yes, but like you said, I didn't make it clear that I didn't want him to tell anyone."

"From what you've told me, your husband is a very intelligent man. I'm sure he was aware that telling his mother something like this wasn't what you wanted. And given how well he knows his own mother, he had to have known she'd tell others."

He did, and he still told her. But that doesn't mean Ethan's intentions were bad. Maybe he told Rose to keep quiet about it and she just didn't listen.

"You said you wanted me to meet them," Edward says. "Let's do it tomorrow. I'll come there for dinner."

"Tomorrow? That's soon. Sometimes Ethan works late. I'll have to check with him to make sure he'll be home."

"I think it'd be better if you didn't. If his mother finds out I'm coming, she might try to stop it. She wouldn't want someone showing up there who's on your side. Don't you agree?"

"I hadn't thought of that, but you're right. Okay, I won't tell them you're coming. Could you be there at seven? Ethan should be home by then."

"Seven is fine."

"Thank you, Edward," I say with a relieved sigh. "It's helped to be able to talk to you."

He uncrosses his legs and leans toward me, looking at my face. "Are you feeling okay? Physically?"

"Not really. I haven't been sleeping. I've been having headaches, stomach aches."

"You don't look well. Would you like to go rest for a bit in the guest room?"

"I can't. I need to get home. But thank you again for letting me come over."

"Of course. And don't worry about this. I'm sure it'll all work out." He walks me to the door. "Goodbye, Anna."

"Bye, Edward. I'll see you tomorrow."

I feel better after talking to him and I'm glad he's coming to dinner. It's not going to change anything, but it'll be nice having him at the house. Living there, in that neighborhood, I feel like everyone is against me, sometimes even Ethan. With Edward there, I'll finally have someone on my side.

30

"What are you making?" Ethan asks, arriving home from work and joining me in the kitchen.

It's Monday night and Edward will be here soon. He texted earlier to confirm he was still coming, but I did as he asked and didn't tell Ethan or Rose.

"Pot roast and potatoes," I say, opening the oven to show him.

"It looks delicious." Ethan waits for me to close the oven, then gives me a kiss.

When I got home yesterday after my visit with Edward, Ethan was back from his golf game. He was sitting on the couch with Rose, watching a baseball game on TV. He wasn't at all angry that I'd gone into the city and left Rose on her own, which surprised me, but I didn't want to question it and stir up trouble.

I decided not to tell Ethan what had happened that morning with Liz and Kelsie. For one, I wasn't sure Ethan would believe me, given how he's always on Rose's side. And two, I wanted to wait for Edward's visit before deciding my next move, just in case he had any advice.

"We're having a guest tonight," I say, taking glasses out of the cupboard.

"And you didn't tell me?" Ethan asks.

"I'm telling you now." I fill the glasses with water. "It was kind of last minute."

"Is it one of the neighbors?"

"No. Edward's coming."

"Edward," Ethan says, seeming confused. "From Adore?"

"Yes." I go past Ethan on my way to the dining room, holding two glasses of water.

Ethan follows me in there. "Why is Edward coming?"

"Because I wanted him to meet you. You are my husband, after all. I felt it was time you meet the people I work with." I go back to the kitchen to get the other glasses of water. "He was free tonight so I invited him over."

"Anna, I really wish you'd told me. I'm not prepared to have company tonight."

"You seemed fine with it when you thought it was the neighbors coming."

"Because I know them. I've never met Edward."

"Well, now you will." I bring the remaining water glasses to the table, noticing Ethan didn't follow me this time.

"Will Mother be joining us?" Ethan asks as I return to the kitchen.

"Of course. Why wouldn't she?"

"I'm not sure she'd want to. This seems more like a business dinner than a casual dinner with friends."

"Edward is a friend. I've known him my entire life."

"But all you do is complain about him. Why would you want him to come for dinner?"

"Edward and I disagree on things," I say, taking the roast from the oven. "And yes, he does make me angry sometimes, but so do you." I smile at him. "And yet I still love you."

The doorbell rings.

"That must be him," I say, wiping my hands on a towel.

"I'll go up and change," Ethan says.

"Ethan, no. Just keep the suit on." I motion him to follow me to the door.

"Edward, welcome," I say to him. He looks very distinguished in his black suit, crisp white shirt, and silver tie. He hands me a bouquet of flowers. "For you."

"Thank you. They're beautiful. Edward, this is my husband, Ethan."

Edward smiles and shakes Ethan's hand. "I've heard a lot about you. Well, as much as one can hear in a very short time."

Ethan chuckles. "I suppose Anna and I did move rather quickly, but as they say, when you know, you know."

"Please, come inside," I say to Edward.

Edward comes into the house and glances around. "It's very nice. Much different than your apartment."

"We need to get that listed with an agent," Ethan says to me. "It shouldn't just be sitting there, unoccupied."

"Perhaps she'd like to keep it," Edward says to Ethan. "Not to live in, of course, but as an investment. Manhattan real estate is an excellent investment, as I'm sure you're aware."

"We've already decided we're selling it," Ethan says. "We'll use the money for other investments."

Edward nods. "Yes, well, just a thought."

"Let me give you a tour," I say to Edward.

I show him the downstairs, except for Rose's room, since she has the door closed. We go upstairs and I show him the master bedroom, the office, and the room that's meant to someday be a baby's room.

"And that's Rose's room," I say as we come down the stairs. Rose is coming out of her room using her walker.

"Good job, Mother," Ethan says. "It's good to see you out of the wheelchair."

"She's getting stronger every day," I say, hinting she could go home soon.

"Edward, this is my mother, Rose," Ethan says.

Edward smiles at her. "It's a pleasure to meet you."

"Anna says you run her company," Rose says.

"I'm the CEO, so yes. I took it over when her father died."

"You and him were good friends?" she asks.

"We were. For many years."

"Let's go to the dining room and sit down," I say. "Dinner is ready. I just need to plate it. Ethan, could you get everyone some wine?"

"Of course."

I go into the kitchen and put the flowers in some water, then plate the food. I bring the plates to the dining room as Ethan pours the wine. As I set Rose's plate in front of her, I prepare for her to criticize my cooking, but she doesn't, probably because of Edward. I like having him here. I feel like the balance of power has shifted and I finally have someone on my side, which is kind of sad when I think about it. As my husband, Ethan should be on my side, but I don't always feel like he is, especially after Rose moved in with us.

Ethan and I take the seats at the end of the table and Edward and Rose sit across from each other. I keep noticing Edward staring at Rose and squinting his eyes, something he does when he's thinking.

"So when did you start working there?" Rose says to Edward. "At Adore?"

"It was after it took off. I wasn't there for the early years. I started out working at an investment firm, but didn't feel it was right for me. When Gerald offered me the job as chief financial officer, I took it and never regretted it."

"And now you're running the place," Ethan says. "It's good to have friends in high places."

Edward stares at Ethan the same way he stared at Rose. "I'd like to think my knowledge and skills also played a part in my current position."

"Yes, of course it did," I say. "Edward is extremely smart and has really helped grow the company."

"You said you started there after it took off?" Rose says, cutting into her roast. "What does that mean?"

"The company struggled in the beginning, but after Adore, our signature fragrance, came out, everything changed. The company became an instant success."

"How does that work?" Rose asks. "Making perfumes. I've always wondered."

"I've wondered that too," Ethan says. "I assume you hire chemists?"

"Yes, ones who specialize in fragrance development," Edward says. "It's not an easy task. There are many things to consider, most importantly how the fragrance will react on the skin."

"Your father must've been very smart," Rose says to me.

"He didn't actually develop the fragrances. Like Edward said, we have chemists to do that. My father studied science in college, but he wasn't a chemist. But he knew enough to be involved in the development of our fragrances."

"But a fragrance alone doesn't make a company successful," Edward says, eyeing Rose. "You have to market it. Use the right packaging. Make ads that convince women to buy it. Gerald, Anna's father, had exceptional skills in those areas. That's really what made Adore such a success."

Rose nods and takes a bite of her roast.

"How's dinner?" I ask. "I found the recipe online."

"It's very good, sweetheart," Ethan says, gazing at me from the other end of the table.

"So Ethan," Edward says. "Anna said you're originally from New Jersey."

He laughs a little. "No. Indiana. Mother lives in New Jersey. I moved her there when I got the job in New York."

"Yes, that's right," Edward says. "I remember Anna

mentioning that. So tell me about Indiana. I've never been there."

Ethan clears his throat. "There's not much to say. It's mostly farmland."

"I'm sure you could tell me more than that," Edward says with a laugh. "What school did you go to? What high school?"

High school? Why is Edward asking him that?

Ethan smiles. "I don't know why that matters. You wouldn't know the school."

"I'll look it up. I've found you can learn a lot about a person by knowing what high school they attended. So what was the name of it?"

Ethan clears his throat.

"He was homeschooled," Rose says.

"Mother, I—"

"Yes, I know it embarrasses you, dear," Rose says to Ethan, "but it shouldn't. There's nothing wrong with being homeschooled."

"You never told me you were homeschooled," I say to Ethan.

"Like Mother said, I'm not proud of it. I wanted a more traditional education."

"And why did you go into law?" Edward asks Ethan. "Specifically corporate law?"

"I didn't want to spend my days in a courtroom. An office job was better suited to me."

"Was your father a lawyer?"

"No, he was a—"

"Engineer," Rose says, interrupting Ethan. "He worked for the railroad."

"I didn't know that." I look down the table at Ethan. "I guess I never asked what your father did for a living."

"Ethan doesn't like talking about it," Rose says. "He blames his father's job for causing his death."

"And why is that?" Edward asks.

"All the time and hours he put in," Rose says. "It takes a toll on the body."

"Which is why I keep telling Anna to stop working so much," Ethan says. "She doesn't need to. She has a beautiful home and a husband who needs her attention." He smiles at me. "And soon she'll have little ones to care for."

Edward shoots me a concerned look. "Are you expecting? Already?"

"No, he means sometime in the future."

"Hopefully the near future," Ethan adds.

The dinner continues and Edward keeps drilling Ethan with questions in his attempt to get to know him better.

"Would anyone like dessert?" I ask as I clear the plates from the table. "It's from the bakery in town. A chocolate-raspberry torte."

"I'll have to pass," Edward says, pushing out his chair. "It's getting late and I've got a long trip home."

We all get up from the table.

"I'm still not used to the commute," Ethan says. "That's another reason I keep encouraging Anna to quit working. There's no reason both of us should have to suffer with that commute."

"I don't see Anna giving up her job," Edward says as we reach the door. "She's not someone who can just sit at home all day. She takes after her father that way."

"I do get bored easily," I say.

"You won't be bored when we have children," Ethan says, putting his arm around me. "You'll be like all the other mothers on our street, barely having time to get your errands done."

Is that how he sees my future? Taking care of the kids and running errands all day?

"It was nice meeting you all," Edward says. "Thank you for dinner."

"I'll walk you out." I follow Edward to his car. "So what did you think?"

"Ethan seems smart. Sophisticated."

"Yes, he's both those things," I say, glad that Edward approves of him. I assumed he would, not that it really matters, but part of me seeks his approval on things like this.

"He's also very controlling," Edward says.

"What do you mean?"

"Telling you to quit your job. I'm sure you've told him that's not what you want and yet he acted as though it was a given."

"We just need to talk about it. I told him I wasn't sure what I wanted to do when we had children. He took that to mean I'd be willing to stay home."

Edward rubs his jaw. "Did you find it all odd that Ethan didn't answer right away when I asked about his high school?"

"No. Not after he said he was embarrassed about being homeschooled."

"That's a rather unusual thing to be embarrassed about, especially now, when he's a grown man and quite successful."

I laugh a little. "I think you're reading too much into it."

"There's something else that bothered me," Edward says.

"About Ethan?"

"About Rose."

"Well, yeah, she's crazy," I say, keeping my voice down. "But I'm surprised you could tell that from having dinner with her. She was on her best behavior tonight."

"She's a very smart woman. Very clever. What did she used to do for a living?"

"Just odd jobs. She didn't go to college. And she didn't work until after Ethan's father died."

"I see." Edward opens his car door. "I should get going. I assume you'll return to the office next week?"

"I don't know. It depends on how Rose is doing."

"That woman doesn't need your help. And if she tells you she does, she's lying."

"You think so?"

"I know so. It's clear as day." He points to me. "I want you back in the office, at least part-time."

"You seem to forget you work for me, not the other way around."

"I know my place, but I also know yours, and it's not sitting around in that house all day. That's not you, Anna. You know that as well as I."

Edward gets in his car and drives away. He's right. I don't belong here. I don't even like it here. But what can I do? I chose this life. I said this is what I wanted. And now that I'm here, I don't know how to get out.

31

"Edward doesn't seem that bad," Ethan says as I come back into the house. "At least not as bad as you made him sound."

"My complaints about him strictly relate to the office. Outside of work, he's a very nice man." I walk to the kitchen with Ethan. "So you liked him?"

"I haven't decided. He seems very smart, which I admire, but I didn't like his constant need to disagree with me when it comes to you."

"He's just looking out for me," I say, rinsing the plates in the sink.

"It's not his job to look out for you. It's mine."

"Or I could look out for myself." I put the plates in the dishwasher. "I'm not helpless." I close the dishwasher and turn to Ethan. "And I'm not sitting around this house anymore. I've decided to go back to the office."

"Anna, we discussed this and decided you'd stay home with Mother."

"Your mother doesn't need me. She'll be fine here on her own. And if she needs anything, she can call up one of the neighbors. Kelsie would do anything she asked. Same for Liz and Sharon."

"I don't want the neighbors caring for my mother. I want my wife to care for her."

"I'm sorry, Ethan, but I can't do it. I'm going crazy being here all day."

He purses his lips and I notice his neck getting red. He's angry, but he'll have to get over it. I'm not changing my mind.

"How about this?" He takes my hand. "You stay with her just a couple more days. By then she'll have had practice with the walker and I won't be as worried about her falling."

I consider it a moment. I guess I could survive two more days with Rose.

"Okay, I'll stay with her until Wednesday, but Thursday I'm going back to the office."

"Thank you." He smiles. "How about some dessert? Mother brought it to the dining room and plated it for us."

We have dessert, then Rose goes to her room and Ethan and I go to ours. I'm proud of myself for standing my ground with Ethan and not letting him talk me into staying home. I want to be a good wife, but there's only so much I can take, and I can't take any more of Rose.

TUESDAY MORNING, I wake up feeling dizzy and lightheaded. I've been feeling this way on and off for a week. I wonder if I'm dehydrated or if it's something more serious.

When I go downstairs, I find Rose in the kitchen. She's got the mixing bowls out, along with the canisters of flour and sugar.

"What are you doing?"

"Making cookies. I told the children I would."

"And their mothers approved? They're so strict about their diets, I can't imagine them agreeing to this."

"I approved the ingredients with them." She points to the

flour. "Gluten-free oat flour." She opens a drawer. "Where do you keep the measuring spoons?"

"Here." I pull out a drawer and show her.

She takes them out and sets them on the counter. "Someone should show you how to organize a kitchen."

"My system works just fine for Ethan and me." I smile at her, refusing to engage in an argument with her. I only have to put up with her for two more days, which has put me in a very good mood. I'll still see her at night, but Ethan will be here. He can deal with her.

I go to get a glass of water and stumble as another wave of dizziness hits me. I grab hold of the counter to steady myself.

"What's wrong?" Rose asks.

"I'm dehydrated. I need some water." I take a glass from the cupboard, fill it with water, and gulp it down.

"Can you get me the eggs?" Rose asks.

"Yes." I take the carton from the fridge.

"Get the butter too."

I set the eggs and butter on the counter. "How are you going to do this with your walker?"

"You're going to help me."

"I can't. I need to log into work."

"For heaven's sake, it won't take long. And this is for the children. Don't you care about the children, Anna?"

"I'm sure they'll survive without cookies." I sigh. "But fine, I'll help."

But instead of helping, I end up doing all the work while Rose orders me around.

"I need to use the bathroom," she says as I'm mixing the dough. She leaves the kitchen using her walker, but it doesn't look like she needs it. She's walking better than I am today. I keep getting dizzy and stumbling on my own feet.

The water helped a little with the dizziness, but now I have a headache. I'd like to go back to bed, but I have a meeting soon.

When Rose returns, I'm portioning the cookie batter onto the cookie sheet.

"I've got it from here," Rose says. "Go ahead and do whatever you were going to do."

I take my laptop into the dining room since I can't work in the kitchen. Rose starts singing to herself and I cringe, but remind myself it's just two more days. I can survive being with her for two more days.

At ten, I call into my meeting. When it ends, Rose comes into the dining room with a plate of cookies.

"I brought you a snack," she says.

"I'm not hungry. I think I'm going to go lay down."

"You don't even want to try one?"

"Okay, maybe just one." I bite into it. "It's not very good."

"Because it's healthy. Healthy stuff's never as good as the real stuff. But the kids around here are used to the healthy stuff. They're going to love them."

"Are you taking them over there?" I ask, finishing the cookie.

"How? I can't go that far with the walker. And how would I carry them?"

A simple 'no' answer would've been sufficient, but that's not Rose's style.

"Would you like me to drive you down to Kelsie's house?" I ask.

"I'm going to Liz's house. She invited me to lunch. Kelsie's picking me up. She'll come by around noon. I'm going to go watch my program."

"Aren't you going to clean up the kitchen?"

"In my condition? How could I?" she huffs, then hobbles away.

Rose's doctor's appointment is next week. I'm hoping he

says her ankle is healed to prove my theory that she's exaggerating her injury. I keep catching her putting weight on her ankle when she thinks nobody is looking.

As I clean up the mess in the kitchen, I call Candace.

"Hi, Anna!" she answers, sounding happier than usual.

"Hi, I just wanted to let you know I'm silencing my phone for the next hour. I need to lie down. I'm not feeling well."

"Again?" she says, sounding concerned. "This happened last week too. Maybe you need to see a doctor."

"I think I just need to rest. I haven't been sleeping well and I think it's finally catching up to me."

"You should just take the rest of the day off. I can cancel your afternoon meetings."

I notice my headache getting worse and say, "Yes, go ahead. I think I will take the afternoon off. Did Edward tell you I'm coming back on Thursday?"

"No. You did. You told me this morning."

I did? I don't remember telling her that.

"Are you sure you want to come back that soon?" she asks. "It seems like you've got a lot going on there."

"I can't sit around the house anymore. It's driving me crazy."

She laughs. "I understand. It'll be nice having you back. I'll take care of cancelling those meetings. You get some rest."

"I will. Thank you."

It's almost lunch time and I haven't even had breakfast other than the cookie I ate. I have another one, along with a glass of water. I'm too tired to make an actual lunch. Going up to my room, I collapse on the bed and fall asleep.

I WAKE up to the sound of loud voices coming from downstairs. I get up from the bed and glance at the clock on the nightstand. It's two in the afternoon. I'm surprised I slept that long.

Leaving the bedroom, I walk down the hall, stopping at the top of the stairs.

"Where is she?" a woman yells. It sounds like Liz.

"She's upstairs resting," Ethan says.

What is he doing home from work?

"Wake her up!" Liz demands. "I want to talk to her and ask why she tried to poison my child!"

Poison her child? What is she talking about?

"I'm sure it wasn't intentional," Ethan says. "Anna would never do anything to harm a child."

"Then how do you explain this? Anna's the one who made the cookies! And she put peanuts in them, knowing my son has a life-threatening peanut allergy! She could've killed him!"

I didn't put peanuts in the cookies. I know I didn't. I followed the recipe exactly and there were no peanuts in it.

"She didn't kill him," Ethan calmly says. "Gabe is fine."

"Only because I gave him epinephrine the moment I saw he was having a reaction. What if I hadn't been there? What if he'd been out back with the other kids, eating those poisonous cookies?"

"I understand what could've happened," Ethan says, "but it didn't, so let's all try to calm down."

"Calm down?" Liz yells. "A mother doesn't calm down when her child was almost killed! I can't believe you'd even say that!"

"He's only saying it so you don't scare the kids," I hear Kelsie say. "They're already scared after seeing what happened with Gabe. We don't need to frighten them even more. They take their cues from us and I think it's best if we do as Ethan says and try to remain calm."

"Okay, yes, but the children aren't here right now," Liz says. "So I'm not going to be calm! I'm furious that Anna's just allowed to get away with this! The woman is dangerous! She needs to be locked away!"

"She simply made a mistake," Ethan says.

"It wasn't a mistake! She knew what she was doing. She knew my little boy could die eating peanuts."

"It *is* really concerning she would do that," Kelsie says. "It doesn't make sense."

"It does when you consider that she's crazy!" Liz yells. "Ethan, the woman is deranged. You have to get her help."

"I'll talk to her about seeing a counselor," Ethan says, "but I can't force her to go."

"A counselor can't fix her," Liz scoffs. "The woman needs to be locked away in a mental hospital!"

I drop to the ground, sitting on the top of the stairs, listening to this and wondering how it happened. Did I really do what Liz is saying? Did I really put peanuts in the cookies? Why would I do that? To get back at Liz for flirting with my husband?

No. I'd never do that. I'd never do something to harm a child. So then how did this happen? The only other person who could've done this is Rose, but she didn't make the cookies. I did. And Rose loves those children. She'd never hurt them.

Rose saw me make the cookies. She knows I didn't put peanuts in them. She was there the whole time, except when she left to go to the bathroom. Is that when it happened? Did I sneak peanuts into the batter while Rose was gone?

Oh, God. What if I did? I don't remember doing it, but what if I forgot? Like I forgot that I told Candace I'd be coming into the office on Thursday?

"I'll talk to her," Ethan says. "And again, I'm very sorry this happened."

I hear the front door opening.

"If you don't lock her up," Liz says, "I'll be taking legal

action against her. She can't be allowed to keep doing this. It has to stop."

"Liz, let's go," I hear Kelsie say.

The door shuts and I hear Ethan walking around. I slowly get up and make my way down the stairs. Ethan's standing in the living room, looking at his phone.

"I didn't do it," I say.

Ethan looks up from his phone. "Anna. How much did you hear?"

"Everything." I walk up to him. "I swear to you, I didn't put peanuts in those cookies. I would never do something like that."

He sighs and looks down.

"You believe me, right?" I ask, my heart pounding in my chest.

He doesn't say anything. Why isn't he saying anything? He can't possibly think I did this.

"Ethan, answer me!" I yell. "You believe I didn't do this, right?"

He looks at me. "I want to believe you, Anna, but..." He shakes his head. "But if you didn't do it, I don't know how to explain it."

"Rose was there," I blurt out. "Maybe she did it."

"Anna, you know my mother. She adores children. She sees the neighbor kids as her own grandchildren. You know she'd never harm them." He pauses. "And, well, it's not as though this hasn't happened before."

"What are you talking about?"

"The dinner you made. The one that made me sick."

I walk past him and sit down on the couch, too weak and confused to stand. "I didn't try to make you sick, Ethan. You know I wouldn't do that."

He walks over to me. "But again, how do you explain it? You knew I had an allergy to seafood. There's even a note in the kitchen to remind you. And yet you still made me that dinner."

My mind is spinning, trying to figure this out. Do I have two personalities? Is that what's happening? Is there a good Anna and a bad one?

"Sweetheart, I know this is confusing," Ethan says, sitting next to me. "It's confusing for me too. I don't want to believe you'd do anything to harm someone, but I also can't ignore what's happened."

"So what are you saying?" I look at him. "Are you going to do like Liz said and lock me up?"

"Of course not, but I don't think you should be going back to the office this week. I don't think you should be working at all, not until we figure this out."

I nod, agreeing that's probably for the best.

"Why don't you go upstairs and rest?" he says. "We can talk about this later."

He helps me up to our room and I get into bed. He gives me a pill to help me sleep and I feel my eyes getting heavy, my mind groggy.

"Goodnight, Anna," Ethan whispers, kissing my cheek. "This will all be over soon."

32

When I wake up, it's morning and I'm alone in the bed. I blink a few times, trying to adjust to the light. I shove the covers back and slowly get up, my muscles achy and stiff from being in bed for so long.

I go into the bathroom and see a note taped to the mirror. It's from Ethan and reads, *I had to go into the office. I asked Candace to come and stay with you. Please don't be mad. I thought it would help to have someone there. I love you. Ethan.*

Candace is here? To babysit me? I can't believe Ethan did that. I know he's worried about me, but asking my assistant to come watch me is making this whole situation worse.

I go to the bathroom, wash my face, and change into jeans and a t-shirt. I'll shower later, after I deal with Candace.

Going downstairs, I see her on the couch.

"Anna!" She jumps up when she sees me. "How are you feeling?"

"Not great," I say. "I'll feel better after I shower and get something to eat."

"What would you like?" She comes up to me. "I can make you something."

"Candace, it was nice of you to come here, but Ethan never

should've asked you to do that. It's not appropriate, given that you're my assistant."

"Anna, I'm more than your assistant. We're friends."

"Yes, but still, it doesn't feel right having you here. I'll be fine. I don't need any help."

"Are you sure?" She crinkles up her nose. "Because you don't look so great. You're really pale and you look really tired."

"I told you I haven't been feeling well. I probably have some kind of virus." I walk past her, not wanting to be mean to her but wishing she'd leave.

She follows me to the kitchen. "Why don't you sit down? I'd be happy to make you something."

"Candace, really, you don't have to stay." I open the fridge, but don't see anything I want to eat. "And if whatever I have is contagious, it'd be better if you go."

I shut the fridge and lean back against the counter as a wave of dizziness hits me. I close my eyes, hoping it'll pass.

"Anna, are you okay?"

Feeling Candace's hand on my arm, I open my eyes and see her in front of me, looking very concerned.

"I'm fine," I say. "Just a little dizzy."

"Anna, please let me help you. You almost fell down just now."

"Okay, you can stay for an hour or two, but after that, you should go back to the office."

"Come sit down," she says, taking my arm.

We go back to the living room and I sit down on the couch.

"Where's Rose?" I ask.

"In her room. Ethan asked her not to bother you today."

"He did?" I ask, surprised he'd do that.

"She was fine with it. She's watching TV. And later, she's going to your neighbor's house. Kelsie? Is that her name?"

"Yes." I look up at Candace as she stands in front of me. "Did Ethan tell you what happened? With the neighbors?"

"Yes, but we don't need to talk about that."

"I think I need to," I mutter.

Candace sits down beside me. "Go ahead."

"I don't understand what happened. I know I didn't put peanuts in the cookies, but then how did it happen? How do I explain it?"

Candace shrugs. "Maybe she made it up."

"Who?"

"The kid's mom. Isn't she the one who doesn't like you?"

"I don't think any of them like me, but yes, Liz seems to hate me. And I think she has a thing for Ethan."

"So maybe she made it all up. To make Ethan, and everyone else, turn against you."

"I think she's capable of that, but there were other people there. Rose. Kelsie."

"Maybe they were in on it too."

"I could see Rose doing that, but not Kelsie. I don't know her that well, but I can't see her doing something that evil. I think she actually has a good heart. Plus, the children were there when Gabe reacted to the cookies. There were too many witnesses for it to be a hoax."

"Huh." Candace chews on her lip. "Well, I don't know what happened, but it's over now and it sounds like the kid is fine. Anna, you should really try to eat something."

"I know, but nothing sounds good."

"What about pudding? My mom used to make that for me when I was sick. I brought some over, just in case you wanted some. It's from a box, but it's really good, or at least I think so."

"What kind?"

"Banana, or I also have chocolate."

"Banana sounds good."

"Great! I'll be right back."

When she's gone, I turn on the TV. Rose must've been the last one to watch it because it's really loud. I turn it down.

I'm surprised Rose agreed to stay in her room. Maybe after the cookie incident, she's afraid of me. Maybe she thinks I'll try to poison her too. I wouldn't, of course. I wouldn't poison anyone, which is why the cookie thing doesn't make sense.

Candace returns with a bowl of pudding and a spoon. "I hope you like it."

I take a bite. "It's good. I haven't had pudding since I was a child."

"I have it all the time." She sits next to me, gazing at the TV. "Wow, I haven't seen a soap opera in forever."

"Is that what this is? I wasn't paying attention." I give Candace the remote. "You can find something else."

"My mom used to watch these all the time," she says with a laugh. "The stories never made sense to me. Like, how does someone come back from the dead three times?"

"That really happened?"

"Not on this one, but a different one. My mom didn't watch this one." Candace flips through the channels.

"So what did Ethan say to you? When he called?"

"Just that he was worried about you and wanted you to be with someone you trusted and considered a friend. He said he didn't know who else to ask."

"Yes, unfortunately, I've lost touch with everyone I used to know. They all got married and moved away." I eat more of the pudding, hoping I can keep it down. I'm feeling sick to my stomach, but I think it's more because of what happened yesterday than from an illness.

"Ethan really cares about you," Candace says. "He's such a good husband."

"That's what everyone says," I say, laughing a little.

"Why is that funny?" Candace turns to me. "You don't think it's true?"

"I don't know. I just wish he'd take my side more. Sometimes it feels like he's against me."

"What do you mean?"

"Like how he doesn't believe me about the cookies."

"He believes you. Ethan doesn't think you did it."

"Did he tell you that?"

"No, but I know he doesn't think that. He knows you, Anna. He knows you wouldn't do that."

"He's only known me a few months. He still has doubts about me. He'd never admit that, but it's true. I have doubts about him too sometimes." I sigh. "We shouldn't have rushed into getting married. I wish we'd waited."

"But you don't regret marrying him, do you?"

"What's done is done. I can't change it. I just wish we'd taken more time to get to know each other before getting married. Like Ethan and his mom? I never knew they were so close. I didn't know he'd want her living with us. And I never would've imagined he'd make me care for her."

"You could've told him no."

"I tried, but he really wanted me to do it. I was trying to be supportive. Be a good wife. And I still feel guilty for not doing more for my own mother. Caring for Ethan's mother made me feel like I was making things right. But I can't do it anymore. I wish I could, but I can't."

"I'm sorry things didn't turn out the way you wanted."

"I am too. This was supposed to be my dream life, and instead it feels more like a nightmare."

"Is there anything I can do to help?"

"No, but I feel better after talking to you." I hold up the bowl. "And the pudding was really good."

She smiles. "I knew you'd like it! It always makes me feel better."

"I'm going to go upstairs and shower and then I might lie down again."

"Okay. Whatever you need to do. I'll be here if you need me."

The shower saps what little energy I had, to the point I can barely make it back to the bed. I fall asleep, hoping when I wake up I'll feel better.

33

"Please, Anna," my father begs, reaching for me. "Help me."

I stare down at him, at the man who never felt like a father. He was almost never around, and in the rare times he was, he'd put me down and tell me I was a disappointment.

My father always wanted a boy. A girl to him was useless. Women don't run companies. Men do. Or that's what he believes. He wanted a son who could take over his business someday, but instead he got me, a worthless girl.

When my father is dead, his company will to go to Edward, my father's closest advisor and the only real friend he ever had. It should've gone to my mother, but due to my father's sexist belief that women have no place in business, he made sure his will excluded my mother from getting even a small part of Adore. She'll still get my father's money, but not the company he built.

Edward doesn't agree with my father's decision to leave him the company. He feels it's only right that my mother should get it. But he's never told my father that. He's only told my mother. I know because I overheard their conversation.

It was late at night and I'd left my room to go to the kitchen. I heard Edward telling my mother how much he loved her and would always take care of her. He promised her the company would be hers when my father passed. He said he'd sign it over to her—all of it—but she insisted he keep a few shares.

I have no doubt Edward will follow through on his promise. He'd do anything for my mother. He truly does love her. And I love him for always treating her well, far better than my father ever did. Edward cares about her, and about me. He's never put me down or told me I'm worthless. Sometimes he's tough on me, but it's only because he believes in my potential and wants me to succeed.

"I'm sorry, Gerald," I say, watching him clutch his chest. "But this is the end."

"Why are you calling me that?" he demands. "I'm your father, you disrespectful brat!"

"You're not my father," I say to him as he slumps to the ground.

"If only that were true." He falls onto his back, staring up at me with dark, narrowed eyes. "I wish you'd never been born, you stupid girl. You're nothing. Of no value. A waste of my time and money."

Even in his last dying breaths, he's criticizing me, telling me I'm worthless. Perhaps he's realized I'm not going to save him so he doesn't feel it matters what he says to me.

I kneel down and look into his eyes. "I'm not yours, Gerald. I never was." I smile a little. "Edward is my father. Not you."

"You're talking nonsense!" he scoffs. "Stop wasting time! Call a doctor!"

"Mother and Edward are in love. They have been for many years. While you were off working, pretending Mother didn't exist, she was spending time with a man who actually loved her. And long ago, they had a child."

Gerald's struggling to breathe, still clutching his chest. "Stop talking and call a damn ambulance!"

"I always thought Edward felt more like a father than you," I continue. "And it turns out I was right. Mother finally told me the truth. Just last week."

"Edward is not your father! Your mother is crazy! Always has been."

"Knowing you're not my real father makes doing this so much easier."

"No! Anna, listen to me," he says with panic in his eyes. "What your mother told you isn't true! I'm your father! You have to help me!"

I slowly stand up, keeping my eyes on him as he remains on the floor. I feel nothing. No emotion.

"Help me!" he begs, his body weakening, his clenched hands falling to his side. "Call an ambulance! Hurry up!"

I do nothing. I just watch, waiting for it to end. Waiting for this man I hate to finally die.

He chokes on his final breaths and his body goes limp. I kneel down and check his pulse to make sure he's gone, then I pick up my phone and call for an ambulance.

I don't regret what I've done. The man deserved to die. He was a horrible person. A horrible father. A horrible husband. The only time I'd use good to describe him is when it came to business. He was a good businessman. He was tough and shrewd, and most of his employees hated him, but he grew Adore into a very successful company.

"Anna?" I hear a man's voice and feel someone touching my face.

"Leave her," a woman says. "Let her sleep."

I was asleep? So that was a dream? What about now? Am I dreaming or is someone really talking beside me?

"She needs more pills," the man says.

That sounded real, but I can't open my eyes to check. I'm too tired to even lift my eyelids.

The voices around me fade and I drift back to sleep.

"He's gone," my mother whispers as we stand beside my father's grave. Everyone's left and it's just the two of us. The funeral was well attended, with hundreds of people showing up. None of them were my father's friends. Most of the people there probably hated him, but they showed up. Because that's what you do.

I didn't cry during the funeral. My mother shed a few tears, but only because she felt she had to, knowing people were watching her. She had no real tears for my father. How could she? He was cruel and abusive to her for their entire marriage.

"He's finally gone," my mother whispers, gazing at the grave.

"You're free now," I say, putting my arm around her. "He can't hurt you anymore."

"Is she talking?" a voice says. It sounds like it's coming from right in front of me.

I try to open my eyes but can't. They're too heavy.

"She must be talking in her sleep," a man says.

What's happening? Am I awake or asleep? I can't tell. That dream about my father seemed real. It *was* real. It actually happened. Whoever's talking around me seems real too, but I think it's a dream.

Someone pokes my arm. "Anna."

That definitely felt real. I must be awake, but I can't seem to open my eyes.

"She's out cold," a woman says, then I feel her poke my arm again.

"How was she this morning?" the man says. It sounds like Ethan.

"She seemed okay. Just tired," the woman says.

Now that I'm more awake, I recognize the woman's voice.

It's Candace. She's still here? It must be late in the day if Ethan's home. He should've told her she could leave.

"She wanted to talk," Candace says.

"About what?" Ethan asks.

"You. She thinks you don't believe her about the cookies. She thinks you have doubts about her, that you don't believe what she tells you."

"Poor little Anna. So paranoid. How very sad," he says, but he doesn't sound sad. He almost sounds happy.

I try really hard to open my eyes, but they won't budge. Why do my eyelids feel so heavy?

"I started telling people at the office," Candace says.

"I told you to wait."

"Why? This is what you wanted. And if it's happening this week, we can't wait. We have to get people thinking she's losing her mind and that it's been going on for a while."

"What did you tell people?"

"That she's forgetting things. Acting paranoid and delusional. I told them what's been happening, like with her trying to kill that kid. I didn't say 'kill' but I made it sound serious."

"How many people know?"

"I only told a few, but they're the people who love to gossip. I'm sure half the company knows by now."

"Then we need to hurry this up. I don't want anyone coming here and checking on her."

"They won't. I told them not to. I said she doesn't want people knowing she's suffering and to keep it quiet."

"What about the will? Did you bring a copy?"

"Yes, it's in your office, in the locked drawer you told me to put it in, behind the folder with the revised prenup. I sent you the electronic version as well."

"And everything's signed, correct?"

"Of course. Anna never even looked at it. I hid it in a stack of paperwork she had to sign and made sure to give it to her when she was in a hurry and didn't have time to read it. Just like I did with the paperwork to change her name."

"Good. Very good. You've done an excellent job, Candace."

"I always do when I'm being paid well. So what happens now? Your psychiatrist friend labels her crazy and admits her to the psych ward?"

Ethan clears his throat. "Yes, something like that."

"You and your mom were really smart to come up with this. It's almost too easy."

"This wasn't my mother's idea. It was all mine, but Mother did an excellent job following through with her part. You did as well. I commend you on your performance as Anna's trusted friend."

She laughs a little. "It was easy. I just smiled a lot and told her what she wanted to hear. Oh, before I forget, you need to reimburse me for the pudding."

"What do I owe you?"

"I'm kidding." She laughs again. "It was only a couple bucks. I can afford it given what I'm being paid. So when will I get the rest of the money?"

"On the date we agreed on. I know you want it sooner, but we need to let some time pass or it'll look suspicious."

"No one's going to find out. You're paying me in cash."

"Still, I'm not taking any chances. I've worked far too hard on this to risk being found out."

"Look at her," Candace says. "She looks so peaceful. She's been sleeping for hours."

"It's good. It'll support the theory that she's terribly depressed and can't get out of bed."

"Is that what you told everyone?"

"Yes, I told them she's been silently suffering for years with a multitude of emotional issues and that I've tried to help her but don't know what to do."

"The doting husband with the sick wife. You play the role perfectly."

"Thank you, although I didn't do it without help. Mother did most of the work convincing everyone that Anna is crazy. She even broke her own ankle so she'd have a reason to move in."

"She must really want the money."

"It's more than that. She wants what Anna's father took from us. I want that too."

"You'll have it soon," Candace says. "We should go. With all the drugs I put in that pudding, she'll be out for a few more hours."

Drugs? What drugs? I try once again to open my eyes. They flutter open just enough for me to look around the room. It's empty. Ethan's not here. Candace isn't either.

But I heard them. It wasn't a dream. Or was it?

I can't tell what's real and what's not. Were Ethan and Candace really here? Talking about drugging me? Putting me in a psych ward? Setting me up to make people think I'm crazy?

No. That can't be right. Ethan wouldn't do that. Candace wouldn't either. It must've been a dream.

But it seemed frighteningly real.

34

I wake up to Ethan sitting next to me on the bed.

"Hello, sweetheart." He brushes his hand over my cheek. "How are you feeling?"

"Tired. What time is it?"

"Just after eight."

"At night?"

"No, the morning. You slept most of yesterday."

"What's today?"

"Thursday."

"I'm supposed to be at work. I have to call the office."

"Anna, we discussed this. We decided you'd take some time off. You agreed that'd be best after what happened with—"

"Yes," I say, not wanting him to bring up the cookie incident. "I remember. But I still need to call the office."

"I already did. I told them you're ill and need to rest. I took the morning off to be with you."

"So Candace is gone?"

"I told her not to come today. I wanted to care for you myself. I might take the afternoon off as well."

"When did Candace leave?"

"Yesterday."

"I mean, what time?"

"I'm not sure. I think in the afternoon. She was gone by the time I got home."

So Ethan wasn't here with her. The conversation I heard wasn't real. I assumed it was a dream, but it seemed so real that I thought it might've actually happened.

I roll onto my back, feeling weak and lightheaded. "What's wrong with me?"

"I believe it's some kind of virus. That's what my physician said when I called and described your symptoms to him." Ethan feels my forehead. "You don't have a fever so that's good. The doctor said to keep giving you water and pain relievers and let you rest."

"I feel like I can't even get up. I didn't feel this bad yesterday."

"Yes, the doctor said it would probably get worse before it gets better." Ethan leans down and kisses my cheek. "I'm sorry, sweetheart. I wish there was more I could do. I hate seeing you this way."

"Is Rose here?"

"She's downstairs. She made you some more pudding if you're able to eat."

"Not right now."

"I understand. But you should try to drink some water and take more pills."

I sit up as best I can as Ethan hands me the glass of water that was on my nightstand. I take a few sips and he hands me the pills. I swallow them, then hand him the glass and fall back on the bed.

"Get some rest," he says. "I'll check on you later."

"Ethan?" I say, as he gets up from the bed.

"Yes, honey?"

"I love you."

He smiles. "I love you too."

I fall back asleep.

When I wake up later, I hear voices talking. They sound distant, but then get closer, like whoever's talking is here in the room.

"Mother, stay out of here," I hear Ethan say.

"Relax. I'm just checking on her." I feel someone sit on the bed. I can't force my eyes open to see who it is, but I can smell her perfume. It's Rose.

"Mother, leave her be," Ethan says.

"She looks nothing like Gerald," Rose says. "She must take after her mother."

"She does. She's shown me photos of her. The two of them look very similar."

"Good. It'll help sell the story. Like mother, like daughter."

"Except poor Anna was even more damaged," Ethan says, "and couldn't stand to live with herself and the pain she was causing others."

"It sounds poetic when you say it that way. You should remember that for the funeral."

Funeral? What funeral? What are they talking about?

"We really shouldn't talk about this in front of her," Ethan says.

"Why? It's not like she can hear us. Even if she could, she'll never tell anyone. She can't. She'll be dead."

Dead? Am I that sick? What's wrong with me?

"It's really quite sad," Ethan says. "I must admit, Anna was starting to grow on me. I could even imagine us being together for real."

"Stop that right now!" Rose says. I feel her get up from the bed. "Don't you dare even think of her that way! She's the enemy. She always has been. She took your father from me. From both of us."

"It wasn't Anna who did that. It was her father."

"And since he's no longer here, she has to pay for his sins. Don't you go changing your mind now."

"I'm not. I'm fully committed to this. It was my idea. It's just a shame it has to be this way. I was hoping it wouldn't come to this. I thought the insanity route would be enough to get us what we wanted, but it's too risky. All it would take is for some doctor or counselor to say there's nothing wrong with her and she'd get the company back."

"I liked the kid idea," Rose says, "but that's just me wanting to be a grandma."

"The child was simply a backup plan in case something went wrong. Insurance to make sure someone in our family got a piece of Adore."

"I really thought Anna might be pregnant."

"If she had been, it still would've gone as planned. I would've raised the child on my own."

"With my help."

"Yes, Mother, of course." I hear Ethan walking around, coming closer to my bed. "Look at her. She has no idea what's about to happen."

"Don't be feeling sorry for her. Anna deserves this. That little bitch grew up in a life of luxury while we struggled to put food on the table. What we're doing now is getting back what we should've had the last thirty years. We can't get your father back, but we can at least get back what he created."

"You're right, Mother," Ethan says. "It's time for Adore to go back to its rightful owner."

Rightful owner? What are they talking about? I wish I could make myself wake up and find out what's going on here. Am I dreaming this or is it real?

"When's she supposed to be up again?" Rose asks.

"Soon," Ethan says. "Probably within the hour."

"I'll go get the pudding."

"Don't bother. She won't eat it. I'll just give her the pills."

"And what if she refuses the pills? She's eventually gonna put it together that the pills are what's making her this way."

"Don't worry about it. I'll take care of it."

The doorbell rings from downstairs.

I hear Rose sigh. "It's those damn neighbors again. Don't those women have anything better to do with their lives than bother me all damn day?"

I flutter open my eyes enough to see Rose going over to the window. She's not using her walker or even a cane. My heavy eyelids fall shut again and I wonder if what I just saw is even real.

"Stop complaining," I hear Ethan say. "The neighbors will be quite useful to us when she's gone. Now hurry up and get down there. Tell them Anna is more confused than ever today. Tell them I'm so concerned about her that I insisted on staying home."

"Fine, but I'm getting tired of playing the sweet old granny. This needs to end."

"Soon, Mother. Very soon."

The doorbell rings again.

"I'm coming!" Rose says, using a high-pitched, cheery voice that's far different than the deep, angry voice she was using just moments ago.

I feel the mattress sink down as Ethan sits beside me on the bed.

"Anna," he says in a soft voice, gently shaking my shoulder.

I open my eyes just enough to see Ethan's face above mine.

"That's good, sweetheart," he says, his hand moving over my cheek. "Open your eyes. Try to wake up. It's time to take your pills."

"No," I whisper.

He leans down to me. "What was that?"

"No more pills," I whisper, my eyes fluttering open.

"Anna, you must take your pills. They help you sleep, and sleep will make you better."

I look into his eyes. "What are you doing to me?"

"Taking care of you." He smiles. "Like any good husband would."

"I heard you," I say, my voice now more than a whisper, but hoarse and very weak. "You're trying to hurt me."

He frowns. "I'm sorry you think that, dear. It's your paranoia. Your mind telling you I'm trying to harm you. You see, darling, it's not your body that's sick. It's your mind." He smooths my hair. "I'm here to help you. To put you out of your misery."

"No. Please. Stop doing this. I want out of this bed. Out of this room."

"I'm afraid that's not possible. Your mind is far too ill for me to allow you to be around others. Just think of what you've done. How you nearly killed me, then almost killed one of the neighbor children."

"No." I grab hold of his arm, using all the strength I have. "I didn't do those things. It was Rose. She did it. It wasn't me."

"My mother would never harm me, and she certainly wouldn't harm a child."

"She would. She's evil. Please, Ethan. You have to believe me."

"The fact that you believe my mother would do those things just shows how disturbed you are." He takes a pill bottle from the nightstand, removes the cap, and pours some of the pills into his hand. "These will make you feel better."

"No." I shake my head. "No more pills."

"Anna, take the pills," he orders, his tone now angry and harsh.

"No." I turn my head away.

"If you don't take them, I'll have no choice but to do this the hard way."

Suddenly more awake, I realize this definitely isn't a dream. It's real. What Ethan and Rose said about me being dead soon... it was all real. They're trying to kill me. Whatever is in those pills is going to kill me.

"Anna, don't be difficult," Ethan scolds. "Open your mouth."

I keep my head turned away and purse my lips.

"Fine. But you made me do this." Ethan turns my face toward him and yanks down my chin, forcing my mouth open and dropping three pills on my tongue.

I cough, causing two of the pills to fly out of my mouth.

Ethan smiles, a sick, sinister smile. "You really shouldn't have done that." He picks up the pills, then uses both his hands to pry open my mouth and shove the pills down my throat, nearly choking me.

He takes the water glass from the nightstand and hands it to me. I drink it down, having no choice but to swallow the pills that feel like they're lodged in my throat.

"That's a good girl," Ethan says. "Perhaps now you'll have learned your lesson and won't be so difficult." He takes the glass from me. "I'll let you rest."

I look over at the nightstand. "Where's my phone?"

"You don't need it." He sets the glass down. "I'm answering your calls for you, letting people know you aren't well and need your rest."

"For how long? How long are you keeping me here?"

"Not much longer. Just one more day, if all goes as planned."

"And then what? What happens next?"

He gets that sick smile on his face again. "Then you return to your family. To your mother and father."

"Why?" I look at him, my heart pounding as I realize what he's saying. He's really doing this. He's really planning to kill me. "Why are you doing this? I don't understand."

"Your father took something. Something very valuable that gave you a life of unlimited wealth and left my mother and me penniless. I know that's not your fault, but someone has to pay, and unfortunately you're all that's left."

"What... what are you talking about? What did my father take?"

"It doesn't matter. You don't need to know. Just take comfort in knowing you'll soon be back with him. And your mother."

"No. Please. I don't want to die."

"I tried to spare you, Anna. I was going to have you declared mentally unsound. I even had our prenup amended to deal with such a scenario. But I decided it was too much of a risk and far too complicated. This way is so much easier. And better for all of us."

"No. Please. Don't do this."

"I have to, and honestly, I'm doing you a favor. Your life here is sad and pathetic. You have no friends, no family, and you married a man who doesn't love you. By doing this, I'm putting you out of your misery."

He runs his hand along the side of my face and I cringe at his touch. How could I have ever loved him? Trusted him? Told him my secrets?

I don't even know this man. I loved him, married him, lived with him. But I have no idea who he really is or why he's doing this. And I have a feeling I'll be dead before I find out.

35

EDWARD

"You wanted to see me?" Candace asks, coming into my office.

"Yes. Sit down," I tell her.

She takes the seat across from my desk, sitting up straight, her hands in her lap, like she's a student who's been summoned to the principal's office.

"Am I in trouble?" she asks.

"I don't know," I say with a slight smile. "Are you?"

She nervously laughs. "I don't think so. I mean, I can't think of anything I might've done wrong."

I look at her across from me. Young. Beautiful. Ambitious. Why is a young, beautiful, ambitious woman working as an assistant? She has a college degree. She could do better than this.

I'm letting my mind wander. I need to remember why I called her in here.

"I wanted to talk to you about Anna," I say.

"What about her?" Candace asks.

"I haven't heard from her in days and she's not answering her phone."

"It's because she's ill. I sent everyone an email about it. Did you not see it?"

"I did, but even if she's ill, it's unlike Anna to cut herself off like this. She at least checks her phone."

"Maybe she's sleeping and hasn't had a chance to check messages."

"Have you heard from her?"

"No. I mean, not since she got sick."

"Which was when? Do you know?"

Candace shrugs. "Wednesday, I think."

"You spoke to her Wednesday?"

"No, I just mean that's when she felt ill. She sent me an email saying she wasn't feeling well and would be out of the office the rest of the week."

"So when was the last time you spoke to her?"

"Um... I think it was on Monday? Or maybe Tuesday. I can't remember."

"That's interesting," I say, leaning back in my chair.

"What's interesting?"

"You're Anna's assistant and closest friend and yet you can't remember when you last spoke to her?"

"I've been really busy this week. I'm getting my days confused."

"I see." I rub my chin, my eyes locked on Candace, knowing she's lying and wondering if she'll tell me the truth if I wait long enough.

Why would she lie about seeing Anna? This is unexpected. When I called Candace in here, I assumed she'd tell me about going to see Anna and give me a clue as to what illness Anna may have, be it the flu or something else. But instead, she's hiding the fact she was there, which I find quite disturbing.

There's something seriously wrong here. It's Friday, and Anna hasn't checked in with me all week. I haven't even received a text. When I heard someone in the office saying Candace went to see her on Wednesday, I became concerned. If Anna was well enough to have visitors, she'd be well enough to send me a text or give me a call. But I've heard nothing, and now I find out Candace is lying about going to see her.

"Am I excused?" she asks.

"No," I say, and leave it at that, giving her yet another chance to tell me she went to see Anna on Wednesday.

She's uncomfortable with the silence, her hands fidgeting in her lap, her eyes bouncing around the room.

"Mr. Beaumont," she finally says. "I don't know what's going on here. Did I do something wrong?"

"You're very concerned about that. About having done something wrong. Is that because you *did* do something wrong?"

"No," she rushes to say. "It's just I've never been called into your office before and it seems like the only time you have people come see you is when they're in trouble."

"I called you in here to talk about Anna."

"And we did. I don't know what else to say."

"Is that so?" I pause. "You have nothing else to tell me? Not even about going to see Anna?"

Candace looks down, her shoulders slumping. She knows I've caught her in a lie, but will she admit to it or keep denying it?

"Okay, yes," she says. "I saw Anna. I spent the day with her. At her house."

"Why didn't you tell me that?"

Candace looks up at me. "Because she didn't want you to know."

"And why is that?"

"She, um... she hasn't been well. Mentally."

"And how do you know this?"

"She told me. And Ethan told me. Actually, he's the one who called and asked me to stay with her. He was worried about her."

"For what reason?"

"He thought she might be developing what her mother had. I don't know that much about it. I just know Anna's mother suffered from mental illness. Like delusions. Paranoia. That type of thing."

"And you believe Anna has similar issues?"

"I don't know. I mean, maybe. She forgets things a lot."

"Many people are forgetful. That doesn't make them mentally unsound."

"Yeah. You're right," Candace says. "I'm sure she's fine. She's probably just stressed with everything going on at work and taking care of Ethan's mom."

"Rose. I met her last week."

"Yes, Anna mentioned having you over for dinner." Candace smiles. "Isn't Rose just the sweetest lady? I hope someday to have a mother-in-law just like her."

"Yes, she seems very nice."

Now I'm the one lying. The moment I met Rose, I felt something was off with her. The feeling became stronger as we had dinner. I felt the same way about Ethan. When I asked him about his past, it was clear he was hiding something. He kept hesitating before he'd answer, or he'd glance at Rose and she'd answer for him.

I don't know what they were hiding, and I don't have the time or skills to find out, which is why I hired a private investigator. It may seem extreme, but I have strong instincts when it comes to people, and my instincts told me there was something not right about Ethan and his mother.

There was also something very familiar about Rose. I feel as though I've seen her before, but when? I rarely go to New Jersey and have never been to the town where Rose lives, so I can't imagine how it would've been possible for me to have encountered her before. Even if I had, it's unlikely I'd remember her.

"So when you went to see Anna," I say to Candace. "How did she seem?"

"She was tired and said she didn't feel well."

"Mentally or physically?"

"Physically. She didn't have much of an appetite and she kept going to her room to lie down. She was like that yesterday too. Ethan stayed home with her."

"You spoke with Ethan?"

"Um, yes. I called Anna's phone to see how she was and Ethan answered. He said she didn't feel well and was resting."

If Ethan is answering Anna's phone, why hasn't he picked up when I've called? Is he avoiding me?

When I met Ethan last Monday, I immediately had a bad feeling about him. He was polite, but it didn't seem sincere. It's as though he was putting on a show for me. And he was very controlling of Anna. When I suggested she return to the office, he made it clear that her job was to be his wife, not work at Adore.

"What about today?" I ask. "Have you spoken to Anna?"

"No. Ethan texted this morning that she still wasn't feeling well and would be spending today resting."

I fold my hands and place them on the desk. "How much do you know about Ethan?"

"Not much."

"I'm sure Anna has told you things about him. After all, you are her closest friend."

"She said he treats her well and that she really loves him."

"That's it? She said nothing else about him? About his past?"

"She might've, but I don't remember."

"You were at the wedding, correct?"

"Yes." She smiles. "It was beautiful. Well, not the city hall part, but the dinner afterwards at the hotel."

"Tell me about the wedding. The ceremony. Was Anna at all nervous?"

"No, not at all." Candace looks away as she says it and her hands are fidgeting again. She's lying, but I'd know that even if her body language wasn't giving her away.

Anna always gets nervous before a big event. Her anxiety gets the best of her, sometimes to the point of her having a panic attack. Even if she was thrilled to be marrying Ethan, her anxiety over making such a huge life decision would make her nervous before the ceremony, maybe even sick to her stomach.

Why would Candace lie to me about this? Did Anna tell her to do so, in the off chance I asked about the wedding? No, that wouldn't make sense. Anna wouldn't mention me to Candace, not for something personal like that. It would give us away, which is why I didn't make an appearance at Anna's wedding or the dinner that followed. I desperately wanted to be there, but couldn't. But I regret not meeting Ethan before Anna married him. If I had, I would've expressed my concerns, not that it would've made a difference. Anna seemed determined to marry him, and I accepted that, as long as the prenup was in place.

"We're done here," I say. "You're excused."

"Oh. Okay." Candace jumps up from her chair.

I wait until she reaches the door, then say, "And Candace?"

"Yes?" She turns back.

"Clean out your desk. You're fired."

Her jaw drops, then snaps shut. "I don't understand. You said I wasn't in trouble."

"You weren't. Until you lied to me."

"But... but I only did that because of Anna. She told me not to tell you I went to see her."

"Anna wouldn't do that. Trust me, I know her far better than you do."

Candace stands up straighter, her shoulders back. "You can't fire me. I work for Anna. She owns the company."

"And I run it. I can fire whoever I want. And I can assure you, Anna wouldn't want someone she can't trust working as her assistant."

"Of course she can trust me," Candace says with a huff. "I'm her best friend."

I pick up my phone. "I'll have security escort you out of the building."

"Wait—what? Are you serious?"

"Yes, this is Edward Beaumont," I say as one of the men on the security team answers. "An employee has just been terminated and I need you to escort her out of the building."

Candace runs out of my office and back to her desk to collect her things. I've interacted with her very little in the time she's been working here. I trusted that Anna's assessment of her was correct. That she was hardworking and dedicated to her job. I did have concerns when Anna became closer to her. I warned Anna never to mix her personal life with her professional life. But Anna has so few friends—none really—that I let her have this relationship with Candace, but clearly I should've intervened.

I don't know what the story is with Candace, but I know Anna would never tell her to keep something from me. If it were someone else? Yes. But not me.

36

ANNA

I've been lying in this bed for what seems like forever. The room-darkening drapes are shut so I can't tell if it's day or night. I assume it's day because Ethan was in here earlier to take me to the bathroom and force more pills down my throat.

I now understand why he's doing this. He wants Adore. If I die, it goes to him. But why does he want it? Is he planning to sell the company and take the money? That's the only thing that makes sense. He's not going to take it over. He's not a businessman and he has no interest in perfume. Whenever I talk about it, his eyes glaze over, which means he must be planning to sell the company and make himself rich. But why? He's already rich. Being married to me, he has access to my money and the money I receive from Adore. He could buy whatever he wants. He doesn't have to kill me to do it.

My throat is dry, but there's no water in my glass. I must've drank it all the last time I woke up. I'm never up for very long. Ethan seems to know when I wake because the moment I do, he reappears with more pills to knock me out.

He'll be in here any minute so I don't have much time. I'm very weak and very tired, but I have to get out of this bed. I have to try to save myself.

Pulling myself up to a sitting position, I shove the covers back, then rest a moment. I take a breath and force myself to get up. My legs wobble and I fear I might fall so I sit back down on the bed, then slowly lower myself to the floor. I rest again, then get in a crawling position and feel my way around the room.

I crawl over to the window that faces the front of the house, feeling a surge of victory as I yank the drapes aside. No light comes in and I notice there's a blind blocking the window. Ethan must've installed it to make the room as dark as possible, or maybe to make sure nobody can see inside. I pull on the blind. It races to the top of the window, snapping against the rod and making a very loud sound. I hope Ethan didn't hear that. I think he's downstairs, but I'm not sure.

The sun pouring through the window blinds me. After days of darkness, the bright light hurts my eyes and makes me see spots. As I wait for my eyes to adjust, I pull myself up enough to look outside. The spots in my vision fade and I'm able to see the street and the yard. Two children I don't recognize are running down the sidewalk. I wave at them, but they don't see me. I try to open the window so I can yell for help, but the window won't budge. I unlock it and it still won't budge. I think Ethan glued it shut to make sure I couldn't open it.

Why? Why is he doing this? He said he loved me. He said he'd always be there for me. I thought I'd found the perfect man. A man who was nothing like my father. But it turns out Ethan is just another version of Gerald. An evil man who will do anything to get what he wants.

My heart races when I notice Kelsie coming down the sidewalk. She's pushing the stroller, almost about to pass by my house. Piper is skipping behind her, her tiny arms flailing around.

"Kelsie!" I whisper, frantically waving at her. She doesn't see me. Why would she? She's looking straight ahead, not up at the house. I tap on the window, but not too loud. I'm worried Ethan or Rose might hear.

Kelsie's now at the part of the sidewalk that's directly in front of my window. I wave with both arms. She doesn't look up. But Piper does! She stops and stares up at me. I wave at her, a distress wave, not a 'hi, there' wave, but little Piper doesn't know the difference. She waves back, then does that jumping-up-and-down thing that used to drive me crazy, but now I'm thrilled she's doing it. It gets her mother's attention and Kelsie stops and turns back.

This is my chance. Kelsie will see me and save me. I use all my strength to pull myself up to standing and wave my arms. But Kelsie's not looking. She's talking to Piper, who's no longer jumping, but her tiny arm is pointed my way. Why isn't Kelsie looking?

I have to get her attention. I bang on the window as hard as I can.

"Anna!" I hear Ethan's voice behind me and feel his arms yanking me back the moment Kelsie looks up.

Did she see me? I don't think she did.

"You little bitch!" Ethan says as he drags me away from the window. "I told you to stay put!"

"And you thought I'd listen? You're going to kill me. What do I have to lose?"

He picks me up and brings me back to the bed.

"Even if someone saw you," he says, "they'd never believe you. Mother and I have convinced the entire neighborhood that you're crazy. People at your office think so too. And I've told everyone I work with how concerned I am about your mental health. The night you didn't show up at the charity event, I told them you were having one of your breakdowns. One of many you've had since we got married."

"So it was you who made sure I wasn't there that night? So you could tell people lies about me?"

He smirks. "I had Mother silence your phone and turn the alarm off. The point is, no one will be surprised when they find out what happened to you."

"No one at my office thinks I'm crazy. And they're not going to keep believing your lies that I'm sick. Someone will show up here, asking about me."

"They won't. Candace has told them to leave you alone. She's also told them how disturbed you are, and how you've been that way the entire time she's known you."

"Candace would never say that. She's my friend. She wouldn't make up stories about me."

"She would if I paid her enough."

No. He's lying. Candace wouldn't do that. She wouldn't betray me like that. Would she?

I think back to the other day, when I thought I heard Candace in here with Ethan. I thought it was a dream, but what if it wasn't?

"Was she here?" I ask. "In my room?"

"Yes. We were talking. We assumed you were asleep."

"I wasn't asleep," I mutter.

"Good. Then you know what I'm saying is true." He laughs a little. "Did you really think I was making that up?"

I feel sick, like I'm going to throw up, although there's nothing in my stomach. I can't remember the last time I ate.

"How long?" I ask. "When did you start paying her?"

"A few months ago. She set us up, actually."

"What do you mean? We met by accident."

"No. That was not an accident. It was carefully planned out. Candace told me where to go and when to be there. She also told me everything about you so I'd know what to say to make you think we were a perfect match." He laughs. "You were so taken by me. Like I was your dream man, the one you'd been waiting for but didn't think existed."

That's exactly what I thought. But I didn't know it was

fake. I thought Ethan was the real deal, the man I was meant to be with forever.

"Candace told me how desperate you were to get married. I probably could've proposed the night we met and you would've said yes, but I didn't want anyone questioning my motives so I erred on the side of caution and waited to propose."

"I had a date with someone else the night we met. Are you saying Candace made him up?"

"No, you definitely had a date. And from what Candace told me about him, he seemed like quite the catch. But she messaged him that morning and told him you'd found someone else and needed to cancel the date."

"I can't believe she did this," I say, my heart aching as I realize my one and only friend was never my friend at all.

"You should know better than to trust people. You're a wealthy woman, Anna. You should know that people will only pretend to be your friend to get to your money. Or, in my case, pretend to love you."

I swallow past the lump in my throat. "You really never loved me? Not even a little?"

"Oh, my dear, Anna. This was never about love. It was about getting what you took from me. What I deserve."

"I didn't take anything from you."

"But your father did. He was a very selfish man. He took advantage of people. Stole from them for his own gain."

"I don't know what you're talking about. I'm not saying my father was a good man, but I don't know why that has anything to do with you."

Ethan sighs. "I wasn't going to tell you this, but since you'll be dead soon, I suppose I could be generous enough to share what's behind this so you can leave this world with at least a little peace."

He pauses and I wait for him to continue.

"Harold Krum," he says. "Does that name sound familiar at all?"

"No. I've never heard of him."

"Harold was my father. He worked at Adore when it was still Montgomery Fragrance. He was a chemist."

The moment he says it, I know what this is about. I was very young when it happened, but I heard my father talking about it. All I know is a man who worked for the company got fired, then sued my father, demanding he give him money and part of the company. My father won the lawsuit and life went on. I was too young to know any details about the man or the lawsuit and I never asked my father about it. In fact, I remember him telling my mother after the lawsuit was settled to never mention it again. So she didn't, and neither did I.

"My father developed Adore perfume," Ethan says. "It was his creation. He worked day and night in that lab, tweaking the formula, perfecting it, until it was exactly how he wanted it. And then your father stole it!" Ethan yells. "He denied my father was even involved in it!" Ethan leans down and talks over my face. "You know what that did to him?"

"No," I whisper.

"It drove him into a deep depression. He couldn't work. Couldn't eat. He couldn't even get out of bed. Meanwhile, Adore was taking off, making your father millions, making the company a huge success."

"Ethan, I'm sorry. But that isn't my fault. I didn't—"

"It doesn't matter if it's not your fault. Someone has to pay for what your father did. You got the life I was supposed to have. You didn't have to suffer like I did." Ethan slowly backs away from me. "Gerald Montgomery stole from my father. He profited off of my father's creation. He murdered him! You really think I'm just going to let that go?"

"My father didn't murder anyone," I say, although I'm

certain he was capable of it. He would've done anything to protect his company.

"When my mother and I finally convinced my father to get out of bed," Ethan says, "do you know what he did?"

I don't answer, so Ethan continues.

"He turned on the TV and the first thing he saw was an ad for Adore. The product he developed. The one inspired by MY mother, not yours. The one that should've made him millions." Ethan takes a breath. "Then he went into the garage. With a gun. And shot himself in the head."

"Ethan, I'm sorry. I didn't know."

"Your father killed him!" Ethan yells. "He took him from my mother. I was left without a father. We had no money. We were forced to live with my uncle, a raging alcoholic who would beat me just for the hell of it. My mother had to work three jobs to pay the bills. I worked my way through college, then law school, determined to find a way to sue Adore for stealing my father's work. But I couldn't find a way." He pauses. "So here we are. I had to marry the daughter of the man I despise in order to get the company back."

It was never Ethan's company. It was never his father's company either. Harold Krum was an employee, and when you work for someone else, they get to take ownership of whatever you create for them. Ethan knows that, but he's too emotionally invested to see the situation logically. There's nothing I could say that would change his mind about this.

Ethan and his mother are determined to get revenge. And I'm the target. Killing me gets them what they want. Their plan started long ago, and now it's about to finally come to an end.

37

EDWARD

At four, I leave the office to meet up with Harlan, the man I hired to get me information on Rose and Ethan. I considered doing a background check on Ethan's family when Anna told me about their engagement, but I didn't see a reason to, especially given that Ethan had no objections to the prenup. If he was marrying her for her money, he would've had an issue with it. Since he didn't, I assumed he was harmless. Now I regret not being more cautious.

I called Anna's phone earlier today, but she didn't pick up. I asked around the office to see if anybody had been able to reach her, but nobody had. The only person who heard from her this week was Candace, who I no longer consider Anna's friend. The woman is clearly up to something or hiding something, or both.

When I reach the bar, I give Arman, the bartender, a nod as I head back to the private room. Arman owns the place. We've known each for years. He used to be in the perfume business until he decided to get out and do something else. He lets me use the private room whenever I'd like, knowing there are times when such places are needed. The room has a back entrance, which is useful when the meeting doesn't go as well as you'd hoped. Today's meeting isn't that type of meeting, but it does require privacy, which is why Harlan is meeting me here.

"Edward," he says, coming into the room. "It's been awhile."

"It certainly has," I say, shaking his hand. "Care for a drink?"

"I'll take what you're having," he says, noticing the glass of bourbon I poured for myself as I waited for him to arrive. I slide the bottle his way as he gets a glass.

"You're not going to like what I found out," he says, pouring his drink.

"I didn't think I would." I take a seat on the black leather chair and take a long sip of the bourbon. "How bad is it?"

"She could be in danger."

"Danger?" I set my drink on the table and race over to him. "What the hell do you mean?"

"Hey, easy," he says, backing up. "I don't know if it's true. I'm just being extra cautious. They could wait months before something happens."

"Before WHAT happens?" I grab his glass as he goes to take a drink and slam it down on the table. "Tell me what you know. Now!"

He looks me in the eye. "Harold Krum."

The name brings back memories. Bad ones. Ones I'd rather forget.

"What about him?"

"Turns out this Rose Halstrom woman is really Roslyn Krum, wife of Harold Krum."

"No. It can't be." I shake my head. "You must be mistaken. The woman is Rose Halstrom."

"Halstrom was her maiden name. She changed it after her husband died. She changed her son's name as well."

Roslyn Krum. I never met her, but I saw her on the news

once, along with her husband, after he'd filed his lawsuit against Adore. She was much younger then, and very thin, with long, jet-black hair. She looked nothing like the Rose I met last Monday at dinner, except for her eyes. I remember the way her eyes looked when she stared into the camera as a reporter interviewed her husband. *Eyes that could kill*, I said to Gerald. He laughed and said Roslyn was the ugliest woman he'd ever seen. A perfect match for Harold, who himself was quite unattractive.

"Roslyn wasn't from Indiana," I point out, trying to prove what Harlan's telling me can't be true. "Rose lived there for many years. She had a house there. I looked it up."

"That was her sister's house. Same last name, Halstrom, but her sister is Rhonda. She sold it around the time you say Ethan moved Rose to New Jersey. The truth is, she was already living there, just in a different town."

"So she never lived in Indiana?"

"She grew up there. She moved to New Jersey for college but only lasted a semester. She dropped out when she met Harold. They got married soon after that, but it took them a few years before they had their son. Then later, after Harold died, Roslyn went back to her maiden name and moved to a different town."

"It can't be her. It's not possible." I return to the table where I left my bourbon and drink what's left of it. "Gerald said he took care of her. After her husband died, Roslyn blamed Gerald for his death. He was worried she'd try to get revenge through either another lawsuit or some other means. So he hired someone to make sure that would never happen."

Harlan shrugs. "I don't know what to tell you, because everything I found says this is her. Maybe whoever your boss hired didn't do the job."

"Or never got the message," I say, remembering back. "Gerald died the day he was going to give the order. He was sick of her threats. Sick of worrying she'd do something to convince the media that Harold was the rightful owner of Adore. I assured Gerald it didn't matter what she said. Anyone with half a brain would know Harold never owned that formulation. Anything he developed while working for us was the property of the company, not him. But Gerald didn't want to take any chances. Years had gone by since Harold's death, the lawsuit was settled, yet Roslyn wouldn't give up. She convinced a writer at a very small and insignificant paper to write a story about Harold being the creator of Adore, and that's all it took for Gerald to decide to end her."

"But you're saying he died before he gave the order?"

"I'm not sure," I say, trying to remember that day. "Gerald and I talked that morning. He told me what he was going to do. I tried to talk him out of it, saying it wasn't worth the risk, but his mind was made up. He had to get rid of her. He went home later that day to make the call. He wanted to do it at home, in his study, where there was no possibility of anyone overhearing him. Then later that afternoon, I received the news that Gerald had died. Between the shock of his death and all the things I had to do to keep Adore running, I gave no thought to Roslyn. I assumed she'd been taken care of."

"You can never assume," Harlan says.

"Yes, well, I didn't want to think about it. I've done some bad things in my life, but when it came to this woman, I thought Gerald was taking things too far. And even if his plans for her hadn't been carried out, I assumed she no longer posed a threat with Gerald dead. Her issues were with him more than the company. When Harold spoke up about wanting a piece of Adore, Gerald fired him. And less than a year later, Harold committed suicide. Roslyn blamed Gerald for that. She saw him as the reason her life turned out the way it did and she wanted revenge."

"It sounds like she hasn't given up. And now she's got her son involved."

I look at Harlan, my heart pounding as I realize what he's saying. "Anna! They've got Anna!"

"Do you want me to go there?"

"No. It has to be me. They know me. They'll let me in the house."

"You'll need a gun."

"I came prepared." I tug up the leg of my pants, letting him see the ankle holster that holds my gun.

"When's the last time you used that?"

"If you're implying I'm not properly trained on how to use this, I can assure you I am."

"I'm just saying, you might only get one chance to take her out. Your aim has to be perfect."

"Yes. I'm aware this won't be easy."

"You sure you don't want me to take care of this? I've got a guy I could call right now. He could be over there within the hour."

Harlan isn't the typical private investigator. He's the kind that knows people, the kind of people that get rid of problems. Problems like Rose and her son. If this didn't involve Anna, I'd hire someone to take care of this for me and keep my hands clean. But this is personal. It involves my daughter. My pride and joy.

"No," I tell him. "It has to be me."

"How are you going to get away with this? It'll still be light when you get there. And they're in a neighborhood. You're gonna have people watching."

"I'll figure it out."

"Then I guess we're done here." He extends his hand. "It was good seeing you again."

I shake his hand. "You as well."

He leaves out the back, while I go out the front, through the bar.

"Ed," Arman yells, smiling and giving me a wave. "Got time for a drink?"

"Not tonight," I tell him. "Maybe tomorrow."

If I'm not in jail tomorrow. This is risky, but I have to do it. I have to save Anna. I have to get rid of Rose. Maybe Ethan as well.

I just hope it's not too late.

38

ANNA

"Where's Ethan?" I ask, my eyes flickering open as I hear Rose come into my room. She's walking just fine now, as though she was never injured.

"It's Friday. He's at work."

"What time is it?"

"Almost six. Why? You got plans?" She laughs, a hideous, evil laugh.

"When will he be home?"

"When it's over." She leans down to me and whispers in my ear, "When you're dead." She backs away, a smirk on her old, wrinkly face.

"No. Please. Rose, don't do this."

"Sorry, dear, but you're wasting your breath. Ethan and I have been planning this for years. We're not stopping now."

"You'll both go to prison."

She laughs again. "You think we're that stupid? If we were just going to shoot you, we would've done it by now. But we're smarter than that. It was Ethan's idea. That boy is a genius. Takes after his father."

"What..." I pause, my voice shaky and weak. "What are you going to do to me?"

"It's not what *I'm* going to do to *you*. It's what you're going to do to yourself."

"What does that mean?"

She stands by my bed, staring down at me. "Ethan and I have convinced everyone you're crazy. We told them about your mother and how you're becoming just like her, forgetting things, having delusions. They've heard about the strange things you've done, like when you bought me all the foods I hate or when you gave Ethan lobster. And you're clearly a danger since you tried to kill a small child by sneaking peanuts into his cookies."

"I didn't do those things. You did. You set me up."

"And yet you wondered, didn't you? You wondered if you were really doing those things. Maybe you still do."

"I don't. I know it was you. All of it, even that dinner I made for Ethan. How could you tell me to give your own son something he was allergic to?"

"That was Ethan's idea, not mine. But I knew he'd be fine. Ethan made sure to only take a small bite."

The lobster ravioli was Ethan's idea? He was so determined to make me think I was crazy that he was willing to put his own health at risk?

I look up at Rose. "What about Gabe? You added peanuts to those cookies, knowing it could kill him. How could you do that? You almost killed a child. The same child you let call you grandma."

She smiles. "I put on quite a performance, didn't I? Everyone here loves me, and Ethan. They believe whatever we tell them about you. We've told them you don't mean to do such evil things. You're just crazy and don't know how to control it. A person like that often can't live with themselves. So they end it."

"Wait, what do you—" I stop and watch as she walks to the closet.

She comes back, holding a gun. "You took it from the safe, even though Ethan told you never to touch it. But you had no choice. You couldn't take being like this anymore. You couldn't take living with yourself, knowing you were causing others so much pain and suffering. You felt this was your only choice."

"No! I'm not doing it. I won't!"

"You don't have to, dear. I will. Then I'll put it in your hand, positioning it just like Ethan showed me. He's such a bright boy. So very clever."

"The police will know what you've done. They'll figure it out."

"I'm afraid not, dear. After all, I can't even make it up the stairs. How would a frail, old lady who can barely get around with her walker make it up a flight of stairs? And even if I were able to, a sweet, little granny would have no clue how to use a gun. When this is over, I'll get my walker and go outside, yelling for help, saying I heard a gun go off upstairs. Ethan will be home by then and will race into the house, worried his poor disturbed wife has taken her own life. When he finds out it's true, he'll come back outside, sobbing over the loss of his wife. The neighbors will have gathered by then, witnessing the tragic effects of what you've done. The pain you've caused us. And once again, you'll be the one they despise for putting Ethan and his dear, sweet mother through so much trauma. They'll assure us we did all we could to help you. You just couldn't be saved."

Rose positions the gun by my head.

"No," I beg, my heart pounding. "Please don't do this."

"Just relax, dear. It'll be over soon."

I squeeze my eyes shut, preparing for the gun to go off, then hear someone running up the stairs.

"Ethan?" Rose says.

Opening my eyes, I see Rose looking back at the door, the gun still aimed at my head.

"Put it down," a deep voice says. I follow it to the door and see Edward standing there, holding a gun, aimed at Rose.

What is Edward doing here? And why does he have a gun?

I must be dreaming. Or maybe I'm dead. This can't be real. Edward didn't know about Rose and Ethan and what they were planning.

Edward steps into the room. "Put the gun down, Roslyn."

Roslyn?

"Who told you?" she asks, keeping the gun at my head.

"Put the gun down," he says, stepping closer to her.

"And what? Let her take what belongs to my son? Never." Rose looks back at me. I see her finger on the trigger.

The shot fires.

My ears are ringing. My eyes are squeezed shut. But I don't feel pain.

"Anna?" I hear a voice but it's muffled. "Anna, say something! Open your eyes!"

I blink open my eyes and see Edward standing over me.

"What happened?" I ask. "Where's Rose?"

He glances down at the floor. I look and see Rose lying there.

"Is she..."

"Yes," Edward answers. "Can you get up?"

"No." I try to lift my arms, but they feel like lead weights. "They have me so drugged I can't move."

"What did they give you?"

"Ethan says they're sleeping pills, but I don't believe anything he says."

"Where is he?"

"Rose said he'd be home after she killed me. It could be any minute now."

There's a noise downstairs, a door opening.

"Mother?" Ethan yells.

"Keep quiet," Edward whispers as he backs up to the door, his gun aimed and ready to shoot.

"Mother, where are you?" Ethan calls out.

I hear his footsteps walking slowly up the stairs.

Edward lowers his gun and steps out into the hall. "Hello, Ethan."

"Edward," Ethan says, sounding panicked. "What are you doing here?"

"I came to see Anna. I was concerned."

"She's resting. She's not to have visitors."

"Yes, well, I didn't know."

"You shouldn't have come here, Edward."

"Yes. I see that."

What does he mean? Does Ethan have a gun? Was he going to shoot me if Rose couldn't?

"So how is your mother?" Edward calmly asks. "Roslyn, is it?"

"Rose."

"No, I'm fairly certain it's Roslyn. Roslyn Krum, wife of Harold Krum."

"So you know," Ethan says. "Then I guess there will be two deaths here today."

"I think you're right."

A gun goes off.

"Edward!" I cry out.

Ethan shot him. I know he did. Edward was my one chance to be saved and now he's dead!

There's silence in the hall. What's happening? Are they both dead?

"Ethan?" I call out.

"Yes, I need emergency help right away," I hear Edward say. "I just walked in on an attempted murder."

He's alive! Edward's alive! I listen as he tells the person on the phone that two people have been shot and need immediate medical care. He wants them to think Rose and Ethan are still alive, but seeing the blood pouring from Rose's body, I'm certain she's dead.

When Edward's done on the phone, he returns to my room.

"Is Ethan alive?" I ask.

"No." Edward walks up to me. "And when the police arrive, you need to tell them this was self defense. I shot them to save you, and to save myself. Do you understand?"

"Yes, of course. What else would I say? What you just described is what happened."

"You didn't witness Ethan about to shoot me. I need you to say you did. I can't take any chances here. I don't want to go to prison for this. The police are already going to wonder why I showed up here with a gun. Hopefully, once I explain what I found out about Ethan and Rose, they'll understand why I was forced to assume the worst."

"What do you mean?"

"I'll explain later. First, I need to rearrange some things."

He goes out to the hall and returns with Ethan's body, laying it down at the door. He positions Ethan's gun in his hand, making it look like he was going to shoot me the moment he got to the bedroom.

When he has Ethan just the way he wants him, Edward goes to the bathroom. I hear the water running, then shut off.

He reappears, wiping his hands on a towel. "Are you ready for this? Because if you're not up for it, I can deal with the police."

"No. I want to tell them what happened. I want them to know what Rose and Ethan were doing to me."

"They wanted Adore. That's why they did this. To get the company. Harold Krum, Ethan's father, developed the original Adore fragrance and felt that gave him the right to take the company. It's completely flawed logic, but that didn't stop

Roslyn from thinking she had the right to take Adore." He sighs. "I should've checked that she was gone. I'm so sorry, Anna."

"What do you mean? You thought she was dead?"

"She was supposed to be." Edward looks down, then back up at me. "Gerald didn't want her being a problem anymore. The day he died, he was going to give the order to the man he'd hired to do the job. I thought he'd made the call, but apparently he was never able to."

Because I walked in and interrupted him. The day Gerald died, I went into his study to talk to him. He had his phone in his hand like he was about to call someone. He yelled at me for interrupting him and we got into a fight. Then he clutched his chest, collapsed to the floor, and I watched him die.

"So Rose would've been dead if I hadn't..." My voice trails off as I realize I'm the reason Rose has been alive all these years, convincing her son to find a way to take Adore from me.

If I hadn't walked in on my father that day, would none of this have happened? Would Ethan have left me alone and gone on with his life?

"The police are here," Edward says, looking out the window. "I need to go."

He races out of the room and down the stairs.

I hear loud knocks on the door, then Edward answering it. I hear him talking to the police, telling them what happened. He sounds frantic and shocked, completely unlike how he sounded just moments ago. He was completely calm when he was telling me about Rose. He was even that way when he was talking to Ethan in the hall before he shot him.

Edward is an even better actor than Rose. I never knew that about him, or that he was capable of killing someone.

I guess you never really know a person.

Even your own father.

39

A WEEK LATER

ANNA

I haven't been in this house since the day it happened. The day I was almost killed.

I didn't want to come back, and not just because of what occurred here, but because of the neighbors. I didn't want them showing up at the house, questioning me about what happened so they could gossip about it later.

So I'm surprised when I find myself answering the door.

"Kelsie," I say, trying not to laugh when I see the shock on her face. Like me, she didn't think I'd answer the door. I smile at her. "Did you need something? Or were you just dropping by to collect some juicy gossip?"

She stares at me, not saying anything.

"That was a joke," I tell her, following it with a laugh. "Would you like to come in?"

"Oh, um, no. I just saw the lights on in here and wondered if someone was home."

"Your suspicions were correct," I say in a cheery voice. "Here I am."

"Are you, um... here to stay?"

"No. I've decided I'm more of a city girl. I'm just here to pack up some of my things."

"So you're selling the house?" she asks.

"Yes. The real estate agent will be here later this morning."

"Oh. Well, I'm sorry to see you go."

"Are you?" I ask, cocking my head to the side.

Her lips twitch up to an uncomfortable smile. "I know we didn't always get along, but it's only because of Rose. She poisoned us all against you."

She says this now, after knowing what happened. It took Rose trying to kill me to convince the neighbors I was right about Rose all along.

"You didn't have to believe her," I say.

"How could we not? She seemed so sweet and kind. I still can't believe what she did." Kelsie shudders. "I have nightmares about it. And to think I let her around my children."

"Maybe you'll be more careful next time."

She looks down, then back up at me. "The day before it happened, Piper said she saw you in the window. She said you were waving at her. I didn't believe her." She nervously laughs. "You know how kids are, always making up stories." She pauses. "So how are you feeling?"

"As well as one can after being drugged for weeks," I say, hoping to make her feel uncomfortable and maybe a little guilty. She deserves to feel that way after believing all of Rose's lies, not even considering they might not be true.

"What exactly did they give you?" Kelsie asks. "Was it sleeping pills?"

"Sedatives at the end, but they started with Rose's blood pressure pills. They look similar to my anxiety meds so Ethan replaced those pills with the blood pressure pills. I was taking them without even knowing it. Taking them when you don't have high blood pressure can cause headaches, dizziness, stomach problems, confusion. All symptoms I was having.

They added the sedatives later, when they wanted to confine me to bed."

"It's absolutely horrible," Kelsie says with an exaggerated sigh. "We're all completely shocked. Ethan seemed like such a good man. Almost perfect, really. And to think he was capable of such a thing. It's really unbelievable."

"Not really. I think deep down a lot of us are capable of things we wouldn't want people knowing about." I step closer to her. "Dark, evil things."

She rears back. "Yes, well, I should go. Good seeing you!" She races off.

Maybe I shouldn't have said that, but I needed to get rid of her. I have a lot to do. And besides, I'm sure her opinion of me hasn't changed. If she wants to think I'm crazy, so be it. I'm done caring what these people think of me. I just want to sell this house and forget about the time I spent here.

I was hoping work would take my mind off it, but when I'm there, I'm reminded of Candace and how she was part of this. I can't believe she betrayed me like that. She made me believe we were friends, but just like with Ethan, it was all an act. I'll never know the extent of her involvement with him or the whole situation, and I'd rather not. I'm better off not knowing.

I haven't seen or heard from Candace since the day she was at my house. After she was fired, Allison, an intern at Adore who'd become friends with Candace, went to her apartment and said it was empty. And when Allison tried to call Candace's phone, she got a no-longer-in-service message. I'm guessing Candace left town. Maybe she started a new life with whatever money Ethan gave her.

Janet, the real estate agent, arrives at noon. She sold us the house so she's already seen it, but she wanted to go through it again and take new photos to put on the website. It takes less than an hour and she says the listing should be up by the end of the day.

"I must tell you," she says as she stands at the door, ready to leave. "Given what happened here and how much press it's been getting, the house could be hard to sell. It might take longer than you'd like, or you may have to lower the price."

The story about Ethan and Rose has been all over the news. I don't even turn on the TV anymore because I'm so tired of seeing it. I'm hoping it'll go away soon, but I have a feeling it won't. It's the type of story people love to talk about, which is sad, but it's human nature. People are fascinated by other people's tragedies, especially if they're as dark and twisted as mine.

"I'm happy to lower the price," I say, "if that's what it takes to get it sold."

"Let's start high and lower it as needed," Janet says, not wanting to decrease her commission. "Hopefully, people will see past what happened here and appreciate the house for what it is, as well as the neighborhood. It's a very desirable area, especially for young families."

That's why I moved here. I imagined myself having children with Ethan and us being one of those families. But it never happened. And I'm okay with that. Thinking about it now, that life was never for me. I don't even see myself getting married again. After what I went through with Ethan, I can't imagine starting all over with someone new, someone I may not be able to trust. I didn't think I'd ever say this, but I think I'll be happier alone.

"Yes, I'm sure it will sell," I tell Janet, in regard to the house.

She keeps talking, but I'm not listening. I suddenly feel sick to my stomach.

"Well, I need to do some more packing," I say, hoping Janet will get the hint and leave. "Just call if you need anything else."

"Will do." She turns to leave, then turns back. "Oh! I left my phone in the kitchen." She goes to get it.

"Just let yourself out," I tell her, running to the bathroom. I get sick, and given how fast it came on, I'm guessing it's due to something I ate.

"Anna?" Janet says, knocking on the bathroom door. "Are you okay?"

"Yes. I'm fine. I think it was something I ate."

"Do you need anything?"

"No. I'm good."

"I can wait here. Make sure you're okay."

"Really, I'm fine," I say, opening the door so she can see for herself.

She looks at me, her eyes bouncing around my face.

"What are you looking at?"

"Oh, um, I was just thinking about something."

"About the house?"

"No, about you and... well, your husband. Should I not call him that? I'm not sure of the proper term."

"Ethan. Just call him that. What about him?"

"I was just remembering when you moved in here, how you talked about starting a family right away."

"Yes? And?"

"The way you got sick just now, I thought maybe you were—"

"No. I'm not," I say with a laugh. "It's not possible."

But the truth is, it's very possible. We weren't doing anything to stop it.

Oh, no. What if she's right?

"Well, that's good," she says, smiling. "Can you imagine? After everything you went through with him?" She laughs. "I'm sorry I even brought it up."

"I really should get back to packing," I say, ushering her to the door. "But thanks for coming over. Let's hope it sells fast."

"Yes. Bye!" She leaves and I shut and lock the door.

I go up to the bathroom and open the linen closet. The pregnancy test I bought is still there. There were two tests in the box, but I only used one.

"Please be no," I say as I hold the stick, waiting for the results. I close my eyes, telling myself it'll be negative. It was before. I'm sure it will be again.

The timer on my phone dings. This is it. The moment that could forever change my life. Will I be a mother or not?

I open my eyes and see the answer.

40

SIX MONTHS LATER

ANNA

"She'd be very proud of you," Edward says as we stand in front of my mother's grave. "Doing this on your own."

"I'm not on my own," I say, looking up at Edward. "I have you. You're still going to help, right?"

"Of course." He smiles and puts his arm around my shoulder. "I am his grandfather, after all."

"I want to tell him," I say, resting my hand over my rapidly growing baby bump. "I don't want him thinking Gerald was his grandfather."

"You need to wait until he's older. When he can understand why you were raised by Gerald. When he's old enough to keep a secret like that. You're a public figure, Anna. You don't want this getting out and have to endure the media and all their questions."

"I suppose you're right. It was probably good I didn't learn the truth until I was older."

"You know, your mother and I never intended to tell you."

"Why not?"

"Claire didn't want you knowing she wasn't faithful to Gerald. She thought you wouldn't respect her."

"I understand why she did it. You loved her. Gerald didn't. But she was too afraid to leave him. So what was she to do?"

"She was terrified he'd find out. Sometimes I wonder if the stress of it caused her dementia." Edward kneels down to my mother's grave and sets the flowers on it. "Happy Birthday, my love. I miss you so very much."

Edward and my mother had a secret affair for over thirty years. I didn't know Edward was my father until the day my mother told me. She didn't mean to. I overheard her when she was talking to herself. It's something she often did, usually when she was making something in the kitchen. She didn't like having the radio or TV on while she cooked so she'd talk to herself to fill the silence. One day I got home from shopping and was walking by the kitchen on the way to my room and overheard my mother saying how she wished I knew Edward was my father. She didn't know I was home. Or maybe she did. Maybe she wanted me to overhear her so I'd finally know the truth.

I was 25 at the time, and couldn't believe I'd gone that long without knowing. I was furious at my mother for making us live with Gerald all those years when we could've been with Edward. But then I realized that Gerald would've never let my mother go. She was his, and he'd rather see her dead than with another man. She felt trapped, much like I felt trapped with Ethan.

"Hi, Mom," I say, touching the top of her tombstone since kneeling down isn't possible in my very pregnant state. "Happy Birthday. It's supposed to snow today so your flowers probably won't last." I smile. "But Edward insisted on getting them anyway."

"Because I know how much she loves them," Edward says, rising up to standing. "Claire, dear, we're about to be grandparents. Can you believe it? I must say, I don't feel prepared."

"I think you'll make a wonderful grandfather," I say, looking up at him.

He smiles at that, then glances down at my stomach. "I'm very much looking forward to being part of this child's life."

"He'll be here soon," I say, rubbing my hand over my stomach.

"Any decision on a name?"

"Not yet. And my list of possibilities keeps getting longer, not shorter."

"You'll figure it out."

The wind blows, making me shiver.

"We should go," Edward says, looking up at the sky. "I think I see a few snowflakes."

"Bye, Mom," I say, then I turn to Edward. "I'll go wait in the car."

He nods and I walk away. When I look back, I see Edward talking to my mother, then kissing his fingers and placing them on her stone.

They have the kind of love I wanted for myself. The kind I wished for and thought I had with Ethan. But his love was never real. And now I'm left with his child. A boy, who will one day take over Adore. So in a way, Ethan and Rose got what they wanted. The company will go to their family by way of my son.

"I'm glad you'll never meet him," I say, looking down at my stomach as I walk to the car. "Your father was a bad man. That's why your grandfather killed him. I wish I would've killed him myself, but it didn't work out that way."

I get in the car and gaze out the window at the darkening sky and the snowflakes swirling around as the wind picks up.

"You want to know a secret?" I say, running my hand over my stomach. "I didn't really love your father. I just told myself I did. Because I wanted to. I really wanted to love him. But I didn't. I thought I might feel differently the longer we were together, but I knew when we got married that I wouldn't. I knew when I said my vows. I knew when we moved into that house. I knew when I saw him looking at the neighbor women more than he looked at me. I knew when he took his mother's side over mine, and when he didn't believe me when I told him things I knew to be true."

I pause a moment.

"You want to know another secret?" I slowly smile. "I always knew he was allergic to lobster."

Printed in Great Britain
by Amazon

43323865R00162